Never Say G

A Novel

By

Colin Griffiths

2014

Part One Chapter 1

It was midsummer 1989. Blackpool was bustling, full of hen parties, stag nights, people on their annual holidays. The great British weekend away, and it was raining.

'Always rained in Blackpool' Bill thought, *'always bloody rained'*.

The north of England was known for its wet weather, in spite of it having one of the biggest and most popular holiday resorts which, at one time, held the tallest roller coaster in the world. Blackpool had been neglected over the years, along with the rest of the north of England, in an industrial decline, but, although in decline, it still remained Britain's most popular holiday resort.

Both he and Carol were walking along the sea front, the famous Blackpool promenade. Trams were bustling alongside; the UK's only surviving first generation tramway was on their left, transporting holidaymakers from one destination to another.

As Carol walked with Bill she was excited about where they were going. She had a feeling inside her that something big was about to happen. Something good. She hadn't been to Blackpool since she was a child, except for five years ago, and again this weekend. This visit seemed to have brought out the child in her again.

Bill, well, he was grumpy. Bill was always grumpy; it seemed to be the only mood he knew. Maybe having an unhappy childhood made him that way. He didn't know, but he found it hard work to be happy. He hated smiley people, those that always had a smile on their face.

Carol smiled a lot, but sometimes she could be fiery as well. He was moaning inside himself about the amount of money this weekend had cost.

Okay he thought, *the bed and breakfast was cheap enough, but £3 for a poky hotdog!* When most of it lay in the gutter where he had dropped it instead of covering the only coat he had with him (the only one he had) with mustard and ketchup. Carol had wiped it off but you could still see the stain it had left. Carol had laughed and offered him half of hers.

'I'll starve' he sarcastically said.

'Oh you'll waste away.' giggling as she said it.

Bill had wanted to spend the money on a fishing trip for him and his five year old son Daniel, and then spend some time with his mates at the football before going out on the lash, maybe smoke a bit of dope, cop off with some slag from Newport, just get wasted and have some fun. Bill loved to take Daniel fishing. He sniggered to himself as he remembered his son struggling as he caught his first trout, the look of excitement on his son's face as they reeled it in, the look of utter disbelief as he gutted the fish.

Fishing would have been so much better he said to himself *fishing and then getting wasted.*

But Bill was here for Carol, the only girl he had ever had feelings for. Was it love? He wasn't sure what that was, having felt very little of it in his own life, but he loved what Carol gave him. He was unsure what it actually was. He felt secure with Carol. She made him feel safe. Life was good. He had a trophy wife and a trophy son.

As they walked, Carol had popped into the arcade to use the toilet, the third time she had been since they set out. This was annoying Bill. But this time he had promptly bought five donuts from a stall, giving the seller a growl as he paid. He scoffed all five before Carol had returned. Carol had pretended not to notice the sugar around his mouth on her return. 'I bet your starving,' she had said to him 'there's a donut store there. Would you like me to get you some?'

Bill looked at the donut stand, seeing the overweight seller serving up another lashing of donuts to some children

'No I'm fine' he said. 'I'll wait till later'

'I do hope she's there. It's been four years since we last saw her.' mumbled Carol as they walked. Carol, taking in the seven miles of sandy beach, watching the children playing, and the trams passing, she felt like a little girl today and was loving it.

'Five' Bill replied.

'Uh'

'It's been five year. You were pregnant, remember? That's why we're here.'

'Of course it is. How could I forget?' She paused, 'It would be so lovely to have a daughter, Bill. A little sister for Daniel. I really think she made it happen last time.'

'Of course it would,' replied Bill, thinking it really was all bullshit. Just another dose of Blackpool bullshit.

She put her arm in his as they walked, her face beaming with excitement and anticipation of what was ahead. It made Bill feel good, having this beautiful petite lady on his arm. He treated her as if she was his trophy to parade. *Maybe that's what she was to him,* he thought. *His own human trophy.*

'I just so hope she's there.' Carol repeated.

'She'll be there' said Bill. 'Ripping off people for a few years yet.'

4

They both smiled as they walked, happy, content and very, very wet as the rain still fell and the wind blew. The sea looked murky as the waves pounded the beach, which was not empty in spite of the weather. Children still played, and people walked their dogs, Blackpool was like that. Whatever the weather it never deterred holiday makers. The three piers were very busy as people held on to their hats and umbrellas. It felt more like a November day, but this was not stopping people enjoying the sights of Blackpool. The place was heaving.

Earlier on they had been to the pier, when the rain eased for a little while. They had gone to the central pier, which was always the best one, but there was so much pushing and shoving that they had decided to head to Marie Rose earlier and visit the pier later, weather permitting. This suited Carol down to the ground as all she really wanted to do was visit Marie Rose. After all that was the only reason they had come. They would give the waxworks a miss, perhaps go tomorrow. When they had wanted to go, the queue was massive and they didn't fancy queuing in the wet.

Standing outside the waxworks entrance was a life sized Simon Cowell. Carol had insisted she had at least four pictures taken standing beside the waxworks model. Bill didn't get it. 'It's a wax model for shit's sake.' he had said, but pretended that everyone would think she was stood by the real Simon Cowell because it had looked so life-like. Carol had said that when people saw the photos they would think she was with him.

Will the real Simon Cowell please stand up? Bill thought to himself and smiled as he thought it.

It was five summers earlier, on the same weekend trip to Blackpool, the same Blackpool, that Hitler had bombed in 1940. The same grotty bed and breakfast, the same hideous rain that seemed to stick to the north side of the British Isles like glue, the same sea front as they walked along now, though neither of them could remember if Simon was outside the waxworks that long ago. Somehow they doubted it.

Yes, five years ago, in what was not much more than a tent on the sea front, surrounded by queuing customers was Marie Rose, Blackpool's finest clairvoyant, at a ridiculous £2 a go for ten minutes, £3.50 for couples. Yes, your future dreams and aspirations will be unfolded in Marie Rose's famous crystal ball.

'That's at least £12 an hour, Bill had thought, *not bad for a bag full of bull shit.*

'This is a waste of money' he had told Carol, but Carol had pleaded and pleaded, and she gave Bill her puppy dog eyes look, a look she knew that he could just not refuse, Carol never overused that look, but certainly knew when to use it to her full advantage. She also knew how to play Bill and this time it had worked out very well.

The young couple had set up home together and married. They fell for each other at a barn dance in Newport, South Wales, where Bill had put his hand up Carol's blouse. She had slapped him and called him 'a bloody pervert'. No one hit Bill Fenton without facing the consequences. His reputation as a hard man and a nutter, which had grown over the years, was not to be reckoned with. He was feared by many. Maybe that's what attracted Carol. After that day's events she would never really know. Bill had simply laughed at the slap, apologised and bought her a drink. He won her over that night and they had been together ever since and here they were.

After four minutes of complete nonsense and the clairvoyant telling them stuff about when they hurt themselves as kids 'What kid didn't' Bill had said. *If only she knew* he thought. Bill had insisted that they leave and demanded his money back saying that it was complete rubbish and she should be taken to the trade's description act or whatever act they took dodgy clairvoyants to when Marie Rose blurted out those words that changed their life forever.

'You're pregnant and it's going to be a boy' she had said. 'Bloody rip off' Bill responded as he stomped towards the exit, not really listening anymore to the dodgy clairvoyant.

'Shut up Bill, you're demanding nothing. Why have you always got to spoil things?' said Carol as she dragged Bill by the sleeve, back into the tent. He was strong but he didn't resist. Turning her gaze to the clairvoyant, their eyes met.

'Are you sure?' she asked.

Marie Rose looked stone faced at the two of them. 'Yes my dears' she said without breaking her expression. 'You are bearing a baby boy, you are going to have a son.'

'How do you know that?' Carol had asked.

'It's in the ball.'

'Are you sure?'

'It never lies.'

'A load of balls to me.' Bill had said.

They both then left the clairvoyant, Bill shouting about what a rip off. Carol in stony silence, was thinking about what she had just been told, feeling scared then. *A child*, she thought, *a baby boy*. How would they cope? Or more like, how would Bill cope? She had never regarded him as the fatherly type and in a strange way, though she wanted children desperately, she somehow thought it wouldn't be with Bill.

7

Chapter 2

Those five summers ago, immediately after leaving the clairvoyant, Marie Rose, in her dodgy tent on the sea front, Carol had nipped into a chemist to buy a home pregnancy test kit. Bill was thinking at the time, that Carol was going to use it in the shop; such was her eagerness to find out. She told him not to be so silly and headed back to the b & b. Carol ran all the way back, a good mile away. Bill had come in two minutes later. When he got there, Carol was already in the bathroom, and sure enough, a 'quick piss on a stick 'as Bill called it, there it was. What Marie Rose had already told her? Carol indeed was pregnant.

How they hugged, kissed and laughed. It was probably the greatest Blackpool weekend they had ever spent.

'It's fuck all to do with her though,' Bill had proclaimed 'if she tells everyone that, she's bound to get one right!'

Deep down Bill was impressed. His life was beginning to take on a meaning; the next five years would be his happiest ever. He never heard any voices. He never heard his father. That day, deep down, Bill was impressed.

'Marie Rose, I love you!' he had shouted, dancing on the bed, and they laughed until Carol wet herself, thinking maybe it wouldn't be so bad after all.

'Fucking hell! She's got a gypsy caravan now.' Bill said, as he could see it in the distance. It was just past the tower, big letters announcing: 'Blackpool's most famous clairvoyant, no extravagance spared.'

'She must have earned a few quid since we last saw her, ripped off a few million I reckon. How many people visit Blackpool each year, and each one a £2 rip-off?'

Carol wasn't listening. She ran ahead, almost pushing people away

'She's here!' she cried.

Bill laughed at her eagerness. Some people turned to stare at her, one man giving her a glaring look, as she brushed past him. Bill wanted to punch his lights out, but he always did when it came to his Carol. He watched her legs skipping along, remembering the first time they met, and how she had not changed one bit, still that hidden child inside her. He loved that about her. How lucky he was to have her. How she had put him on the straight and narrow. *Who knows where I would be now if not for her.* He thought. He felt like he could give and receive all the love in the world, a feeling that would never return after today's events.

Carol had reached the caravan, and she looked behind her to see Bill lagging in the distance. She started jumping up and down, waving, and beckoning Bill to hurry up. As they approached each other, both were smiling. Carol briefly reflecting that it was his smile which had first won her over at the barn dance. His smile and his charm. *He very rarely smiled, but when he did it lit up her world,* she thought. Suddenly Bill's expression changed to shock. His smile turned into a frown. His eyes wide, his mouth open. Carol felt concern at the sudden change. Bill put his hand to his mouth and gave what appeared to be a gasp.

'Five fucking quid!' he said.

Carol laughed as Bill took his place beside her in the queue.

'A fucking queue!' he said.

They knew Carol wasn't pregnant this time, as she had taken a test only yesterday, the day before they arrived at Blackpool. The purpose of the visit was that Carol was convinced that the

9

clairvoyant would be able to tell them the sex of their next child. Carol so wanted a girl.

Bill thought it was a stupid idea. She had got lucky last time. No person in the world could tell the sex of a child that hadn't even been conceived. Of course there was always a fifty per cent chance you would get it right. They had been taking precautions. Bill's work at the warehouse had dropped to three days a week and, although it looked like things were beginning to pick up, Carol wanted to make sure, and try again, when Bill was on full time. Things had been tight, but when her mother offered to take Daniel to Malta with them, she missed two weeks rent, and organised this trip as some 'us' time.

She had said 'The council can wait for their rent.'

She had never missed the rent before, but she controlled the household bills and knew she could make it up, and there was always her parents. She never liked to ask them for anything, but knew it was there if she needed it. Bill had never been convinced about Marie Rose's abilities, constantly reminding Carol that if she was really that good, why would she be working in Blackpool at £2 a time.

They were now next in line. They both had to admit that the gypsy-style caravan was a great improvement from the previous time they had visited, and it looked quite convincing, *'And it's best to be convincing when you're conning the British Public.'* Bill had thought.

'Come on in, my dears' said the old lady, as they walked up the two caravan steps and entered the caravan through two small double doors. The old lady was sitting there in her glitter, the caravan spruced up with heather, candles, and mysterious figures of serpents and ghouls. Carol recognised her, thinking she hadn't changed much. *In fact she had looked younger then,* she thought, *and less scary.*

10

Marie Rose put her hand on her crystal ball and looked up at Bill and Carol.

'Hello my dears' she said, then, after a slight pause, 'How's Daniel?'

Bill stood there, unable to say anything for a moment. The look on his face was one of shock. His head started to spin, as if the old lady was controlling it, making his head all fuzzy, then the voices would come back and he didn't want that. He didn't want the voices back. *This shouldn't be happening,* he thought, this *stupid lady. How the fuck does she know his name?*

'He's fine' Carol replied. 'He's in Malta with his grandparents.'

My head's going to explode. Bill thought. *Is this really happening? She's talking to the old woman as if she's asked the most natural question in the world.* He tried to speak but no words appeared. Bill Fenton very rarely felt fear, but he now really felt scared.

Bill shook his thoughts away and looked the witch woman straight in the eyes.

'How the fuck do you know his name?' He put his face close to hers, strangely trying to guess her age and putting her at sixty. Marie Rose was in fact fifty one.

Marie Rose just sat expressionless, not shocked, more dismayed at Bill's attitude. Her stare did not leave his eyes.

'Well, bitch?'

'Bill!' Carol shouted 'Don't be so rude. She was only asking how he was.' then it dawned on her that the clairvoyant had actually used their son's name.

The clairvoyant turned her gaze to Carol 'Would you like a reading?'

'Fuck no.' said Bill.

Hang on, Bill, she's a clairvoyant. She knows his name. That's all, that's what they do'

Bill, freaked out by this, stared at Carol. *No puppy dog eyes,* he thought, *do whatever eyes you want were getting out of here.*

'We're going now!' Bill said, grabbing Carol by the arm, pinching her skin, causing her to wince in pain. 'We're leaving now!' he shouted.

The old lady just looked on.

'Ok ok, I'm coming, just leave go of my arm. You're hurting me.'

Bill released the pressure on her arm, and continued to walk to the exit. Carol rubbed her arm. It had hurt where Bill had pinched her. Carol was still unsure what was happening, but thought it better not to resist Bill. As they were about to leave Carol looked back at the clairvoyant. Their eyes met, there seemed to be a connection. The old lady smiled.

'Goodbye dear,' she said 'enjoy your new baby.'

With Bill's grip loosened, Carol was able to free her arm from his grasp. She took two steps back into the caravan, shoving Bill away from her, finding strength she never knew she had. Marie Rose still sat with her hands on the crystal ball, not even flinching.

Carol still did not understand the situation.

'What did you say?' she stuttered.

'You're pregnant.' Marie Rose told her.

On hearing that, Bill turned round, grabbed Carol forcibly by the arm and almost lifted her out of the caravan. He did not let go of her until they had reached the tower, and what he thought was a safe distance from the evil witch of Blackpool.

Marie Rose stood up from her chair, as a young girl was about to enter the caravan, having queued for what seemed an age. The clairvoyant brushed past her table, almost tipping it over, almost pushing the young girl back through the door.

'We are closed' she shouted. She put her head outside the caravan door and looked at the waiting queue 'Marie Rose is done for today.' she said.

'Fuck you!' said the girl who had just been ejected, and gave Marie Rose the finger. The waiting customers were annoyed, angry that they had queued for nothing, and a number of them shouted obscenities at the lady in the caravan.

Marie Rose didn't care. Her job was done for the day. She went back into the caravan and sat on the chair normally used by customers, a small round table in front of her and on it her crystal ball. She picked up the ball and stared into it, hoping she would at last see something, but she knew it was just a glossed up paper weight. She had never seen anything useful from that ball. Well almost never. Not that she wasn't mystic in some way. Not that she didn't have the power inside her. It was just that crystal balls didn't work, well, at least not for her. They had never worked for her. She reached across the table for her bag lying where she usually sat. She put the bag on the table next to the crystal ball. Fumbling in her bag she found her packet of cigarettes and took out an Embassy, which she lit from one on the burning candles on the sideboard. She puffed on her cigarette, blowing plumes of smoke all around the caravan. She could still hear the crowd outside, complaining as they dispersed.

She smiled until her smile turned into a grin. To her own surprise she found herself laughing out loud. She put her hand over her mouth like a naughty child who had been caught doing something wrong. She took a long puff on her cigarette, over-exaggerating as she inhaled, letting out another plume of smoke before extinguishing it in the ashtray.

No. Crystal balls don't work. She thought. Her face now grew stern, a face that had lived a thousand lives, told a thousand lies. *They've never worked.* She thought. *I've never been able to make them work, not until that first time five years ago, and again today*

She sat back in her chair and smoked another cigarette. 'It's been a good day.' she said to herself.

Chapter 3

Marie Rose had left her place of work, and was now drawing close to her drive in her white Rover 400. She lived a few miles outside Blackpool, in a place called Lytham St. Anne's. Her house, a 1980's build was a five-bedroomed detached property with modest gardens, with rose beds, shrubs that she never knew the names of and trees, plenty of trees. Her nearest neighbours were two hundred yards to the left, and four hundred to the right. Her house was set well back off the busy road, and once inside you would never have thought there was a road there at all. She could not see her neighbours' houses because of the trees in her, and their gardens. She liked it that way. She had seen the neighbours a couple of times but she didn't know either of their names, nor did she wish to. This was an idyllic retreat for her, some place for her to be while she watched.

Lytham St. Anne's was formed by integrating two towns, Lytham and the seaside resort of St. Anne's. The towns are situated on the coast south of Blackpool and, like Blackpool, St. Anne's overlooks the Irish Sea, whereas Lytham overlooks the Ribble Estuary, and is internationally renowned for its golf courses and the British open. Lytham St. Anne's is considered to be a wealthy area with some of the highest earners in Lancashire.

She had moved there just after her second husband had died in the 1980's. Her husband wasn't psychic but he knew she was. They kept it out of their married lives, as much as they could, and her husband had never wished to see that side of her. She had lost two babies, both miscarriages, with her second husband. Something that she never saw coming either time. She never told her husband of any psychic moments she had.

He was a property developer and even when she had seen him, in her other mind, falling from scaffolding hundreds of feet in the air, she never told him. She knew that, although her other mind didn't see very often, it was never wrong. It was always right. The same mind that oversaw the birth of Daniel Fenton and would oversee the birth of his brother. Yes, she had seen her husband on the ground in a pool of blood, every bone in his body broken, as he lay lifeless. She never told her husband this. *It was going to happen anyway* she thought, *so what was the point.*

Instead of informing her husband of his upcoming death, she insured him to the hilt, and within six months of her premonition she had buried her husband, and gathered a very wealthy bank account. The 'business' that she ran in Blackpool wasn't crucial to her finances. It merely just kept her in touch with the real world, and every now and again, a person like Daniel would come along. Someone she knew was special to her, and how she longed to be part of his life. One day she would be, of that she was quite sure. One day they would come calling. It was all she lived for now. She could sense it. She could feel it and one day she would see it.

She parked her Rover, and entered the house through its large, solid wooden door leading to a hallway with oak flooring. Heavy embossed wallpaper covered the walls below ornate coving. The glass chandelier that hung from the high ceiling, rattled in the wind, until she closed her door. She went straight into the living area. This was her favourite room, filled with green leather sofas, dark mahogany tables and sideboards, and had three large windows draped with the finest green satin there were paintings on the walls. Copies of Constable and Lowry, two completely different artists, but brilliant in their

16

own way she thought. She poured herself a large brandy from the decanter standing on the mahogany drinks cabinet. She sat down on her leather sofa with her brandy and lit a cigarette. *Oh it's been a busy day.* She thought, *a busy, wonderful day.* She took a sip of her large brandy, puffed on her cigarette and left it to burn out in the floor-standing ashtray beside the sofa. *It was so nice to see Carol. How wonderful she and Daniel had turned out* she thought, *but that Bill. Yes I know all about that Bill.* Her face scowled. She finished her brandy. 'I need food' she said out loud to the empty house and went into the kitchen.

Chapter 4

'What's up with you?' Carol asked Bill as he planted her firmly on the ground. 'You're acting like a mad man, and you hurt me!'

'Mad? I am mad.' Bill growled. 'Isn't what I just heard mad?' He scowled 'I'm sorry. It was all just weird. She knew our son's name, for fuck sake. She called him Daniel! It freaked me out. I'm sorry babe.'

As he spoke Carol noticed how pale he looked, this big strong man, of whom almost everyone was scared. Now he looked so afraid. What made him like this she did not know? She had never seen him like this before. She knew he had a temper and could flare up at the slightest thing, but to her and Daniel he was nothing but a gentle giant. Now here in Blackpool he looked like a frightened lost boy for all to see.

'Let's go to the arcade for a coffee.' she said, putting her arm in his. 'The bars and cafes will be full now; it's always quieter in the arcade cafe. We can talk over a coffee.'

The colour was coming back to his face as they linked arms and walked the short distance to the arcade. He fancied a beer, but agreed. The cafe would be better. Carol was right. There were about thirty tables in the cafe in three rows each, seating up to four people. Half of them were empty. The others were occupied mainly by adults having a coffee whilst their kids ran havoc in the arcade. It was noisy, but that suited Carol. They needed to talk and she didn't really want anyone listening. Bill hated the noise; the sound of lots of children shouting drove him mad. He hoped he would be okay. He hoped it wouldn't start. He could feel it coming and he didn't like that. Carol told Bill to grab a seat whilst she got the coffees. There was no queue and she ordered two cappuccinos, smiled as she paid the lady, and then she walked back with the coffees. Bill was sitting at a table he had found in the corner. Carol noticed his colour had come back but she still thought he looked as if he'd just lost a tenner and found five pence. She sat opposite him, placed his coffee in front of him, and took a sip of her own coffee. It was hot and she felt her lips burning. She put her coffee down on the table. She needed to make sense of all this. It didn't really make sense to her that this could happen twice, and she was really concerned about her husband's reaction. Why did it freak him so much?

'Right Bill, what just happened to you?' she asked, as she put her hands around her mug of coffee, feeling the warmth of the coffee on her hands.

Bill raised his hands in the air, shuffling in his seat He looked really uncomfortable as he spoke 'She knew his fucking name!' He flopped back in his seat.

'Calm down.' Carol soothed. 'Let's look at this logically, she's a . . .' She paused thinking of the right words. 'She's a wots it,' she continued, 'a medium, psychic person, or whatever you call them. She leaned towards him. Their eyes met, Bill knew it was time to listen now and try to make sense of it. Maybe Carol could make it better, make this feeling go away. His head hurt and he didn't like it when his head hurt.

'Four years ago,' she paused, and then corrected herself. 'Five years ago, that dear old lady told us we were going to have a baby. All that's happened is that it came true. We had Daniel, just like she said. She told us we were going to have a baby boy. Like you say, Bill, it's a 50-50 chance.'

She leaned across the table and held both his hands in hers. Her voice grew softer. 'I always loved that name, and maybe, five years ago when she told us that wonderful news, in all the

19

excitement I probably shouted out what name we would call him. We had often talked about it.'

Bill squeezed her hands. *She made it sound all so simple, so logical,* he thought.

'Maybe I had that pregnant look, and she recognised it. She is a medium. Maybe she has a memory like no other person, and she's not a medium at all. I don't really know,' she sighed, 'she just knew his name, that's all. You know, she continued 'when I told my mother I was pregnant with Daniel she wasn't a bit surprised. And do you know why?'

Bill didn't answer. He knew the answer was coming. Carol went on, 'because she said she could tell, by the way I looked. She told me I looked pregnant.'

Bill wasn't getting it. 'It's women's intuition,' she continued, 'my mum knew. That's the way it goes '

'You're right, I acted like an idiot.' Bill replied, 'She just had a good memory.'

He did not really believe what he said. There was something about that woman that frightened him. She looked familiar. He tried racking his brain for answers, but there were none there. Carol smiled. They let go of each other's hands and both grabbed their coffees which had cooled now. They both took two long gulps feeling the coffee warming their not cold, but damp bodies. They looked at each other and smiled, and didn't say a word until the last drop from their mugs had gone. They sat for a while in silence both trying to take in the day's events. 'Just one more thing,' Bill mentioned, 'she said you were pregnant.'

Carol looked at him from across the table, biting her bottom lip. She was expecting that statement. 'Haven't worked that one out yet.' she replied.

Chapter 5

Daniel had been an easy birth, almost nine months after Bill and Carol's trip to Blackpool. He arrived, not as planned, all a bit rushed and low key, but the bump didn't show at their wedding. A council house was quickly forthcoming with a baby on the way. They were housed on the Ashbourne council estate, just outside Newport, in the county of Gwent. The estate comprised over a thousand houses, with playing fields, a stream and woods behind the estate, half and half of two or three-bedroomed houses which all looked exactly the same. A real blot on the landscape. It was originally developed from a World War Two prisoner of war camp at the end of the war, and the remnants of the camp still survived until the early nineties. Then it was demolished and houses built on the land. It was built in the shadow of a wooded area, all the streets were identical and, if it wasn't for the signs, you would never know which street was which. All the houses had pebble-dashed fronts with picket fences. Some owners had replaced the fences with more sturdy and modern fencing but most still retained the picket fencing. Wooden poles with three sets of wires going horizontally and, somehow, whatever you did to them, they never looked straight. A pristine garden would border a neighbour's with grass four feet tall. Every other house had a satellite dish. An occasional window smashed by kids playing football. All in all, a typical housing estate in Wales.

Bill and Carol lived at 39 Hill Street. Like the other streets it had forty houses, twenty on each side. The Fenton's lived in the last but one on the left as you drove into the street. There was a chip shop between Hill Street and Ash Way, the latter being where Wendy Cross would live, someone that the

Fenton's had yet to meet. In the centre of the estate on a little precinct were two pubs, a social club, a pizza shop, a chemist, a Spar grocery shop, a newsagent, hairdresser, a garage for repairs and petrol, and a communal building used for youth clubs, coffee morning and similar social events. To the left of the precinct stood a church, to the right there was a park, behind which were a football pitch, a school and further derelict land. Everyone knew everybody else in Ashbourne. People used to describe it as a prison camp, which of course it had been, because once you got there, there was no escape from it, but generally most people loved it there. It was their estate and the problems that came with it were their problems. Those problems were dealt with by their people.

It was hot today. The James family had been coming to the same villa in Malta for fifteen years now, each time loving their annual break, to get away from the damp U.K. and soaking up the sun. They did very little on their holidays other than sunbathe eat, relax and, in the evenings, get slightly tipsy at their villa.

However this holiday was different. It was the first time they had ever brought their grandson, Daniel, and how he had loved the flight, marvelling at how that big piece of metal could float in the air, and the excitement of exploring the new apartment when they got there, where he would spend the week and for the first two nights he didn't have any nightmares. He never once thought about his father after he had caught his first fish. Daniel went on his first fishing outing with his dad some weeks earlier. His father hooked up his line from the sea wall in Porthcawl, a seaside holiday resort in South Wales, and it wasn't long before he and his father were reeling in his first ever fish. Daniel was full of excitement and jumped up and down as the fish drew closer. He was expecting his dad to throw the fish back in where it would swim away and continue its fish life, but instead his father had taken his knife out and cut off the fish's head and started cutting the fish open

'This is our tea' his father had said. It was the first time he had ever seen anything being killed, and he didn't want to see anything like that again. The thought of eating it had repulsed him. Daniel didn't cry or say anything. He didn't want his father to see him cry or be upset as he knew dad would get angry. He prayed that he never caught another fish and, as luck had it, he didn't. All the time he couldn't get the image of the fish being gutted out of his mind. He would never want to go fishing again.

From the third day Daniel had grown increasingly quiet. Although a very private child in many ways, Daniel was a chatterbox. He would love to sit and hear his grandfather's stories about when he had been a little boy, and a young man in the army. None of these stories involved killing fish.

Vera and Doug James were sitting on their loungers while Daniel played in the sand for the fourth day running. Daniel was bored by the same routine. They had barely ventured out from the villa except to go to the beach, which was just a few hundred yards away. They had gone to the shopping mall once but didn't stay long, just long enough to pick up some groceries and a case of alcohol. Daniel wanted to explore the mall, and pleaded with his grandparents. Age had caught up with them, and all they wanted to do was sit in the sun. Daniel showed little interest in the bucket and spade with which he was playing. His mind was far more active than either of his grandparents. He wanted adventures, but sadly none seemed to be forthcoming. Both Vera and Doug were in their sixties, childhood sweethearts. Doug had run a bookmaker's which resulted in a chain of five shops. He had been made an offer by one of the leading bookmakers around and he sold up. He hated gambling, which was odd as the benefits of gambling had served him well, but he let others do it and he reaped the rewards. He had never gambled, not even a small flutter on the Grand National.

'It was for mugs.' he would say.

Vera just didn't understand the business he was in, and took little interest, but it was true to say she certainly enjoyed the financial rewards it had brought in. She had been a school teacher for a while but retired early. They had been retired for five years now, not rich by any means, but Doug's business shrewdness had given them a comfortable early retirement, with no mortgage worries and an extremely comfortable life, retiring to a countryside bungalow just outside the capital city of Cardiff. Carol was their only daughter and they doted on her and Daniel.

Daniel loved his mum and grandparents, and was an extremely well-behaved child, very intelligent for his age, and even at four and a half, you could see that he was going to have the strength and build of his father. Other than falling over and scraping knees or bumping his head like any other child, Daniel had never been ill in his short, and yet uneventful, life. Not a cold, measles, chicken pox not even a headache, not one days illness and, at this point, I think it's true to say that Daniel would never be ill right up until the day he died.

Yes, Daniel had gone quiet, Vera thought. Doug had noticed it too. They hoped that it was because he was missing his parents, and of course, they were right about that. Daniel was still playing in the sand on the beach close by, not really doing anything, just digging the same area with his little spade, filling the bucket up, pouring the sand out again, digging, filling, pouring, digging, filling, pouring.

Do they think this is all I want to do? He thought. *Why can't we go on a boat or look around the shops or something.*

Digging, filling, pouring, digging, filling. He was sick of sandcastles and sand. He had wanted to bring some of his action figures with him, but his grandparents wouldn't let him, saying there was no room in the cases, and he would have plenty to do when he got there. *How wrong they were* he thought.

'Are you okay, Danny darling,' Vera shouted.

Yes Gran, I'm having fun.' he lied.

'Okay. Five more minutes, then we'll go back for our tea' *just five minutes,* Daniel thought, *digging, filling, pouring.*

They took Daniel back to the villa, cooked a tea, and had put Daniel to bed just after seven. He had pleaded to stay up longer, as he never went to bed that early at home. The truth was, his grandparents were finding it more difficult than they thought, having a four year old on holiday, having to give him their attention and watch over him all the time. They loved Daniel very much but they were pleased when it was his bedtime, so they could sit and relax without worrying what Daniel was getting up to. They wanted some time to themselves, and Daniel had quickly fallen asleep and began to dream. It was a calm dream at first. He dreamt of building sandcastles on the beach just as he did all day, but in his dream the castles were immense and soon became a fortress with soldiers on the walls, and then..... He saw giant fish jumping out of the sea, the fish had human faces that he recognised from the telly, but he didn't know their names. About twelve were jumping out of the sea, each one looking at Daniel, as they fell back into the sea. Then, as one fish jumped out with a face

25

Daniel didn't recognise, it looked at Daniel, and seemed to hover in mid-air.

In a gargled voice it said 'We're going to eat you up, just like your Daddy eats us up. We're going to chop of your head and....'

That caused Daniel to stir and he altered his sleeping position to lie on his back and the dream went away. He was soon dreaming again, dreaming of his mum and dad pushing him on the swing, then him and dad pushing mum on the swing, and then his mum changed into an old lady with a glass object in her hand. Again Daniel stirred, releasing him from his dream and he turned back on his side. Another dream came to him. Daniel dreamt of his brother, someone he hadn't met yet. That was the last dream Daniel had that night.

Doug and Vera were on the veranda. This is where they spent their evenings whilst on holiday, usually with a couple called Sid and Betty; friends whom they met every year, Sid and Betty lived in Yorkshire. They had met on holiday some six years ago, and every year they had met up. Doug and Vera had visited them in Yorkshire once, and enjoyed the beautiful city of York. Sid and Betty had returned with a visit to Wales, exploring the sights of Cardiff, but they didn't like the wet weather. They now had villas adjoining each other. The men were drinking beer from the supermarket, whilst the women were drinking something that tasted like Martini, only a lot cheaper. It was a beautiful warm evening, with the sun setting and even though the veranda looked over barren land you could still hear the noise of the sea splashing from the south side of the complex. Both couples loved it here and would never even think about venturing to another country or even another part of Malta. This was their idyllic retreat.

It was just after eight pm when Vera got up, a bit wobbly from the effect of the alcohol; Sid grabbed her arm to steady her as she rose from her chair.

'I'm just going to check on Daniel' she said, as she disappeared to the back of the villa.

Vera opened Daniel's bedroom door. It took a while for her eyes to contact her brain, due to the effect of the alcohol, before she realised what she was seeing, or in this case, not seeing. Daniel was not there. His unmade bed was empty. She let out a muffled scream, and then a louder one, and stumbled back towards the others shouting 'He's gone, he's gone.'

Her heart raced, her lips quivered. All sorts of thoughts flew through her head at once, too many for her to comprehend. It made her feel dizzy. She was sure she was going to throw up. The two men had come running in to see what all the noise was about. They both could see the look of panic on her face.

'He's gone, he's gone' she kept screaming as she flapped her arms, and tears streamed down her face.

Doug grabbed Vera by both arms, trying to calm her. Sid had run into the bedroom, and saw that it was empty. He looked under the bed and in the wardrobe but wasn't really expecting to find anyone. A sense of horror came over all of them. Someone had taken Daniel. With Doug and Vera locked in each other's arms, Doug was trying to calm the now hysterical Vera.

'He's gone. He's gone' she kept shouting.

Sid told them to call the police 'Now!' he had shouted, realising that someone needed to take charge of the situation.

Sid went to have a look around outside.

'He can't have gone far.' he said.

The police came very quickly. Holiday resort kids going missing was never very good for the tourist trade, so they always acted promptly. Two officers turned up, a male and a female both seeming apparently too young to be police officers, according to Doug, who was still in a bit of a panic, and struggling to get his words out. Vera sat motionless, staring into space, fearing the worst.

After stuttering out his words, the male officer asked them in perfect English to show him Daniel's room. Vera and Doug escorted the officer to Daniel's room at the back of the villa. Vera saw what she hadn't noticed before, although it now looked so obvious. Daniel's pyjamas were on the floor, the clothes he had taken off earlier were gone.

'He's got dressed.' she said, 'It looks like he got dressed.' Her voice was cold, anxious.

'So he's not been taken,' said the male officer, 'he's left.'

'How can a four year old boy just leave?' Doug shot back at the officer. 'He's gone. Just bloody find him!' he demanded.

By this time the female officer was on her radio, in the other room. The officer began to speak but was interrupted by the sound of Sid approaching the villa.

'I've found him!' Sid shouted. 'He said he was going to the Airport.'

For both Vera and Doug, the worst moment of their long lives now seemingly over, they quickly moved to grab Daniel, hugging him, yet failing to hold back their tears. Daniel stood, looking confused as to what all the fuss was about.

'Why were you going to the airport?' Asked Vera. 'Did you want to go home?'

'My dreams told me to,' he hesitantly said. 'My dreams are always right.'

'What dreams were those?' asked Doug.

'Mummy has something to tell Me.' he said excitedly, mumbling his words, as he tried to get them out. He gave a sigh. By this time Doug and Vera had let go of him. Sid was downing a beer, feeling the need for more than one.

'She's going to have a baby.' said Daniel.

Chapter 6

Carol and Bill had finished their coffee and left the arcade. The clouds were now clearing, and through the gaps came brilliant sunshine which seemed to make the roads glisten through the wetness they had endured. The wind was brisk, so the sun was never out for long, before going behind a cloud again. Carol gave a shiver, but she didn't think it was from the cold. The wet seaside front seemed to have more of a seaside feel about it. People seemed happier now that the rain had ceased and the sun kept breaking out from behind the clouds. Children skipped and laughed, and the music from the bars, piers and fairgrounds seemed so much louder now. Queues were again forming at the attractions, and, in the distance, the piers looked full. They walked past the entrance to the wax works where another long queue had formed. Simon Cowell was having his photo taken with two children as they stood beside the waxworks model but Carol barely noticed. Her thoughts briefly went to her own childhood, how good her own parents had been and the joys she had felt as a child. Only good memories, she thought, although she had longed for a sister or a brother. Yet she remained an only child. Carol somehow thought she had missed out on that. She was determined Daniel would have a brother or sister, and at least one good parent. She thought about Daniel then, how his holiday was going, and how much she missed him, wishing instead that they had taken him with them to Blackpool. He would have loved the fair and the seven miles of sands. They were making their way back to the B & B, a pregnancy kit in her bag, feeling like they had done this before.

Bill lay on the bed of the small room in the B & B. It was a double bed with a small dresser on either side. In the small drawer of one was the obligatory Bible. Both dressers had cheap lamps standing on them, which flickered if they were left on too long. On one wall was a table with coffee-making facilities, standing next to an old wardrobe in the other corner was a doorway leading to the small shower room with sink and toilet. The building was away from the sea front, and offered no views other than the road, and other B & B's. The ceiling of their room was white with mould in the one corner where it had previously been damp, and the owners hadn't bothered to redecorate. It lacked both charm and ambience. These buildings were far cheaper than those by the sea front. All except a few had vacancy signs up, which was probably unusual for this time of year, but Blackpool was suffering from what up to now had been one of the wettest summers on record. The U.K. as a whole was suffering in the tourist trade. Families were choosing sunnier climates.

Carol was in the bathroom. She had sat on the toilet for a good ten minutes before peeing on the tester. She was suddenly overcome with emotion.

'*This morning* she thought, *I was the happiest girl in the world, who just wanted another baby, so why do I now feel so scared?* She asked herself. The only conclusion she could come to was that perhaps Bill wasn't really the most desirable father. Yes she loved Bill, but during this holiday, something deep inside her made her doubt him. Something tugged at that inner doubt. She had thought for a while now, that her marriage was a test, a test of character which Fate had given her. Marry the most fearsome man you can find, and see how you deal with that then Carol.

It was really since she had seen Marie Rose, five years ago. It was all she had wanted to hear. This time, somehow, it felt different. She knew she was pregnant. Marie Rose had told her she was. Her thoughts returned to Bill's reaction and the way he faced up to Marie Rose. But the clairvoyant never flinched. She just stared at him, as though he was irrelevant. There was really more to it than that. What it was she just didn't know.

She came out of the bathroom and lay on the bed beside Bill. 'We will have to wait another five minutes' she said.

Bill grunted and looked at the pregnancy tester gripped firmly in Carol's hand. They lay there for five minutes. No smiles. Not a sound coming from either. Both just lay in dread. Carol already knew she didn't have to look, or take the test. The walk back had only been about twenty minutes. They had both walked in silence as they tackled their inner thoughts. The sun had made up its mind up and decided to shine brightly, as though it was making up for the weeks it had hidden behind the grey clouds. Yes, they had walked in silence, ignoring the hustle and bustle around them that the sun's appearance seemed to have brought. Even if Carol had spoken it was unlikely Bill would have heard her.

The events during this visit to Blackpool had stirred something inside Bill, a feeling he could never fully blank out. For the past year or so he had managed to 'park' the feelings he had first felt when his father was alive, and the times when his father would beat him. The voice in his head would tell him to run, but Bill never ran as he knew that when he was caught again the beatings would be far worse. At night, when he was too scared to sleep, while he waited for his father to pay him a visit, the voice would tell him to 'get there first. Get there first and kill the bastard before he kills you.' Bill put the voice down to his imaginary friend. He said to himself that every kid

32

has one, but he knew that wasn't true. Whatever the voice in his head was, it was real, as real as his father when he used to beat him.

One night when his father had come home drunk, and he was making his way up the stairs to visit Bill in his room, it was the voice that finally told Bill what to do. His father had not expected his son to be waiting, waiting at the top of the stairs. When he did see Bill, a brief moment of sobriety came over him, as he saw his young son hurtling towards him, with eyes as dark as night, his lips curled back over his teeth. In that brief moment, his father thought he was meeting the devil. That was the last thing his father saw, before falling down the stairs and banging his head on the concrete floor, the tumble being the last movement his son would ever see. No life flashed past through his mind, no time for regrets. Just instant painless unconsciousness.

Bill had woken up in the morning to find his father in a pool of blood at the bottom of the stairs. The voice had momentarily disappeared from his head. Bill never remembered what the voices had told him before they had left the inside of his head. He had called an ambulance. When the police came he told them that he woke up and just found his father lying there, which was true because, as far as Bill was concerned, he had never killed his father. The voice in his head had. There was an investigation, and it was presumed that Bill's father had come home drunk and had fallen down the stairs. That's how Bill had to remember it. *Any other memory* he thought *might give him away.* That was how the authorities thought it to be best way he remembered the incident.

That same voice was talking to him now, the voice that had got him out of that mess almost eleven years ago. Or was it the same voice? It had seemed to change at times. All the same, it was just a voice in his head.

'What if she's been playing around?' it had asked him. The voice was taunting him. 'What if the baby isn't yours?' it had asked, hounding him, taunting him, challenging him, laughing at him.

'Fuck you!' Bill had replied.

'And if this one isn't yours, maybe Daniel isn't either.' the voice inside his head kept on, taunting him.

'Get the fuck out of my head!' Bill angrily demanded of the voice that was hounding him.

It did, for most of the way back, but every now and then, in the back of his mind, the voice questioned 'What if they're not yours?'

He tried to fight it but he thought the voice was winning, as it usually did.

'It's time.' Carol said.

They both sat up and just stared at each other. Bill hadn't heard the voice since he had been lying on the bed which he thought was a good thing, sure that he had put it away, 'parked it.' They both looked down to what Carol had in her hand. For a few moments neither was taking in what they were seeing, not saying a word, just staring at the stick, which told them that Carol was pregnant.

'I'm pregnant' Carol simply said. *Of course, how could I not be?* She thought, *I really didn't need the test to tell me that.* Her mind wandered to Marie Rose. *She knew,* she said to herself.

Bill said nothing for a few seconds, his gaze fixed firmly on what Carol had in her hand.

'How is that possible?' he asked.

'When we tested yesterday, maybe the eggs, or sperm, or whatever, was still working away.' she said. 'Anyway, what does it matter? I'm pregnant.'

She suddenly felt an overwhelming sense of joy, which surprised her considering the thought she had when she was sitting on the toilet. Her mind felt confused. *A sister or even a brother for our Danny,* she thought. Then why did she still feel scared? She stared at the man she once loved, sitting beside her on the bed. She wanted him to tell her it was okay. Everything would be all right. But he didn't. Bill just sat on the bed, his mouth wide open. He could feel the demons inside his head escaping from where they were parked. He knew the voice was there. He knew it would tell him what to do. 'Get her an abortion' the voice said 'No no no!' Bill said out loud, and then realising what he had said, he held his head tightly as if that would squeeze the voice from inside him. Carol became concerned, looked open-mouthed, her bottom lip quivered.

'Bill.' she simply said, eyes wide, mouth open, startled by his reaction

'Oh I'm sorry.' Bill apologised, coming to his senses. 'It's just hard to take all this in.'

He lowered his hands. Their eyes met. *He looks so lost.* Carol thought. She took his hand, held it in hers lightly. She put her other hand on top of his, and clasped his hand in both of hers.
'It's weird. I know Bill, let's go for some dinner and talk about it.'

Bill gave her an approving smile. He had regained his composure somehow. He felt he now had some degree of self-control. They got up and grabbed their coats which were hanging on the back of the door, slipping them on before leaving. As Bill locked the door behind them and put the key in his pocket. Carol stood at the top of the stairs waiting for him. She gave him a smile before descending the stairs.

'Push her down the fucking stairs' the voice said. 'Just like you did to your father. We can say she tripped. Push her. Push her now!'

The pain in his head was intense. He tried hard not to show it to Carol.

'Push her. Push her.' the voice demanded, but now the voice in his head was different. For the first time ever he recognised the voice that was in his head. It was no longer just a voice, it was a being. Not a living being, but a being from beyond the grave. It was clearly his father telling him what to do.

'I fancy a Harry Ramsden's' Bill said as they descended the stairs and into the early evening sunshine. 'You're weak!' his father's voice told him.

Nine months later, their second son was born. They called him Todd.

Chapter 7

Bill was five years old when his mother left them, or, as he had always thought, his father had killed her. As the years went by, Bill barely remembered what she looked like. The only memories he had of her were ones showing her with a swollen face and black eyes. On one occasion, he remembered, his father had kneed her so hard in the stomach, that his mother wet herself. Bill had also wet himself as he watched, not so much in fear for his mother but for himself. Only once had Bill tried to stop his father. He was only five. That was when his father had held a knife to his mother's throat. Bill had screamed and clung on to his father's leg. His dad had turned away from his mother and put the knife to Bills throat. He never heard voices in his head in those days. They came later. As a five year old he thought he was going to die. But even without the voices Bill knew how to run. He ran upstairs and locked himself in the bathroom, just listening to the screams of his mother, as his father beat her. He never saw his mother again. His father told him she had left. Bill hated her for that. He thought she must have deserved the beatings. She had been a bad mother, and that was what bad mothers deserved. It was after that, his father turned his attentions to Bill. He would often beat him, but cleverly enough so that the marks wouldn't show. No teachers could see them, or if they did, they took no notice. No neighbours could hear them, and Bill knew the consequences if he dared ever tell anyone.

Then the beatings stopped, because his father took other interests in Bill. No more beating, but 'visits' that hurt him more than any beating could. He used to lie there in tears, praying that his father would just beat him. He could handle the beatings, the cuts, the bruises. They would eventually heal, but this, he thought, would never ever go away.

The day he thought the voices had killed his father, was the day Bill had become free of the violence and pain. Now the only violence and pain he would be involved with, was any that he inflicted.

Daniel was six and Todd was one the day there parents split up. It had been a lovely, sunny day in their council home. The two boys had been running around the garden, Todd chasing Daniel. Todd, falling over more then he ran, spending more time pulling himself to his feet then actually running. Daniel teasing him, goading him to catch him. Todd laughing as he tried. Carol was watching from the kitchen window as she prepared tea. She laughed at their antics and felt herself to be the proudest mother in the world.

Bill was due home from his work at the warehouse. The bus would be pulling up in five minutes. Daniel had always somehow known the time his father would be home, and every day around this time he would race to the front room window, waiting for the bus, waiting for his father to come home. 'I can see him. I can see him, he would shout to Carol before opening the door and running to greet his father. But Danny hadn't done that for weeks now, Carol had noticed, but she didn't think Bill had.

Their marriage had been on the rocks ever since that day in Blackpool. Both Carol and Bill knew it, but neither had mentioned it. Bill's drinking had got heavier, and although Bill had never hit her, never raised a hand to her, nor even threatened to, Carol grew scared of Bill, and as the weeks and months passed, her fear grew greater, as if she was expecting an explosion. She couldn't make any sense of this. She just knew the fear was real. She heard the door open as Bill walked in on time.

'Going up for a shower.' he called.

'Okay. Tea's nearly ready.' she replied. 'It's spag Bol.'

Bill went to shower without bothering to answer. Today had not been a good day. He had got an order wrong at the warehouse, and had to unpack and repack it. He was given a reprimand at work. He wanted to hit the team leader who gave him the warning, and was sure that if there hadn't been any witnesses he would have done so. His work was suffering lately. He'd been fine since the birth of Todd, although he and Carol were not particularly close, but they had a routine, and Bill thought a routine was good at the moment. It suited him. He could do what he wanted. All Carol was interested in was the boys. She didn't have much time for him anymore.

As the shower ran over his naked body, the steam filling the room, feeling the water that was too hot, almost burning his skin. He remembered that had been a trick his father would do, making him stand naked in the shower with the water very hot, but not quite hot enough to burn, and how he had cried while his father would laugh, knowing that if he stepped out, there would be far worse to come. There would be no crying today. He let the water run cold, as cold as it could get, still standing there. Another trick his father had taught him. He dried himself off, got into his 'best gear' as he had no intention of staying in tonight. He'd had enough of that. He had stayed in last night. He walked down the stairs, smelling the spag Bol. on the stove, tempted to stay and have some, but he didn't want to do the family thing tonight. He needed to get out. He saw Carol in the kitchen from the bottom of the stairs.

She's still beautiful he thought, and indeed she was with her long, dark hair shining in the evening sun which came through the window, wearing tight jeans that almost fitted like a second skin, showing off her peachy bum, her nose a perfect profile to her face. She turned around saw him standing in the passage by the front door. Their eyes met.

'I want a paternity test.' he said, 'for both of them!'

He turned around and shut the door behind him as he left. Carol stood there, motionless for a while, the spoon with which she had been stirring the spaghetti bolognaise still in her hand. She turned her head slightly and saw the two boys standing by the back door.

'You okay, mum?' Daniel asked.

'Bah.' said Todd.

She looked at her two sons standing there, concern on both their faces. Putting down the spoon, she moved to them, bending down in front of them, putting an arm round each. She hugged them, a tear appearing in her eye.

'I'm fine, sweethearts, I love you both so much.'

Daniel, still hugged against his mother's chest gasped, 'We love you too, mum.'

'Bah.' said Todd.

She released her grip on them and stood up. The boys' eyes followed her movement.

'Tea's ready' she said. *They're mine. That's all that matters.* She thought.

As he saw Bill walk out through the door, Daniel knew that he would probably never see his father again. Even at that young age he felt an overwhelming responsibility towards his mother and brother.

Bill left the house, walked down the short path, opened the gate and turned left. He could see the chip shop in the distance with three or four children outside. There was a Burger King further down. That was what he fancied. Two minutes later he was inside. There were about three people in front of him. He waited patiently for his turn. The young lad, who was serving, looked no more than sixteen. He was wearing a cap on his head and showed signs of acne around his chin.

'Yes sir?' the young man said when it was his turn.

'Big Mac and fries.' said Bill.

The boy looked at him very strangely, a look which Bill wanted to wipe off the young lads face.

'This is a Burger king, McDonalds is in town.'

'You trying to be fucking funny?' Bill scowled.

The young lad saw the scowl on his face and for the first time saw the size of Bill, a big powerful man, with an angry face. The boy had the feeling he could be snapped in two with one arm.

'No sir!' He stuttered 'I'm sorry sir. I didn't mean anything sir. I just.......'

'Just give me a cheeseburger and fries.' demanded Bill, staring at the young lad, daring him to say another word.

'Certainly sir. Would you like to go large with that?'

'Do I look like I want large?'

The young lad thought there was no answer that would be a safe one, so he made Bill up a large cheeseburger and fries, for which he would only charge for a regular, just to be on the safe side.

'Make it two.' Bill said.

'Certainly sir.'

Bill walked out of the Burger King eating his burger and fries. The day was still warm. It had been nice... The sun was still shining, but was losing its strength as it headed towards sunset. He walked down the street, eating his burger and fries, looking forward to the beer he was heading for. As he walked his father's voice spoke to him. *You did the right thing.* Bill didn't reply. He just carried on eating until the food was almost gone. The main street to the pub was quite busy. The houses were now behind him, and the shopping centre a hundred yards ahead. It wasn't big, but more was being added to it all the time, as the estate was on route to the capital city. In not so many years it would become a small town. Already there was a supermarket, chemist, newsagent, butcher, a hairdresser's, a cafe, a take away Chinese, an Oxfam shop, a pub and a restaurant just behind. Between the last two buildings was a community hall and behind that a church and doctors' surgery. There was a lady on the other side of the road walking her dog. A cocker spaniel, it looked like to Bill. *What a lovely dog,* he thought. He'd finished his last chip and threw the wrapper to the floor in spite of there being a series of bins ahead of him in the direction that he was going. The lady saw this and gave Bill a disapproving look as they passed.

'You got a fucking problem?' Bill shouted

The lady quickened her step until Bill was out of sight.

Bill was never to return home again. That evening he sat in the pub which was relatively quiet for that time of day. But as the time went by more and more people were coming in. Bill was sitting there, but he wasn't alone. He never seemed to be alone these days, not since the birth of Todd, and perhaps before that, during the time in Blackpool and the visit to Marie Rose. No he was never alone lately. He always had his father with him, the father he had killed when he was just a little boy. Yes, he had had many 'fathers' since going from home to home, foster parent to foster parent. Seven foster parents in total, and only two had abused him like his father had.

He finally thought he had lost his demons when he met Carol. He somehow hid his past life from both Carol and himself, but his father had come back, his real father.

'I will never leave you.' his father had said. 'I will always be here'

He had tried ridding his father from his mind. When that didn't work he tried to 'park' his father. That worked okay for a while, but now his father was here in his mind, and this time he knew he was here to stay. That day Bill drank his beer, not setting out to intentionally hurt someone. He wanted a beer, lots of beer, and maybe he would pull. *Yes that's it,* he thought, *beer and sex.* As the night went on the place filled up. Bill continued sitting underneath the front window in a U shaped cubicle with another five places alongside him and three on either side. He sat alone, with his father's voice, getting drunk. After about an hour or so, two couples had taken seats either side of Bill. A young couple in their twenties, enjoying a night out, had put some songs on the juke box and had sat down. They were closely followed by a couple in their thirties. 'Wrecking ball' was playing on the juke box. Bill sat there with an empty bottle of Budweiser.

By the time the Police came, a lot of damage had been done and a lot of blood lost. None of it was Bill Fenton's. Bill had gone to the bar and whilst slipping past the young couple Bill had trodden on the young girl's toe hard enough to make her yell.

'Stop your fucking whinging.' he had told her.

43

Her boyfriend, a young man of twenty three, out with his new girlfriend, and wanting to make an impression, couldn't let it go. No one would speak to his girlfriend like that, without him at least saying something. Barely before the young man had stood up, the beer bottle in Bill's hand had crashed against his head. As he went down, he slid between the chairs and table onto the floor, an instant pool of blood forming around his head. The couple opposite just looked on in horror, and the young girl shrieked in terror. The bottle had now broken from the force with which it had been wielded. It took the two bouncers, one of whom had received severe lacerations, together with a number of customers to finally get Bill to the ground, where they sat on him until the police came. It then took five policemen to get him into the van. The young boy had not died instantly. It was three days before he died. It was seventeen years before Bill was released from prison.

With the dishes washed, Todd fallen fast asleep, Carol and Daniel sat on the sofa watching Toy Story 3

'I think Daddy's in trouble.' Daniel said to her completely out of the blue.

An hour later the police knocked the door.

Chapter 8

Seventeen Years Later

The twenty three year old drove up Hill Street in his three year old Mercedes S class. Daniel had just finished work. It was mid-May, a pleasant day with hazy sunshine. Daniel had made one of his visits to a client this morning, and with Becky not home yet he thought he'd pop in to see mum and his brother.

See what I can scrounge to eat. He thought.

Becky was his wife to be. They had met at a bowling alley three years previously, when Daniel had misjudged a throw so badly that it had ended in the next alley, the alley where Becky and her friends were playing. They hit it off immediately. Daniel had tried to apologise, amid tears of laughter running from Becky's eyes. In spite of doing very well as an accountant, with top market businesses requiring his services, (Daniel was highly sort after with his shrewd business head,) he was officially employed as an accountant. He had a natural and remarkable ability in being able to invest money without paying taxes. His skills were tax avoidance and his customers included a lot of celebrities, even a top lawyer and chief inspector.

Daniel and Becky had chosen to live on the council estate just around the corner from his mum and Todd. They were still very close, and he needed to be close to his mum, even more so with his father out of prison. They had done the house up nicely, after purchasing it from the council. They both loved it there. Daniel funded his mum and brother in many ways, and his wife to be realised this as a natural thing to do. Becky was never kept short; indeed she could have almost anything she wanted.

As Daniel drove through the council estate, two streets away from his mother's he saw Stephen Jenkins. *The twat!* Daniel thought, as he pulled up outside the house where Stephen was cleaning the windows. Stephen wasn't a small lad. He was about twenty two years old, but compared to Daniel he was small. Daniel had grown into a huge hunk of a man just like his father. Stephen hadn't noticed Daniel, and didn't know he was there, until the ladder he was standing on suddenly moved away from the wall where it had been leaning. Stephen found himself in mid-air. He shrieked! *A little too girly.* Daniel thought.

Stephen, clinging on for dear life, regained his balance and managed to look down to see what was happening. He saw that Daniel was holding the ladder in mid-air.

'What have I told you?' Daniel shouted up.

'Please just put me down!' he shrieked.

Daniel placed the ladder against the wall, both his arms aching through the strain. When it was against the wall Stephen began to climb down. He was feeling a bit queasy and started to shake. When he reached the bottom, he turned to face Daniel with his shammy still in his hand. Remarkably, the buckets had managed to stay hooked to the ladder 'I'm sorry. I was only doing a couple.'

Daniel could see Stephen was shaking.

'This is Todd's round.' he said, and took the shammy from his hand and rammed it into Stephen's mouth until he was choking. Tears were running down his face, noises coming from a mouth full of shammy. It had only been in his mouth for a short while, but Stephen thought he was going to die. He gasped for breath. He began coughing. Daniel released the shammy, put his arm round the window cleaner's shoulder. A plastic-handled cleaner lay on the floor beside them. Daniel pointed to it.

'See that?' he said.

Stephen had stopped choking but he was clearly still shaken up

'Yes...yes' he stuttered, still with Daniel's arm around his shoulders

'If I catch you again, I'm going to shove that up your arse'

'I promise.' Stephen said, 'I promise.'

As Daniel approached his mum's house Todd was up the ladder, cleaning his mum's windows. Daniel parked the car outside his mum's house, opened the gate, still grinning at the thought of Stephen Jenkins shaking up the ladder.

'Hey, bruv!' he shouted up to Todd.

'Danny Boy!' Daniel hated that, and Todd knew it. 'Be down in a min, bro.'

Daniel opened the front door. "Mum!' he shouted.

'In here.' came her voice from the kitchen

Daniel walked into the kitchen, took hold off the petite lady who stood before him, and hugged her.

'Hi mum, anything up?' he asked as he released her.

She gathered her breath. She always loved it when Daniel did that.

'Nothing up, as you would say.' She smiled. Carol knew exactly what he meant. It meant, had she heard from his dad.

'Good. Now, you got anything to eat?' he asked as he opened the cupboard doors.

'Doesn't that lady of yours ever feed you?'

'She does, just not enough!'

Todd came into the house and into the kitchen. His mum was making Daniel a sandwich. Daniel stood there with a box of

Pringles, ramming half a dozen at a time in his mouth. Carol got more slices of bread for Todd.

'Just caught that Jenkins kid cleaning windows.'

'Not again.' said Todd 'I'd warned him once.'

'Well, let's just say he won't be cleaning anymore' said Daniel and laughed.

Todd laughed with him. Carol gave a disapproving look to the pair of them, but as she turned away she smiled to herself.

Todd had been academically bright, just like his brother. He liked to write short stories and poems, and had a fascination with crosswords and quizzes, but he had chosen a window cleaning round on the estate where he lived. He loved the fact that you only worked when the sun was shining, and he met lots of people. He wouldn't do it forever, though it would do for a few years .Of course he still spent some time in his wardrobe. For an eighteen year old, he was big in build, though not as big as his brother. Daniel had his father's build and the rugged looks that all the girls fell for. Daniel was always perfectly groomed, with a smart suit when in work, but Todd always looked a bit unkempt, hair slightly too long, jeans a bit too frayed, and a vast collection of T- shirts ranging from Disney characters, to the Walking Dead series. Yet he was handsome with it. He wasn't money orientated, nor did he wish for fast cars. He liked life just as it was.

They sat at the kitchen table eating their sandwiches, while Carol loaded the washing machine, made herself a coffee, and sat with them. It was three pm

'What you doing?' Daniel asked his Brother.

'Wendy's working till eight. She's on a break soon. I'm going to have tea with her.' Todd said with his mouth full. 'I've done enough windows for today.' he had in fact only done his mother's.

'I'll come with you. Have something more to eat.'

They finished their sandwiches, and kissed their mum goodbye, but not before Todd got the £5 from his mum for doing the windows

'I pay my keep; she can pay for the windows.' Todd had said when Daniel questioned his mother paying.

They were all laughing, and then the boys left the house. They entered the cafe on the estate, which was set out more like an American Diner with a long counter going the length of the room, stools beside it and some four-seater tables with chairs, running along the front of the diner, which had vast windows looking outside. Red and white table cloths adorned the tables, on each of which stood a little trestle full of sachets of sauces, a triple burger being their speciality. They took a table by the window, Todd giving Wendy a wave and blowing her a kiss when he saw her behind the counter. His heart melted a little. It always did when he saw Wendy, especially wearing her uniform. Oh how he loved that uniform. Wendy blew one back and made a gesture that she would be two minutes.

Todd was eighteen and Wendy seventeen. They had been together less than a year. Todd had once described her as having a face ready to live a life.

'A life of adventure and fun.' he had said, 'with the softest lips I will ever kiss.'

Wendy was never sure how to take that but she knew he meant it well. Today she wore her uniform, the American style pink baseball cap, with Ashbourne Cafe printed on the front. Her long hair pony-tailed at the back, a blue top and trousers and a pink apron. She wore no make-up. She very rarely did. She had a natural beauty. She lived in the next street to Todd, just past the chip shop. His mum knew her mum, that kind of thing. She was in the year below Todd in school and they had never really got to know each other in the early years, and the day Todd cleaned Wendy's mother's window was the first time he really noticed her. Todd was washing the upstairs windows of the house, which he later found out to be Wendy's bedroom. Wendy had just taken a shower, and walked into her bedroom. Although her dignity was covered with a towel, the shock at seeing the window cleaner's face at the window, caused her to jump, and for a split second the towel dropped. At that moment Todd stood on the ladder in a trance, motionless, his hand in the air, still holding the shammy, his mouth wide open in total amazement at what he had just seen. Not the fleeting sight of her naked body, just a brief second, before Wendy had managed to "re-towel" herself. It was her beauty that he noticed. Her wet hair, all scuffed up as she had been drying it, her unmade-up face, showing more beauty then any make-up kits from the world's top models, he had thought. He was in such awe of her beauty that he fell off the ladder, just hearing Wendy shriek as he went past the window. One minute he was there, the next he was gone.

Todd had landed in hedge running alongside the path below the windows. He had been scratched and shocked, but his pride and dignity was hurt more than himself. Wendy had come running down the stairs, still in her towel, and out through the front door. Her mother, Helen, heard the commotion and followed. Todd was still dangling half in and half out of the hedge as the mother and daughter came outside. He got himself free, struggling to stand. He looked at Wendy standing there, a raven-haired beauty with just a towel around her.   'Are you okay?' she asked 'You frightened me to death'

Her mother went back into the house. Neighbours looked from across the street. Todd wasn't sure if they were looking at him or the beautiful image of this admirable girl wearing only a towel.

'I'm fine. I'm sorry I didn't recognise you without your clothes on.'

Wendy blushed but smirked. Todd checked again that he hadn't been cut.

'I think a thorn has pierced my heart.' he said. 'You know, in order to thank me, you can take me out tonight.' he added. 'Thank you?' came the reply. 'Thank you? I ought to bloody well slap you, for peering at me like that. I should report you!'

'Okay then.' Todd replied

Wendy looked a bit shocked. 'Okay, I'll phone the police now.'

'No, I don't mean that. I mean I'll take you out.'

'What makes you think I want to go out with a peeping tom?'

'You don't. You want to go out with me.'

Wendy smiled, smitten by his charm. Todd smiled too. *How beautiful this girl is.* He thought. *Don't blow it now.* He said to himself.

'I'm Todd. I live in the next street.'

'I know. I'm Wendy. I live here.'

'I know. Pick you up at seven?' he asked.

'I'm washing my hair.'

'You just washed it.'

'Seven?'

'Seven.'

'Okay.'

Todd's face beamed. Wendy's face glowed. Todd gathered his cleaning stuff, lowered the ladder, placed it on his shoulders, smiled at Wendy and said, 'Tell your mum there's no charge.'

That evening they went bowling, and then to Nando's for Wendy's favourite chicken. They never stopped talking or laughing, and fell in love with each other that night, and have been inseparable ever since, both knowing there was something different about each other, not sinister, just a sense of being someone special. Wendy loved song writing and she played an acoustic guitar. Todd had shown Wendy his poems, and she loved them, putting a few of them to music. Many a night was spent sitting together, singing the songs that they composed. They were only six weeks into the relationship when Todd told her about his wardrobe.

'It's where I see things, and find answers.' he had told her. 'That's cool.' was all that Wendy said, thinking that it was the most natural thing in the world.

Wendy sat down opposite Todd and beside Daniel. The table next to them was occupied by a couple in their twenties. The red-haired man was wearing a seventies style suede jacket which looked as if it was about to fall off him, the girl had her hair tied back, acne round her nose, she wore jeans and a T-shirt with ' my parents still love me' written across the front. In front of them were two coffees that had been standing there for an hour.

Although there were only occasional strangers came to the cafe, Ashbourne had grown over the years. A motorway link had been built nearby, and with new private houses springing up around the estate, it had become a regular stop-off for motorway drivers on their way to Cardiff, or maybe travelling over the bridge to England. They were used to strangers as the cafe became more popular and far cheaper than the motorway services, but mostly the customers were from the estate. Wendy took no notice of them at first, but the length of time they had been there made her feel suspicious.

She leaned over to Todd. 'Don't look now,' she said, 'but the couple behind you have been there for what seems like hours, and have only ordered two coffees.'

Todd looked behind him.

Wendy frowned. 'What did I tell you?' she said.

'Sorry, it's instinct. As soon as someone says, 'Don't look now' you have just got to look.'

Wendy and Daniel laughed. Daniel was facing the couple and could see what they were doing. The boy had his back to him but the girl was in full view.

'Want me to ask them to leave?' he said.

'No, it's okay.'

The couple, Katy and Mickey, got up and left the cafe. Once outside the girl turned to Mickey saying, 'the waitress, that's Daniel's wife?'

'Yep!' said the red-haired man.

Chapter 9

Carol is panic-stricken. Kevin will be here in a minute. The baby-sitter's late, and she can't find her earring, one of her favourite pair. They were on the table by the window and now there's only one.

Ten year old Daniel and five year old Todd were playing computer games on the X box.

'You two, please help me look for my earring.' Carol said.

'Okay mum.' said Daniel.

Daniel started looking behind the cushions on the sofa. Todd left the room and they could hear his footsteps running up the stairs.

'Where's he gone now?' Carol asked impatiently.

'It's okay, mum' Daniel replied

The babysitter walked in, a scruffy-looking girl with clothes that didn't match, but she was reliable, and the boys liked her. She was munching on a Mars bar.

'Hello Mrs. Fenton.' she said,

'I can't find my earring.'

As she spoke there was a toot from a car horn outside. Kevin had arrived.

'Shit!' Carol exclaimed, then put her hand over her mouth having realised what she had said.

Daniel laughed. He had stopped looking for the earring knowing there was no need. He began showing the baby-sitter his new game.

Todd was in his bedroom, his single bed adorned with superhero figures, his Spiderman quilt cover, and posters of Wolverine, Thor and Iron Man covered the lilac walls. Wolverine, being his favourite superhero. Next to the

Spiderman quilt cover, there was a triple chest of drawers with a Spiderman lamp on it. The room was quite tidy for a five year old. On the main wall was his wardrobe, a piece of furniture that used to be his mother's, and her mother's before that. Old in age, but sturdy in construction, it stood tall and wide, almost touching the ceiling, and with double doors on the front, the old oak-looking wardrobe looked out of place in the superhero bedroom and seemed to fill the whole room. Todd stood before the wardrobe, its big double doors waiting to be opened. He opened the doors, and stared a while.

The floor of the wardrobe was clear, as it always appeared to be. His clothes hung high, so there was plenty of room for a five year old to hide. Even an adult could hide in there easily, Todd had always thought. He got into the wardrobe, sat sideways on the floor, pulled his knees to his chest even though he needn't have done, as there was plenty of room. He pulled the one door shut and heard it click. He pulled the other door halfway shut, hesitated, then pulled it again. He heard it click shut. Now he was in complete darkness.

Kevin beeped again, as Todd came running down the stairs into the living room. He went straight over to the table where the earring was; he bent down and lifted the bottom of the curtain behind the table. Stuck in the hem of the curtain was the missing earring, which had fallen off the table as the boys had played.
'Here it is, mum' Todd said

Chapter 10

It all happened very quickly. Daniel and Todd had left the Cafe and gone back to their mum's. As Becky, Daniel's fiancée, was still at work, Wendy had remained at the diner until 5.30.

Now, as she lay on the back seat of a car, still semi-conscious from what she thought must have been chloroform; she vaguely recalled who her attackers were, the red-haired guy and the girl who had been in the cafe earlier. She had left by the staff entrance at the back, which was not overlooked by houses, and there was no more than a dirt track, which had at one time been the access road to the church. As she left work, with a bag of rubbish to bin on her way out, all she could remember was a hand going over her mouth. She recalled the smell of body odour. She had no memory of screaming or fighting back, just that awful smell of disinfectant that made her feel drowsy. She barely remembered being bundled into the car that she thought must have been parked on the lane behind the Cafe. She didn't hurt in any way, as she lay on the back seat of the car. She could hear the driver and passenger talking but could not make out the words. She realised that her hands were tied, and she was gagged. *Maybe I'm dreaming.* She thought, her mind confused as she drifted in and out of consciousness.

Bill Fenton sat on the plastic two-seater sofa, the air filled with smoke fumes as he sat waiting, chain-smoking and drinking cans of Fosters. It was still daylight, barely 6.30, but he had received a call from Mickey saying he and Kate had got her.

Bill knew his dad would have been proud of him. The voices in his head would be good ones.

He had been out of prison for six months. He did not have a parole officer as he wasn't on parole, having served his full term plus two years more for various episodes of bad behaviour, He was, however, assigned to an assistance officer, whose job it was to introduce him back into society and the changes that had taken place in the last seventeen years.

It was a three month assignment, and the officer had found him a council flat on the tenth floor of a block of council flats, where the lifts never worked and the stairs always stank of shit and piss. It was in the St. Paul's area of Bristol, a run-down council area, mainly inhabited by West Indians and illegal immigrants. There were frequent knifings in the area, and every night, at one time or another; you would hear sirens from police cars or ambulances. There was very rarely a day went past without something untoward happening in the area.

His time in prison had been hard. It was a category A prison, but he soon became recognised as an inmate who could look after himself and was very rarely bothered with in prison, other than when he was jumped by two Jamaican guys who put him in the hospital wing for a week. Within two days of him being back in the wing one Jamaican guy had suffered both legs broken and the other had lost an eye. Bill was never bothered after that nor did he choose to bother anyone. He didn't serve any extra time for that. He was never charged. The two he injured were refusing to co-operate. The worst part of it was the amount of time he was actually locked away.

For the first three years he shared a cell with a convict who had committed armed robbery on a post office. As time went by, he earned his privileges. He was given a cell of his own, only three paces wide and four paces long, with a bed, sink, toilet and a cabinet with a shelf and a door. He was allowed a telly in his cell. He was locked up for nineteen hours a day, only being allowed out to collect his meals, forty five minutes in the yard a day, and an hour a week in the prison gym, but he was prepared to wait. He had never seen his sons since he committed murder. Carol had got a divorce and he had only seen her once in that seventeen years.

Seventeen years was a long time. A long time to wait for revenge. He would hurt the only girl he ever loved, by hurting the things that she loved. His flat was in a run-down complex and the views through the dirty windows were of similar buildings all in a similar state. The walls were thin and the rooms were cold. It didn't remind Bill of prison. In prison it had been warm, he was well fed and he felt safe. Here was worse than prison.

Daniel and Todd walked, both having given up on any kind of work for the day. Daniel was going home, as Becky would be home now. Todd just strung along. He wouldn't be seeing Wendy tonight, as she was spending time with her mum; bottle of wine, and watch a movie, Wendy's father had left them when she was seven. He had not kept in touch for very long, but that neither bothered Wendy, nor her mother. He had worked away a lot, so Wendy never got to know him. Now Wendy had no idea where he was. She had thought that one day she would track him down, and ask him all the questions she wanted answering. Then she met Todd, and her priorities changed. He was the only man she wanted in her life, the only man she needed.

Daniel offered Todd a juicy fruit. Todd declined.

'He's been out six months now, you know.' said Daniel as they walked

'Who?' asked Todd, knowing full well who he meant? Todd stopped walking, looked at Daniel. 'What does it matter?' he asked.

There was a slight breeze in the air, the sun went behind a dark cloud. Todd had been expecting this conversation. That didn't mean he wanted to hear it. He had put his father out of his life, and really didn't want to acknowledge his existence.

'Do you remember him Todd?'

'Not at all, but that might be a good thing.' They continued walking. Todd spoke again, 'Life is okay at the moment. Why bring him into it? Why even mention his name?' He sounded annoyed. His brother could sense it.

'I remember him well. I loved him at one time.'

Todd tried to digest that, unsure whether to be jealous of Daniel. For at least a short time he had a father. *Was that good or bad?* He thought. 'Do you miss him?'

Daniel paused, ran his tongue over his lips, let out a sigh. 'I hate him.' his voice sounded creaky. 'I wish he was dead.' Todd noticed his change of voice. 'But do you miss him?' They walked for a minute in silence.

'I need to find him, Todd.'

Todd stopped, grabbing Daniel's arm.

'Why?' he simply said.

They continued walking.

'To make sure he can't hurt us. Hurt you and mum, hurt what we have. It took mum years to get over what he did. She has a new life now. We all have new lives. He's not just going to

Leave us to live it. I can feel it. I can smell him.'

'And what makes you sure he will want to find us?'

Todd was not surprised by Daniel's comments. He had sat in his wardrobe only two nights ago and had a feeling that something was about to happen.

'I know him. '

'You were five, Daniel. You were just a kid.' They were walking past the Roundabout pub.

'Let's grab a beer.' said Daniel.

'Okay, as long as we talk about something else.'

They ordered two pints of John Smith's and sat in a corner. The pub was quiet. It was still early. In a few hours the place will be full.

Daniel took a sip of his beer. 'Don't you think it's funny that we never knew any of his family?'

Todd put both hands round his pint glass, as if to stop anyone from taking it. He released his grip, sat back in his chair, looked at Daniel. They made eye contact for a few seconds. Todd thought how much he loved his brother, but something was troubling him.

'You know when you do your thing,' Daniel said. Todd's eyes widened. He knew he had a 'thing', where sometimes he remembered things, or he found things, or he saw things. Daniel continued. 'Years ago, I was in Malta with Nan and Gramps. I tried to catch a plane home without them knowing. It frightened them to death. I was five, I think.'

'Why, you idiot? You loved them.'

They both sipped their beers, Daniel taking a large gulp. He wiped his lips with the back of his hand.

'I knew mum was having you. I had this feeling. Sort of a sixth sense.'

They had rarely talked about this sixth sense before, but both knew that they were somehow different. When unexplained incidents happened they would both realise what had happened, it required no explanation, and they would just accept it.

'So you loved me before I was even born.' Todd smiled.

Daniel laughed. 'If I knew what a pain you were going to be, I would have stayed in Malta.' They both laughed. Daniel finished his beer. 'Want another?' he asked. Todd gulped his beer. 'Sure, if you're paying.'

Daniel sat down with the two beers. Each took a sip. 'Six months ago,' Daniel said, 'he was released after seventeen years. I knew that, the day he was released, before mum told us.'

'What's this about, Daniel?'

'I don't really know, Todd. I was hoping maybe you might make sense of it'

'Me?' he looked startled. Todd didn't want to tell him about the night he sat in his wardrobe, the feeling of despair that came over him whilst he sat in the darkness.

'What do you think?'

'He knows where we live, Daniel. If he had wanted to find us he would have come by now. There will be injunctions and all sorts of things against him'

'Do you think an injunction is going to stop him coming?'

'No.'

'I don't necessary want to find him. I need to know.'

'Know what?' asked Todd

'Where this gift came from, because, Todd, if it comes from him it's more evil then we think.' Silence.

'Leave it, Dan. Some people in this world have odd powers. Some gift, that's all it is, and let's be honest, it doesn't amount to much.' He took a sip of beer. 'Don't involve him'

'For my little brother, you talk a lot of sense, and you're probably right.'

'Probably?'

Daniel leaned forward, his face inches from Todd's. 'I have this feeling that we aren't going to have a choice!' The funny thing was Todd had that feeling too.

Chapter 11

They had driven over the Severn Bridge towards Bristol, Mickey driving, Kate in the passenger seat, Wendy semiconscious on the back seat. The kidnappers in the front seats were on a high. They had taken the gag off Wendy, scared that she was going to vomit and choke, as she didn't seem to be too well. Katy hoped that they hadn't overdone it with the chloroform. Wendy grabbed the air in her lungs as if it was her last breath, breathing heavily. She was scared. She shivered. *Where is Todd?* she asked herself. Bill had promised the two of them a spliff each if they managed to do this one thing.

Mickey and Kate lived together on the same floor as Bill. They were both drug users, whom Bill had quickly befriended. The lovers were scared of Bill. He had built a reputation as a hard man in what was really a tough neighbourhood, so that had been no easy feat. It was rumoured that he was a leg breaker for the local drug lord, who called upon Bill's services when debts needed to be collected. This paid handsomely; breaking legs was something that he enjoyed, amongst other things.

'Bill's going to be so pleased.' Kate said with a smile upon her grubby face. As she turned towards Mickey, revealing two missing teeth.

'Sure is.' Mickey looked in the rear view mirror. Wendy was stirring on the back seat. *She's hot.* He thought. 'If I pull over, will you drive?' Mickey asked Kate.

'Why?'

'She's hot! I want to do her before she wakes.'

'Aren't I enough for you? She thumped Mickey in the arm. 'You always let Bill fuck you.'

'That's just to keep him sweet. Anyway, Bill will go mad.'
'He won't know. She's still out of it. She won't feel a thing.'
'I know what that's like.' she replied, and burst out laughing.
'Fuck you!' He ripped through the gears. Katy looked at the
back seat. Wendy was stirring and trying to sit up.

'Better not.' she said, 'looks like the bitch is awake. Maybe
Bill will let you, as a reward.'

They drove a further five miles, Wendy gaining her senses
all the time. She could hear them talking, something about
doing her. Wendy shivered. She wasn't sure whether that was
because she was scared, cold, or the effect of the drugs used
on her. She began to cough, and sat up slowly. Things were
becoming a bit clearer now. She remembered putting the
rubbish out, then being bundled into a car. *Have I been
kidnapped?* She asked herself. Her mind was confused. Her
head hurt. She wanted Todd. She wanted to know what was
happening.

'Who are you? Where are you taking me?' she stuttered
Katy looked around, smiling her toothless smile. 'Just be a
good little girl and you'll be okay. Just be quiet or I will let
Ginger-top here fuck you.'
Both kidnappers laughed. A tear trickled down Wendy's
cheek.   They pulled up outside the block of flats where Bill
was waiting. A tower block which looked as if it was standing
on waste ground. A twenty-storey block of flats which at one
time had been the answer to Britain's housing problems.

'We build them high. Create a hundred homes on one site.'
the people responsible had said, 'a new wave of living. A life
style to be savoured. The answer to all our housing problems.'
More than thirty percent of them had been torn down since the
sixties' revolution of high storey homes. Most had never been

64

maintained; some would no longer comply with current health and safety regulations. This particular block consisted of a hundred and eight homes, less than sixty were occupied. There was rubbish strewn everywhere, and several members of gangs were wandering around, smoking and swearing. Outside the tower block stood a burnt-out car, with a group of young children playing on it. The gangs were familiar with the car, familiar with the occupants.

No one seemed to really notice as the kidnappers pulled Wendy out of the car. She was unsteady on her feet for a moment. The fear inside her grew, but she somehow knew that if she was going to get out of this she had to keep her composure.

'Just walk towards the flats, bitch. Any shouting and Ginger top here will slit your cute little throat. We'll be right here with you.'

Wendy surveyed the situation *Even if I shout, I don't suppose anyone would take notice.* She thought, *but if I go in there, then I am finished.*

She looked at her options, whilst both kidnappers stood beside her, running should be easy as she doubted that they'd catch her. They both looked as if their bodies had been racked by drugs. She surveyed the area. The best place to run would be towards the burnt-out car, down the side of the tower block and towards the other tower blocks. Other than the children, there didn't seem to be anyone else around that area. She slowly walked with her kidnappers. She could see that she was about thirty metres from the tower block entry. She could read the rusted sign above the door. It read 'Sandfield Point.' She would remember that, although at that particular moment she wasn't sure why. The car with the kids playing in it, was ten metres to her right. *It's now or never.* She thought. She had regained some strength. She was fit. She trained regularly. Now was the time.

Wendy ran. Her mind seemed to move faster than her legs, she was drowsy, drowsier then she realised. She was afraid, but she ran as if her life depended on it. *Because,* she thought, *it probably did.*

In what seemed no time at all, she was past the car and moving towards the side of the building, before her kidnappers even realised what was happening.

At that particular moment, Wendy thought she was going to make it. She thought she was free. She coughed and spluttered, her head ached, she wanted to be sick, but she still found the strength to run. 'What the fuck!' said Mickey.

'Don't just stand and watch, you silly fucker. Go get her.' Mickey grunted, 'Why do I have to do all the work?' He ran after Wendy not waiting for an answer. Wendy ran as fast as she could. Now she was flagging. Her head felt dizzy and she felt even more sick. She knew she had got a good head start on them so maybe that was enough. She ran round the side of the tower block and round to the back, straight into a closed off area where they kept all the wheelie bins. She immediately noticed the putrid smell.

'Shit!' she shouted, and turned around, not seeing the blow coming, just feeling the pain in her jaw, followed by the pain as she hit the ground and felt the boot connect with her ribs. She screamed out loud, and then vomited.

'Told you not to run, you bitch!' shouted Mickey as he kicked her again in the ribs. 'Now I am going to fuck you!' Wendy still lay on the floor, the pain from her jaw and stomach causing her to scream, not really believing it was happening to her.

But it was real. It was happening, and nobody was going to save her. She curled into a ball, trying to stem the pain. Mickey grabbed her legs and pulled them straight, trying to get to the button on her jeans. Wendy kicked out, he lost his grip. Wendy curled up again. This time Mickey pulled her legs and sat on them. The pain was intense. She was sure she was going to pass out. She could feel the weight of him on her legs.

'Todd!' she cried.

She could feel Mickey tugging at her jeans, but by now she had no fight in her. She tried hitting him off, as he sat on her, but her punches were feeble. She stopped. She didn't want to fight anymore. She couldn't fight anymore. Then, as if by a miracle, she felt the weight go from her legs. She curled them to her waist again, and wheezed as she tried to catch her breath.

'Get off her, you stupid fucker. What the fuck you done to her?'

It was Kate. She pulled Mickey off Wendy, by yanking his hair and pulling as hard as she could. Mickey screamed in pain. Katy had clumps of ginger hair in her hands.
'Do not touch her anymore or I'll kill you!' she screamed. Mickey lay beside Wendy, holding his head. 'Jeez! That fucking hurt. I was only grabbing her.'

'Dirty little fucker! Go tell Bill we're coming. I'll sort this.'

Mickey ran towards the front of the tower block. Wendy now sat up, her knees curled into her stomach. The need to vomit had now passed, but she still hurt an awful lot. Katy sat beside her, stroking her head, thinking about what a sorry mess she had got into.

'It's okay.' she said softly. 'I won't let him touch you. I'll chop his cock off if he does.'

'What's happening?' Wendy stuttered, even more confused, now that one of her kidnappers was consoling her.

'We just need you to meet someone, that's all. He wants to see you' 'Who?'

'Your father-in-law.'

'I'm not married.'

'Yeah, right. I'll help you get up.' Kate said

A woman in her sixties came out with a black sack, looked at the girls, went over to the wheelie bin and put the sack inside. She closed the bin, and stared again. Her eyes met Wendy's. The lady went back inside.

'What the fuck kept you?' Bill was angry, his eyes popping out of his head,

'I tried your mobile. Why didn't you answer?

All three noticed his clenched fists, his red face, and his eyes wide. The three of them just stood there, all afraid, all wishing now that they were somewhere else.

They had finally taken Wendy to the flat, after the initial fight and the carnage that followed. Wendy gave no further struggle; the fight had gone out of her. She needed to keep her energy, for what, she didn't know, but she knew she needed to be strong. She was still unsure what was happening.

I know these people think I am somebody's wife. What would they want with her? She thought.

Now she stood there in a flat that looked as though it should be demolished, her kidnappers beside her, each holding an arm, and a mad man in front of her. She found it incomprehensible. Perhaps it was a nightmare, and soon she would wake up in Todd's arms and he would tell her that everything was fine. A couple of hours ago she had been

68

looking forward to a girlie night in with her mum. Now she was here, wherever here was. She thought of her mum, who would be worried when her daughter didn't come home. She would get hold of Todd, who would find her, and everything would be okay.

She looked around the room. It had very little furniture, the plastic 1970's sofa, the coffee table full of cigarette ends and remnants of spliffs, the television that looked as if it could only ever show black and white, but the smell! That was the worst thing. She thought that whenever she died, she hoped it would be in a field full of bluebells, with Todd by her side. She did not want to die in a place like this. Her mouth was dry. Her body ached. She did not want to die here. Not now. Not alone. Kate spoke first. She sat on the edge of the coffee table which almost tipped over. She slid across a bit, knocking empty lager cans to the floor. She rolled her tongue around her mouth, trying to moisten her lips before she spoke. She was now nervous, perhaps for the first time, comprehending what they had done. To begin with, it just seemed a bit of fun, and the promise of a spliff seemed to make it all worthwhile. Now she was nervous. No not nervous, she was scared.

'She ran.' she said, pointing at Wendy, though it was obvious who she meant. 'I had to catch her, and drag Mickey off her, as he tried to shag her.' She gulped, her eyes went to the floor, 'It wasn't my fault, Bill.' she added.

Mickey couldn't quite believe what he was hearing. He tried to object. He muttered some words that didn't make sense. Mickey was afraid. Bill stood, incensed like a madman. His body shook, his fist clenched.

Your son's wife! You're going to let him get away with that? Asked the voice in his head, the voice of his father, whom he had pushed down the stairs all those years ago and left him to die.

Mickey was just about to protest. As he was beginning to get his words right, the fist hit him in the jaw, followed by another punch full on the nose. He didn't see it coming. As he fell to the floor, he wasn't sure which came first, the pain, or the feeling of his nose splattering across his face.

It had been pure instinct to Bill. His fist flew fast. He had lost none of his speed. He hadn't really known he was going to hit Mickey. It was the voice in his head that had told him, the voice of his dear father who had raped and abused him all those years ago, and had made him the man that he now was. Wendy let out a shriek as Mickey hit the floor, immediately wishing she hadn't. She put a hand over her mouth like a naughty child. Katy got up and rapidly grabbed Wendy's arm, not sure whether she was supporting herself or the girl beside her. She just needed to do it. This reaction shocked Katy. She had seen Bill angry before. She had even seen him knock out a guy with one punch. But this was different. This was like he was possessed. It scared her. Feeling wet between her legs she realised she had wet herself. The girls grabbed each other in fright as Mickey hit the floor. Bill drew his foot back and kicked Mickey in the head as hard as he could. The noise made a sickening sound, and for a moment it looked as if Mickey's head was going to leave his body. The force of the kicked rocked his head. There was no further movement from Mickey. There was no noise. The girls stood, huddled together, for the moment friends, needing each other's support.

Bill told the girls to sit down, which they did, sitting on the seventies sofa. Bill looked at the lifeless body lying on the floor. He nudged it with his foot. He was content that Mickey would no longer bother them. Blood started to pool on the floor

70

from the smashed nose. Bill went over to the sofa; put his hand around Wendy's face, stroking her hair, touching her lips. Wendy sat, scared, but knew she had to keep herself together. Katy just looked on. Wendy didn't speak or move, nor did she try to move Bills hand. She just sat and stared him full in the eye, her lips quivering. She tried to stop the trembling, but realised she had no control. At that particular moment she thought she was going to die. Bill caressed her face. He hadn't really noticed her beauty when she first walked in. but now he could see it, a hidden beauty. When you saw such a beauty, like no other, he realised his son, Daniel, had done all right for himself, a bit younger that what he had imagined, but very tasty.

'If anyone's shagging this bitch it's me.' he said.

'I don't fuck on the first date,' Wendy replied, not believing those words actually came out of her mouth. They sounded clear and confident, but inside she was shivering with fear. She felt as if it was someone else who had spoken those words while she moved her mouth in time. For a stupid moment she thought about a ventriloquist. Why? She didn't know.

Bill smiled, somewhat shocked. 'A feisty one, uh. I like feisty.' He bent down and kissed her. Wendy almost recoiled at the smell of his breath, but she resisted. He stood back up and rubbed his groin.

'Maybe Daniel and I can have a threesome.' he said, laughing rather a bit too loud.

He picked up a cigarette and lit it, blowing a thick plume of smoke in her face.

Oh my god! Thought Wendy, *He thinks I'm Becky. This is Todd's dad.*

She shivered. She couldn't tell him who she was. She would have to play along with it. She mustn't make him angrier. She knew the full history of Bill Fenton. Todd had told her everything, from the visits to Marie Rose, to Bill leaving his wife, and killing a young lad, the time he had spent in jail. She also knew at this moment no one would be looking for him, as he had been freed.

'Take your clothes off.' Bill said.

'No.'

'Take them off.'

'No.'

Bill dropped to his knees in front of Wendy. They were now nose to nose. His breath made her want to vomit. She stared into his eyes defiantly. *Show him you're not scared,* she thought, *if you look away, he'll know you're scared.*

Bill fumbled in his pocket for his flick knife. He took it out, and opened the blade. The swish of it made Wendy jump. Now it was the blade on which her eyes were transfixed. She thought of her mum. She thought of Todd. She thought of her dad. *Where the fuck did that one come from?* She thought.

'I'll say this once, and only once.' Bill said, 'The next choice you make could be the difference between life and death.' He coughed. Spit was on his chin. He wiped his chin with the back of his hand, looked at his hand and wiped it on his trousers. He was having fun.

Katy still sat beside Wendy, more scared then she had ever been. She didn't want to be part of any murder, any kidnapping. She wanted it to all go away like some bad dream. Tears rolled down her cheeks. She was paralysed with fear.

'Now I want you to take your clothes off, all of them. I'll stand back and I promise I won't touch you. I can't have you wearing those clothes. I need them.' The knife was an inch from her face.

Wendy bit her lip until it hurt, tears rolled down her face. She hadn't meant to cry but she had no control over these tears.

'What will I wear?' she said. A small speck of blood appeared on her bottom lip.

Bill stood, withdrawing the knife, he still held it in his hand, the blade open.

'Good point.' he said. 'Can't have you sitting around all naked, can we? Katy!' he shouted.

Katy came out of her trance. She looked as if she had seen a ghost.

'Yes Bill?' she stammered.

'Get in the bedroom, and get her some of that garbage that you wear.'

Katy stood up. *You're such a good dresser,* she thought, wishing she hadn't even thought it. She went into the bedroom, and came out with a sweater and jeans. She handed them to Bill,

'Shoes!' he said.

Katy went back and returned with some trainers.

'Now fucking change!' he said as he tossed the clothes to Wendy

'Can you look away, please.' she asked, trying to be respectful, rather than demanding. He told Katy to get a towel, which she did and held it as Wendy changed. The girls exchanged faint smiles as she changed. *She's scared.* Wendy thought, realising that she had to befriend her, get Katy on her side. That was maybe her only chance, their only chance. The jumper smelled, and the jeans were too big but that was the least of her problems for now, she looked at the grubby sweaty trainers. How she dreaded putting them on her feet.

'No shoes yet,' said Bill, 'sit on the floor in front of the radiator'

Wendy did as she was told. Bill pulled her hands in front of her, cable-tying them together.

'Lie down.' he told her.

She did so. With a number of cable-ties he fastened one foot to the radiator pipe. He sat Wendy up, so that she now sat beside the radiator, her leg bound to it, and her hands tied in front of her. He knelt beside Wendy, the knife in his hand. She wanted to say goodbye to everyone she loved. One leg was still free. *If I'm going to die here,* she thought, *I'm going to give a hell of a kick before I go.*

'Again, this is the most important choice you'll have to make,' he smiled, 'and, you know, keep making the right choices and you'll soon be home with Daniel.'

Somehow she didn't believe it, and it was Todd she wanted. Todd and her mum and where did that feeling of her dad come from?

'I'm going to cut your leg a little, not a lot, but it will hurt. It will not be dangerous, nor will it leave any damage. Do you understand?'

Wendy nodded. Bill had cut her leg, even before she nodded, just above the ankle, a two inch long cut, just deep enough to draw blood. Wendy bit her lip drawing more blood from where she had bitten it earlier. *Be brave,* she thought, *don't cry.* A single tear streamed down her face. Bill then got hold of Wendy's clothes and smothered her blood into the top and jeans which she had worn when she entered the flat. There wasn't a lot of blood, but it was enough for what he wanted. He threw the clothes into the corner. 'Wasn't so bad, was it?' he said.

He told Katy to clean up the cut. Katy did as she was told, using some tissue from the toilet. When she had finished, she asked Bill, 'What do we do now?' her voice shaky.

'You and me, my little scruff bag, are going to fuck like rabbits. We'll show Miss Prim here what she's missing!'

That was the last thing Katy wanted, but knew she had to go along. She was just as frightened as Wendy. It had all gone wrong. Bill had lied. It was never meant to be like this. She thought of her choices, and realised there weren't any.

For the next twenty minutes, Wendy mostly closed her eyes and tried to drown out the noises. The lovers were making out on the settee, and she had to cut it out of her mind. If she looked the other way, all she could see was the lifeless body of her kidnapper. *I hope he isn't dead,* she thought. She sat there, eyes tightly closed trying to think of nice things, but the thoughts wouldn't come. She squeezed her eyes as tight as she could, as if somehow that would shut out the noise as well. With closed eyes she waited. In her mind she could see Todd. Oh how she wished he would visit his wardrobe. The wardrobe would help him, that's what he always told her. The wardrobe could see things.

Chapter 12

It was knocking on for 6.30, when Daniel had made his way home. The effects of the beer were prominent, but in a nice way. Having had more beer then he intended with his kid brother, he was thinking how he enjoyed it, and how they must do it more often. It had been a good day. He had met the Chief Inspector of the Gwent Constabulary, Simon Goldstone. A brilliant name for a Chief Inspector Daniel had thought, like something out of an action movie. The inspector had been thinking of investing in a company up north that specialised in solar panels.

'Solar is the future!' the inspector had said. Daniel advised him against it and said he should keep his money nicely tucked away in that Swiss account, pointing out that the future was orange. The inspector didn't quite get that.

Chief Inspector Simon Goldstone was a betting man, having a few contacts in the horse racing industry. He had given Daniel a tip, a horse called 'Morning Glory' in the 1.15 at Doncaster. Daniel had put £20 on it, and the horse romped home at 4-1, netting him a £100. He had become good friends with the Chief, and respected him for becoming the youngest Chief Inspector in the Gwent force's history at the age of forty six. Now into his third year as inspector, he had been initially concerned about his dealings with Daniel. While tax avoidance wasn't illegal, it was certainly unethical for a chief inspector to avoid his taxes, not paying his share to the treasury, but the assurances Daniel had given, made it quite clear that everything would remain on the quiet. He greatly admired Daniel, thinking he would make a fine police officer or politician.

Daniel and the chief inspector met quite regularly in a Newport Bar for afternoon drinks, along with a sergeant, Tracy Bates, a one-time Olympian at the age of seventeen. She had been a keen cyclist, and that was her chosen sport. Alas, the medals had eluded her, and it was apparent that, although she was a fine athlete, she was never destined to go to the top. She joined the force at the age of twenty. Tracey was a redhead, extremely pretty with boobs that always seemed to arrive before her. She had been a sergeant for four months now, gaining promotion just before her twenty sixth birthday. Daniel was pretty sure that Tracy had slept her way to the top. *And why not,* he had thought, *with tits like hers. I certainly would have.* What Daniel didn't know was that Tracy had earned her promotion the conventional way, through hard work and dedication, and the only person she was interested in sleeping with was Daniel.

Yes, it had been a good day, with an early finish from work. Daniel wasn't office based. He did his business from home, and visited his clients at their chosen venue, which very often was 5 star extravagance. A few pints with Todd, a nice but concerned chat with his kid brother, spending some time with his mum, and now, a bit later than expected, due to one or two extra pints of John Smiths, he was strolling home to Becky, his lovely Becky, oh, and a £100 up he thought. Yes it had been a good day.

That was about to change. He had texted Becky to say he was on his way home. She had moaned about being hungry, as she was waiting for him to come home, so that they could eat together. Now it was late and she didn't feel like cooking anything, so she texted that she was betting he had eaten at his mum's and wasn't hungry. Daniel answered the text, saying he was hungry and telling Becky to get her glad rags on and he would take her out for something to eat. Becky kind of knew that he would do that. She could read him like a book. She was already changed and ready.

Becky was from Devon, having met Daniel at a festival a few years back. The distance between them, while not too great, the road system being such as it was, it could take half a day to get out of Devon, so the travelling had become an obstacle. Finally, Becky made the decision to move to Ashbourne with Daniel, only he had to ask her. After three months of dropping hints he did ask, and she had never looked back. She loved Ashbourne, and they would regularly go back and visit her family. Whilst enjoying the glorious sights of Devon, it was a win win situation, she thought.

About half way through the ten minute walk from his mother's house to his own, his phone jangled. He presumed it was Becky texting, asking where he was. Patience had never been her strong point. He laughed to himself as went to look at his phone, he took the phone out of his pocket; flipped the case, the Blackberry told him it was a picture message.

Chapter 13

Bill had finished his bit of rough and tumble as he called it. Katy was in the bathroom, having a much needed wash. She had slept with Bill many times in the past; to keep him sweet, or in exchange for some dope or E. Sometimes she had even enjoyed it, but today it had disgusted her, making out like that, in front of a stranger tied to the radiator, and probably a dead body in the form of Mickey, her supposed boyfriend. Her feelings for Mickey weren't strong, but she certainly didn't want to see him dead, in this case, literally to see him dead. She thought Bill had changed. He used to be fun, but since they had gone down the road of kidnap, he had changed. She wanted out. Just get out of the apartment, phone the police, tell them about Mickey. Okay, they would probably arrest her for her part in the kidnap, but she would tell them it was all Bill's idea, and if she didn't go through with it, he had threatened to kill her. That would work. She could tell them how she escaped and phoned the police straight away to save Wendy, and maybe Mickey, if he was still alive, although he hadn't moved since Bill had knocked him senseless. *She would be a hero,* she told herself, and the more she thought about it, the more the idea appealed. She smiled to herself. She liked this thought. It was clever. Her head was buzzing now. Oh, how she would love a smoke. She got dressed.

'I'll just bell him, let him know I'm popping home to get some stuff.' and run for it, Why would he think that was strange. It happened all the time. *I am going to be a hero,* she told herself. She smiled to herself. She grew confident. It would all turn out right in the end.

Bill approached Wendy with a big grin on his face, 'Did you enjoy that?' he asked, 'That could be you.'

The thought disgusted her. Her face was tear-stained and she needed a wee. The clothes she wore smelt. She smelt. Bill untied her, told her to go and sit on the sofa. She did as she was told, right to where the bit of rough and tumble had just taken place. She wandered over gingerly. Bill pushed her on to the sofa, his strong hands on her chest, forced her to gasp. For a moment Bill felt one of her small breasts. He liked that, copping a feel when it wasn't expected. Wendy sat, falling onto the sofa, hoping beyond hope that she wasn't sitting in anything that they had just produced. She felt sick again and really thought she was going to vomit, but somehow she kept it down. She had remembered the name of the building she was in, Sandfield Point. If she could get to the phone and just text either Daniel or Todd that name, they would Google it, and come to rescue her. All she would need was five seconds and two words, or perhaps get Katy to do it. She seemed scared now, but she had Bill's trust. If she could just get Katy to send a text, then everything would be okay.

Bill was looking through Wendy's iPhone which he had taken from her when she first arrived at the flat. He was looking through the list of contacts and made an 'ah' sound when he came across what he was looking for. He then turned to the pile of clothes that Wendy had earlier been forced to remove, now splattered with bits of her blood, which had dried a deep crimson on her clothes. Bill took a photo, examined it. 'Yep, that will do' he said aloud.

He typed the following words in the text box 'Do you recognise these, Daniel?' then sent the picture and message to his son.

Katy came out of the bathroom, saw Wendy was now untied and sitting on the sofa, which she thought was a good thing. Bill had his back to her. He seemed to be fiddling with a phone, as if he was taking a photo. She smiled at Wendy, and Wendy swore that Becky had winked at her. *Maybe there is a ray of hope,* Wendy thought. Wendy smiled back, but it came out more of a grimace. Katy licked her lips. Her hands were sweating. She wiped them on her jeans. She rolled her tongue round the inside of her mouth. *I must not sound nervous,* she thought, *this could work.*

'I'm just going to pop home to get some more clothes.' she said, then added 'do you want me to get you anything, my sex bomb?' She liked that. She thought that was good. She felt more confident now. Soon she would be a hero, and, as the brain sometimes works in strange ways, she imagined that when the hero bit had worn off, she would take up acting.

Bill had finished sending the message. 'You aren't going nowhere unless I say so.' he said. Katy sat down next to Wendy, her dream of stardom now faded into the back of her frightened mind. The girls looked at each other, defeat etched on their faces, the dread slowly creeping over them. Bill had locked the flat door with a key, to make sure they wouldn't escape. He got an old rucksack from the bedroom. The girls watched as he filled the rucksack with four bottles of water, a six-pack of Aero's, some cannabis, a bag of white tablets which neither girl was sure what they were for, but what frightened them most was the hand gun that Bill took from a drawer. He checked the chamber, then also put that into the rucksack which he closed. He took his wallet out of his pocket. He looked inside, over £400 in twenties. Nodding, he put it back in his pocket, looked around the room as if surveying what else he needed to pack. *Is he leaving us here?,* both girls

81

thought. Just as that thought crossed their minds, he turned with a big grin on his face. He took out his knife, showing it to the girls, as if to say this is what you get if you mess about.

'Follow me.' he said.

The girls stood and walked slowly towards Bill. He unlocked the door of the flat, opened it and walked into the stairwell. No one heard Mickey stir as they left the flat. The corridor was empty. Even though it was still daytime, it was dark. Most of the light bulbs were out, leaving one just flickering by the stairwell, which made the building seem eerie. It felt like the building was swallowing them up. Wendy thought of the horror films that she and Todd used to stay up late to watch, where the girls would be captured or hunted by the bad man. In those films one always survived. She just hoped it was her. She didn't want to be a star in this horror film. She wanted to run. Surely running would be better than this, but instead of walking down the stairs they walked up. She could smell the stench of urine, vomit and cannabis. She thought that if the people in the building lived like this, then they really had no chance. Bill seemed happy as he took the girls up. He was whistling as he held the knife. This was going well. He was having fun.

Chapter 14

Daniel didn't recognise the phone number, certainly not one of his contacts. He opened the message and found himself looking at a picture of a pile of grubby, stained clothes on an equally grubby carpet. For a moment he thought it was some joke and the caption would explain all. The photo was in colour and the stains looked a bit like dried blood, but he couldn't be sure. He read the text accompanying the picture, 'Do you recognise these, Daniel?'' For a moment he just stood there looking at the picture, the John Smith's still slowing up his thought process. Then his brain seemed to engage and click into gear. His heart skipped a beat. A thousand emotions went through his head. He immediately thought of Becky, but he knew she was safe at home. *Or was she safe?* he thought. It took him less than a minute to run home in a blind panic. He burst into the house. He could hear the radio on in the kitchen, someone singing along to a tune he did not recognise. Within seconds, he burst the kitchen door open causing Becky to scream. This made him feel worse. He looked at his gorgeous wife and hugged her so tightly that Becky thought he was going to crush her. His heart was still racing. For a single moment he had thought the worst. Now she was safe. They were safe.

She struggled to get free. 'You're choking me.' she gasped. 'I can't breathe.' He released her. *She loved all the hugs and kisses but this was going over the top,* she thought.

'What the hell's up with you?' she asked, feeling a bit scared now.

He was shaking, sweating; his eyes looked frightened, as if he had just seen a ghost. For a split second Becky thought he looked like a frightened, lost child. They stood there looking at each other, Becky noticing how vulnerable he looked. He was still shaking. She had never seen him like this.

Daniel struggled with his words. 'I don't know, babe.' was all he could say

Becky drew him closer, put her arms around him laid her head on his chest.

'You sure you're okay? You're frightening me, Daniel. '

For all the years she had known him, Daniel had never shown fear. Nothing seemed to faze him. He was big, strong and handsome. He was a big hitter in the world of tax avoidance and had powerful contacts. Everyone in Ashbourne Estate knew him, and no one would dare cross him. That knowledge made her feel safe. Even when he wasn't there, he made her feel safe. Now she was scared.

Daniel regained his composure. He realised he was frightening Becky and that he probably looked stupid. What Becky didn't know was that he had this inner feeling. His sixth sense had told him something was wrong. Something had gone bad. He had thought his Becky was gone, but here she was, standing in front of him, as beautiful as ever. He felt a fool but he wasn't wrong. He kissed her full on the lips and then he showed her his phone.

Chapter 15

They only walked up three flights and down the corridor, where Bill opened the second door to the left and nodded for the girls to go in. They did, neither girl seeing any option. There was no other option. The man pointing the way with the knife told them there was nowhere to escape to. They were pushed into the living room of the flat, which was a lot better furnished than the one they had just left. A leather sofa, a nice carpet, a sideboard which appeared to be stocked with drinks, and a modern telly was on, showing Coronation Street.   They were met by a black man, six feet two inches. Jezz, who had a smile that lit up his face.

'Yo bro!' he said to Bill. Bill responded with the high five. 'Yo Katy!' Katy did not answer. 'This the chick then, bro, is it?'

Wendy looked at the guy. She noticed his accent was very English.

'That's her.' said Bill

'I'm going to enjoy looking after this one.' he said. He grabbed Wendy and kissed her full on the lips. 'She's cute.' Wendy took a half pace back wiping her lips.

'She's not to be touched, Jezz.' Bill said.

Jezz nodded, smiled an even bigger smile. 'No harm in looking though.' then he laughed.

Jezz told the two girls to sit on the sofa. They did as they were told. Wendy took Katy's hand as they sat, not just for reassurance, but she was sure if she was to get out of this mess Katy would be the one to help her. Katy took her hand. They looked at each other and smiled.

'It will be okay,' Wendy whispered and gripped Katy's hand more tightly.

The two men were talking by the flat door. The girls couldn't hear what was said, Bill had told Jezz to treat Katy as a hostage, because she could not be trusted. He wasn't sure how long he would be, but to look after the two girls until he got back. He handed Jezz £200. Bill left. Jezz locked the door and pocketed the key.

'Right!' he said. The two girls jumped. He went into the bedroom and came out with some clean clothes that he had got earlier for Wendy. Bill had given him the money to get some clothes. That was all Bill told him. It was a good earner for Jezz. Two pairs of jeans, two jumpers, two sets of underwear and what appeared to be a pair of hiking boots. He chucked the clothes to the girls. Wendy got the boots. He pointed to the shower room.

'Take a shower.' he said. 'There's clean towels in there. Change your clothes. You're stinking the flat out. I'll put a pizza in. Sorry, it's only frozen but there's enough for us all. I got a few cans as well, if you fancy one.' He smiled.

'Put your dirty clothes in the washer. You really are stinking my flat out, and I like it nice. Ya know what I mean?'

The girls looked at each other dumbfounded. Katy had seen Jezz a few times. He had been at Bill's when she and Mickey visited. She guessed he was one of the heavies who did the collecting, but why was he being so nice?

'Thank you.' Wendy said, 'that's very kind.'

Jezz flung his hands about as if dismissing it, as if it was the way he always treated people. Truth was Jezz Dwayne was one of life's true gentleman, and a very loyal friend to have. When he did go collecting drug money with Bill, it used to make Bill smile that Jezz would apologise before having to use the baseball bat. A gentleman with attitude and, if he had a weakness, it was girls.

The girls went into the shower room, thankful for having a chance to pee. Wendy sat on the toilet, as Katy stripped and ran the shower, testing the water with her hands before getting in. With the sound of the shower running, drowning out their voices it was Katy who spoke first, as she stepped under the shower.

'I'm sorry for getting you involved in this.'

'So am I.' said Wendy, giving a faint laugh. 'Who's this Jezz?' she continued, 'He seems okay.'

'He is.' Katy said, as she soaped herself, 'but don't underestimate him. You think Bill is bad, well Jezz is twice as worse. The stories I've heard about him would make you cringe.'

Wendy thought for a moment. 'Well, I feel safer with him.'

'I'll never feel safe with either of them.' said Katy. 'If I thought shagging him would get us out, I would.'

She gave Wendy a stare, as if to say don't judge me. Wendy got up from the loo, and started to get undressed. 'If shagging him would get us out, I'd have a threesome.' Wendy said, and both girls laughed.

Whilst they showered and cleaned themselves up, Jezz cooked the pizza and got three cans of lager out of the fridge. Wendy got into the shower. The hot water felt good, as if it were washing away all the bad things she had been through today. She washed her hair with some Lynx. Katy changed into her clothes and sat on the toilet.

'Why did you do this?' asked Wendy, as she towelled her hair dry.

Katy sighed. She really needed some pot. It usually made her feel better.

'He lied. He told me that you were his daughter-in-law, and that he wasn't allowed to see you and he just wanted to meet you.' She rolled her eyes, as if to say what a stupid story she had fallen for. 'The chloroform was Mickey's idea. He had stolen some from somewhere or other.' She wiped a tear from her eye. 'I just went along with it. It's what I do.'

Wendy sat on the edge of the bath, dressing herself. 'Where's your parents? Do you work? Surely you don't have to live like this? Will your work be missing you? Perhaps they'll call.' 'Oh sure, they will be missing me. I specialise in £10 blow jobs. Come on, let's get some pizza.'

Chapter16

Becky looked at the phone, puzzled for a moment, then she realised what Daniel must have been thinking. They were both staring at the picture on the phone.

'Did you think they were mine?' she asked.

'I did.'

'Bless you.' She gave him a hug.

Both were still looking at the phone, reading the message 'Do you recognise these, Daniel'

Becky grabbed the phone from Daniel, used the zoom function to zoom in on the picture.

'They're not mine, but I know who they belong to.' she said.

Todd and Carol were sitting at home, watching the telly. Todd was debating whether to nip out for a pint, or go up to his room and do some writing. Carol was watching Judge Judy, when the front door burst open. They both jumped, Daniel and his wife stood there as if they seen a ghost.

'What's up?' asked a concerned Carol.

Daniel showed Todd his phone, asking him if he recognised the clothes

'Yes I do. They're Wendy's. What the fucks going on?'

Daniel explained the situation. How he had been walking home when he received the picture message. They phoned Wendy's mum, who confirmed Wendy wasn't there, and that she had been trying to ring her and was just about to ring Todd, when he rang her. They tried Wendy's phone which went straight to voicemail, Todd left a voice mail. They explained briefly to Wendy's mum what had happened. Wendy's mum told them she would be over straight away, after she had phoned the police. They sat there, impatiently waiting.

Wendy's mum would be able to confirm whether they were really Wendy's clothes, *and if she did, what then?* Daniel thought.

'Have you texted back?' Sergeant Tracy Bates asked. She was at the station at the time of the call and was about to delegate the call to another officer, until she heard the address, when she promptly took it upon herself. *Another chance to see that hunk, Daniel,* she thought. It was usual for two officers to go, so she took a rookie with her, a nineteen year old, David Stuart.

They were both now standing in Carol's front room. Carol thought the P. C. looked too young to be a policeman, and that he looked young enough to still be at school. 'Big tits' as Becky had named Tracy sat on the sofa, between Carol and Wendy's mum, Helen. Becky was thinking that Tracy was making herself too much at home. She didn't like her, and most of all, she didn't like her flashing her big tits at Daniel. Becky sat in the armchair, ashamed of herself for having those thoughts at a time of crisis. The brothers were standing up beside the window, Todd holding the phone with the picture message. The room looked cluttered with people. Daniel opened the window. A refreshing cool breeze blew in. Wendy's mother had confirmed that the picture was of Wendy's clothes, or at least looked like them. She was sure that Wendy had worn them to work that morning and explained to Sergeant Tracy Bates that Wendy always changed into her work clothes at work.

'I know the place. Lovely food in there.' Bates said, not really realising how inappropriate her words sounded. The rookie cop, Stuart, was standing by the door, taking notes. He was trying to look important, or at least trying to look as if he knew what he was doing.

'No' came the blunt reply from Daniel, Tracy Bates looked at Daniel, and smiled, showing her sparkling white teeth and the 'come to bed' eyes.

No one seemed to notice this except Becky. She noticed it. *Crisis or no crisis*, she thought. *I'll slap her in the fucking face.*

'Are you sure there's not been some mix up, and she's double-booked and just gone out with friends?' asked Bates. Everyone tried to speak at once, but Bates got the message. She leaned forward, put her hands in her lap. She was shuffling her hands, as though she was nervous. Becky noticed this. Becky noticed everything about 'big tits.'

'Todd,' she said, looking at Todd. 'Do you think she could be meeting someone else, and using her mother as an excuse?' Everyone in the room seemed flabbergasted by the question, and they all challenged the absurdity of it. Todd put his hands to his head, which felt like it was exploding. He could feel a headache coming.

'Shut up!' he shouted 'Just go look for her' he added.

'And where would I start?' she asked.

The question made Becky dislike her more. 'You're the fucking cop!' Becky said.

Sergeant Tracy Bates ignored the comment, but stared at Becky, as if to say. *Hey girl, your time will come.* The stare made Becky slightly uneasy. She slumped back in her chair thinking it would be wise if she said no more.

Helen sat in the chair, a tear coming into her eye 'Can we just find my daughter?' she asked.

Tracy Bates asked a few more questions, about Wendy's list of friends, who she may have seen or been with earlier. She explained that she could not file a missing persons report until that person had been missing for forty eight hours, and pointed out that Wendy was of an age where if she just wanted to disappear for a few days, nobody could stop her. Because of the picture, message and the unusual behaviour, a word that made both brothers angry, she would indeed notify her superiors, and in the meantime she would visit the cafe and ask some questions there, and ask to view the CCTV.

She asked Daniel to forward the picture giving him her number. As Daniel punched it into his phone, this exchange infuriated Becky. Tracy's phone beeped as she received the picture. Tracy continued that she would show the picture to the girls at work to see if indeed they were the clothes she had worn to work, Todd protested that all this was a waste of time, and they could do that whilst she could start looking. Tracy reminded him that no crime had been committed, and she was acting above the call of duty and stressed that she would do what she physically could to try and help them. In the meantime this was all she could do, as all she had was a picture of some grubby clothes.

At this point Todd wanted to hit Sergeant Bates, but he said nothing. He just wanted her to go. Wendy's mother began sobbing. Carol got up and comforted her. Tracy moved over so that Carol to sit beside her.

'Everything will be fine' Tracy said, trying to reassure her. This brought a tear to Becky's eyes. *The insensitive bitch* she thought.

The conversation went on for another ten minutes, with the rookie cop trying to keep up with everything in his note pad. As Tracy Bates walked up the path, she was thinking how clever she had been in obtaining Daniel's number.

Wendy's mother had phoned her elderly father, and also her sister who still lived with him. Her mother had passed on long ago with a heart attack. They lived in Marshfield; a picturesque village, about forty five minutes' drive away.

'They'll be here soon.' She told Carol, who took her home saying that she would stay until they arrived, and if they got any info they would contact her immediately. Helen's relations had made good time and Carol was back in her living-room shortly after.

Becky made coffee, still thinking bad thoughts about 'big tits.' She dished out the coffee, and plonked a packet of custard creams on the table. They remained unopened. No one felt like eating. They sipped their coffee and no one spoke for a good five minutes. They were all were trying to take it in. None of them realised that their world was about to be tipped upside down, and nothing would ever be the same again.

Daniel was the first to speak. 'Why send a picture of Wendy's clothes to me? Do you think they got the wrong phone?'

Todd pondered this. He had been deep in thought. He had this deep inner feeling of despair. He had had it before, and it had never been wrong.

He gave a big sigh, then spoke. 'Or the wrong girl!' They all looked at Todd.

'He mentions your name, Daniel. He knows you. He obviously thinks it's Becky he's got.'

Becky put her hand over her mouth, letting out a faint scream, realising the full horror of what Todd was saying. Her mouth had dried up. She tried licking her lips. Her whole mouth was dry. She sipped some coffee, and listened as Todd continued. 'He got your number from Wendy's phone. He's got her phone. That's why we can't contact her. He wants to hurt you, Daniel, and the only way he knows how, is through the people you love. As long as he thinks it's Becky, then maybe Wendy will be okay.'

Becky burst into tears. Carol held her hands, listening intently to what Todd was saying. 'He isn't going to hurt her. He's going to use her to get at you. We need to know what his end game is. Wendy's clever, the cleverest girl I know. She will have realised that telling him her real name will be dangerous. We will play his game,' he paused 'for now.'

Carol looked at her two sons, stunned. How could he know all this, she thought. Her stomach cramped up.

'Who?' she asked. 'Who the bloody hell are you talking about?' The two brothers looked at each other, then at their mother, who was now standing.

'Dad.' Daniel said. 'The bastard is back, just as I thought he would be.' He paused. 'I will kill him!'

Her heart sank. She fell back onto the sofa. She was shaking, not with fear but with anger. 'Becky, get me a vodka, sweetheart.' she said.

Becky went into the kitchen, and was soon back with two vodkas, one for herself.

'I won't let him ruin us.' Carol said.

Daniel went over to his mum, the strongest willed lady he had ever known. He put his arms around her and held her close. Carol could feel the strength of his arms. At that moment it made her feel safe. 'What do we do now?' she asked

'We text him back.' Daniel said, and he took the phone from Todd

'We try to find his end game, and then we finish him.' He hit reply on the phone and typed in. 'Don't hurt her, Dad. I will do whatever you ask.'

He looked at Todd, who nodded. Daniel pressed send.

Daniel took his mother's hand, and then Becky's. 'Whatever you do, don't tell the cops, and don't tell her mother. We've made one mistake already by bringing them in.'

'Do we just sit here and wait for a reply? What if he doesn't reply?' Carol asked.

'He will, eventually, and we don't just sit and wait. I have a friend on the force. He will tell me where Bill lives. I might have to go and pay daddy a visit.'

'Not on your own.' Todd said.

'Definitely not.' Carol said.

'Count me in.' said Becky.

Carol poured another vodka. Becky did the same.

Daniel got his phone out. It was time to call in a favour.

Wendy's mother, Helen, sat at her home with her father and sister comforting her. She had texted Wendy's phone three times now, but, of course, she received no reply. Her eyes were red. She hadn't really approved of her daughter's relationship with Todd. She thought they were both far too young, and she had hoped that Wendy would go to college and try to get a better education. There were murderers in that family, she had told her daughter. How much she now wished she had never said it. If she could just hold her, and tell her how sorry she was.

Meanwhile, forty five minutes away, over the Severn Bridge into England, in a run-down tower block on a council estate in Bristol. Wendy was sitting with two people she hadn't really known before today had begun. She was eating pizza, and drinking lager. Anyone who didn't know her and saw the three of them together, would simply think they were having a good time.

Chapter 17

Tracy Bates left the Fenton's with Stuart, the rookie cop. It was still only just after 8.30. The cafe stayed open until ten o'clock. She was hungry. She was supposed to finish at ten, but eating now would save her having to do something later. It was a lovely summer's evening with a slight breeze. As the sun set behind the church with its high steeple she thought how lovely it looked, and how nice this place was for a council estate. She wanted to take a photo on her phone, but she didn't, with the rookie cop there. She was feeling a bit sad. She hadn't realised that Daniel was married. So she would have to look elsewhere. *There are plenty more fish in the sea* she thought and she did have all the assets to catch them.

They drove the short distance to Ashbourne Cafe, which was fairly busy, with people eating food and drinking soft drinks. The nice evening had brought people out for their tea, or a bite to eat before going to the pub. No one was waiting at the counter to be served. Tracy told Stuart to find a seat while she ordered food. She was still feeling chuffed at getting Daniel's phone number although now she wasn't going to use it. It had annoyed Becky and she liked that. Becky was too big for her boots, and she would have to bring her down a peg or two, swearing at her like she had done, in front of Stuart, just wasn't on. After all, she was the law, and Becky Fenton was not above the law.

She ordered two burgers and fries with diet cokes, and whilst ordering she asked the cashier if the manager was available and could she have a word.

'We don't have managers. We have an owner' came the reply.

Sandy Potts, the forty six year old owner of Ashbourne Cafe liked a man in uniform but, to Sandy, a woman copper, as pretty as her, was just trouble to her mind, and asking questions could only mean one thing. There was going to be trouble on the estate tonight. The customers didn't take much notice of the two uniformed coppers, assuming they had just come in to eat. Although there was no station on the estate itself, the police from Newport very often toured the estate. They suffered abuse, but there was very rarely any trouble on the estate, which made it a favourite posting for the police.

Tracy made her way to the table where Stuart was sitting, the same table that the kidnappers had been sitting, earlier in the day. She sat beside Stuart and they opened their burger boxes and placed the chips in one side. Stuart covered his with ketchup. That disgusted Tracy.

'Takes away all the flavour.' she told him. Stuart just grunted. Sandy Potts soon followed them over, and sat opposite them, with the table now between them. She held out her hand, and introduced herself as the proprietor of Ashbourne Cafe. Both officers took her hand, introduced themselves, Tracy emphasising the Sergeant part. Tracy took a bite of her burger and put two chips in her mouth. This annoyed Sandy, as she was here to talk, not watch a busty copper eat.

When she finally swallowed her mouthful she said to Sandy 'We have come to talk to you about Wendy Cross. I believe she works here.' Sandy Potts was no fool, and Wendy was one of her best employees, and also a good friend. She loved her, and the Fenton's, as if they were her own family. If Wendy was in trouble, there was no contest whose side she would be on. *This cop's getting nowt from me,* she thought.

'And?'

So annoying, thought Tracy. She swallowed what she had put in her mouth. She licked her lips, then wiped her fingers with the paper serviette. 'I just love these burgers.' She put three chips in her mouth and, with her mouth still full, she said, 'Well, the thing is, sweetheart,' she swallowed, 'No one's seen her since she left work. It appears she hasn't arrived home.' Sandy shuffled in her chair. The conversation had taken a worrying turn, she realised.

'I am not your sweetheart.' she said sharply, 'What do you mean, she hasn't arrived home?'

'No one's seen her.' Another chip in her mouth.

'Have you checked her mother and boyfriend?'

'Of course.' Another bite of the burger.

Sandy paused for thought.

'I was on at three. Wendy finished at five. She told me she was having a night in with her mum, a bottle of wine and a DVD. She asked me to get cover and to come along. I would have, but it was too short a notice for the girls. Its summer holiday season, and I ain't hiring more staff. We all just got to chip in'. Sandy stopped, realising all this was irrelevant.

'Did you see her leave?'

'Not actually saw her. She got changed out of uniform, said goodbye, and went out the back way, because I asked her to go out to the bins before she left. She may have come back through, or gone around but that's the long way. Easier to come back through, and go out the front.'

Stuart started to speak, Tracy hushed him. He took a massive bite of his burger, sauce spilling from the sides onto the table. Both women looked at him in disgust.

'What?' he mumbled.

Directing her attention back to Sandy, Tracy asked, 'Do you have CCTV?'

'Not out the back. There's only one window, and that has bars on it. There's only the bins out there. If people are that desperate to rummage through bins, they're welcome to.'
'The front?' Tracy said sarcastically, as if she had already asked.

Sandy had now decided she really didn't like Tracy Bates, Sandy said, in a matter of fact voice, 'We have four cameras in the cafe, at different angles, and two at the front. They give good coverage, I believe. The council has one showing the street, whether it works or not I don't know. You'll have to ask them. If she left through the front, you will see her.'
'Is there anyone here now, who was on at the time? 'Asked Tracy
'No.'
'Can you give me their details? I may need to speak to them.'
'Sure.'
'May I see the CCTV?'
'Sure.'

They walked into the back room, through the kitchen, and into a store room that housed the CCTV equipment. It didn't take long for Sandy to rewind the recording to when Wendy finished. They watched her saying goodbye. The timer said 4.57.

'It may not be exact,' Sandy pointed out, 'but it's within a minute or two.'

They watched the CCTV until 5.15. Wendy was not seen again. It was obvious she had not come back into the cafe. 'Maybe she had closed the door. You can't get back in if you do that. Someone on the inside has to open it for you, or you leave it on the latch, but I tell the girls not to do that in case they forget about it.'

'I'll need copies.' Sergeant Bates said. 'Preferably, all day.'
'It will take ages. Our CCTV is the best, but putting them on disc is slow. The writer is really shit. I'll see what I can do, but I'm not making any promises.'

'I'll call for them tomorrow.'
'Yeah, that can be done. I've only got to set it up. I don't have to stand here and watch it. Can't make it go faster. Once it's done, it's done.'

'Maybe I'll go out the back way. I just want to take a look.'
'Sure, but if you want to come back in, you'll have to come round the front, or knock and hope someone hears you. I'm not leaving the door open.'

Tracy sighed. 'That won't be necessary we will be leaving.'
Sandy looked shocked. 'That's it. A young girl goes missing and that's it.'

The sergeant looked at her, confused. 'It isn't a murder inquiry, sweetheart.'

Sweetheart again. Sandy was annoyed.

'Aren't you going to ask if there had been people acting suspiciously or anything?'

'Well, were there?' Tracy said smugly.

'As a matter of fact, yes. I thought a decent copper would have asked.'

That wound Tracy up big time. She ignored the comment but, mentally, she marked Sandy's ticket.

Sandy gave the coppers a description of two people who had recently been coming into the cafe, ordering a coffee and just sitting for hours, on at least three occasions. Wendy had been on at those times and had told Sandy about them.

'They're on the tape.' she said.

Tracy thanked her, taking the list of employee's details, before she left.

Tracy was annoyed with herself. *Why the hell she hadn't asked that question?* She should have been more professional. Letting herself be caught out by a greasy spoon owner had annoyed her. Stuart had smiled secretly and smugly. It was the question he had been about to ask before Tracy shut him up. 'Fucking amateurs!' Sandy said, as she closed the door behind them, her mind wandering to concern for her best employee.

She phoned Daniel and told him all about her conversation with Tracy Bates, again calling them fucking amateurs as she did so.

Chapter 18

Bill had left the two girls with his friend, now the girl's minder, Jezz. He had one last job to do for the Governor, before he could put his plan into action. Well, it was half a plan really. Bill, not being the most organised, knew he hadn't fully thought this through. He worked on instinct, and instinct had served him well in the past, except for seventeen years in prison. That had been a mere blip. Instinct was what he was good at. The Governor, being Judge and Jury of everything that happened in the St. Paul's area, was a man of great substance. He was feared by everyone, even the police. He was a drug dealer, a loan shark, and had so many cops in his pocket he was impossible to catch. The Governor liked Bill, and Bill liked him.

'Keep going on like this, and you'll soon be my number two.' he had told Bill.

Bill thanked him, but he didn't want to be his number two. He had unfinished business, and when that business was finished he would kill the Governor and be Number One. Bill Fenton would never settle for second. He was a leader, a warrior. No. Number two would never be enough for him. He had told the Governor this would be his last job for a while. The Governor, who was British, born of West Indian descent, stood six feet seven and weighed in at twenty two stone. Being as solid as a rock was okay with him. He looked after his good employees, and, although he was surrounded by good men, he trusted Bill who proved to be one of his best. It was arranged that Bill would give the money to Jess, to pass on, minus the twenty per cent commission that Bill got. Bill thought it was easy money, and would keep him in the groove. He didn't know how long it was going to take, but he wouldn't be doing any collecting for a while. *Maybe never again,* he thought.

The place he was going to, was only a mile away from where he lived. A remarkably improved area, despite the short distance, but the Governor and his mob still had control of the area. Bill drove, and parked four hundred yards away from the block of terraced houses, whose back gardens were overlooked by allotments.

After checking that the coast was clear, he easily made it through the allotments, over the fence and into the back garden of the house he wanted. It would have been just as easy, and less conspicuous, if he had gone to the front door, but Bill liked it this way. It made the job seem more exciting. He had delusions of being a soldier, a warrior. He loved this part of the job, sneaking around unseen, and then arriving unexpectedly. The surprise on the faces was the best thing. Oh, how he loved the look on their faces. Opening the lock would have been easy. He had the tools in his bag, enabling him to do so. Very few locks held him out. It was a craft he had learned in prison, so he was somewhat disappointed to find the back door open. *People are so irresponsible,* he said to himself. He sniggered. He now stood in the living room of the two occupants of the house. It was quite nicely furnished, a large room, quite surprising, as the house had looked small from the outside.

There was a brown, leather three-piece suite, a nice oak dining table with six chairs, and a sideboard. Playing on the forty two inch plasma screen was Sky news. He was never told the names of the people he was to collect from, just their descriptions, where they would be, and what the job actually was, who to hurt and who not to. He could have easily found

103

out their names, but he neither wanted to, nor needed to, another thing the Governor liked about him. The other thing Bill was told, was the level of violence he was expected to use if they wouldn't pay. Bill could never understand the various levels, nor did it bother him too much. Pain is pain, however you look at it. That was his motto.

The first occupant of the house was a pretty blonde girl, about twenty seven years old, wearing jeans and a pink blouse with three buttons undone, showing a bit of cleavage. Bill liked that. She was sitting on the dining chair.

However, her hands were behind her back, gaffa-taped to the chair, each of her legs was also gaffa-taped to a leg of a chair, so if she tried to stand, the movement would topple her over. Her mouth was gaffa-taped, her eyes wide with fright. She breathed heavily through her nose, tears streamed down her face. She didn't even know they owed money, certainly not to the monster who now invaded her home. *But this is what happens when you can't trust people,* she thought.

The other occupant was a forty seven year old man, overweight with greying hair. He stood, frightened. He was standing beside the sofa, where he had been told to, and not to move, whilst Bill tied Blondie to the chair. That's what Bill had called her when he first burst into their home, Blondie and Fatty.

The man was not tethered in any way, nor was he about to be. The man shook as he spoke. Blondie just watched him, cursing under her breath. This was all his fault. *Look at me,* she wanted to shout. *Look at me, and it's all your fault.* She wished he hadn't tied the tape around her mouth so tightly. There was no need for that.

'£400! It was only £100's worth of crack and it's only three days late.' said Fatty.

Blondie looked on in shock and horror, but was relatively calm, given the situation. She had never done drugs, and certainly didn't want to be involved with druggies. *Who was this monster she had living with her?,* she thought. She wanted to pee. *Why does being frightened always make you want to pee?* she thought,

'Look mate,' Bill said, 'I don't make the rules. I'm just a collector. Time is money. There's expenses, my expenses. You were supposed to pay. Now it goes up.'

Fatty's shoulders drooped. He was scared, but £400 seemed way over the top. *I'm not going to pay it* he thought, *no way am I,*

'I've got £200. That's all I've got. I'll get it, then just go.'

Bill had no real patience nor tolerance in his nature. On this particular day he had no real time. He still had things to get for his journey, and he wanted to leave by morning. With this in mind, and with one swift move, he grabbed the man, pulled his hand behind his back forcing the man to his knees, allowing his free arm to stop his face from hitting the carpet.

Bill swiftly produced a pair of secateurs from the bag beside him, and with very little effort he cut off the little finger of the hand he held, Fatty screamed in pain, Blondie wanted to scream but the gaffa tape prevented her. She wasn't really expecting this much violence. She seemed to grunt through her nose, finding it hard to breathe. Bill let the man go, who held his damaged hand with his good one, and sat on the floor crying. Bill liked the sound of him crying, his finger beside him looking lost, as it no longer had a hand and four fingers as companions.

'You made me do that. I didn't want to do that, but you made me. Now I'm angry. It's just gone up to £500. Next it will be two fingers, or maybe even your cock.' He looked at Blondie.

'Then I start on her.'

Blondie nodded her head vigorously. She clearly wanted to say something. He grabbed Fatty by the hair, lifting him and plonking him on the sofa. 'Do not move.' he said.

He took the gaffe tape from Blondie's mouth. She breathed in air as if it was her last breath.

Still gasping, she said, 'There's money in the drawer. Take what you want but please don't hurt me.'

She looked at the drawer in question, guiding Bill to it with her eyes. He opened the drawer. There was about £800. He counted out £500, no more, and put the rest back.

'Sensible move, Blondie.' he said. He looked at Fatty. 'You not going to thank her then?' Fatty was still holding his hand, but the screaming had stopped.

'Thanks.' he mumbled.

'You fucking bastard!' Blondie shouted at Fatty.

Bill laughed.

She looked at Bill. 'There's another £100 if you untie me, and chuck that bastard out.'

Bill was now laughing quite loud; Fatty looked on in shock, but didn't want to protest. He needed the hospital.

Bill untied her hands. 'You can do your legs' he said. 'Can I hurt him some more?' Bill asked.

'You can do what you like to him.' she said.

He grabbed Fatty by the hair, made him hold his injured hand in the air whilst Bill got out his phone and took a picture of the damaged hand. He then escorted him into the back garden and literally threw him over the fence.

'You come back and I'll kill you.' Bill told him.

The man ran as fast as he could still holding the bleeding hand. The missing digit was still on the carpet. Bill said goodbye to Blondie, as he cupped her breast. She hit his hand away. She saw the smile on his face, then she thanked him. Bill left the flat £100 pound better off than he thought he was going to be, and he had copped a feel, and he just loved it when you copped an unexpected feel. He thought that when all this was over he might go back and pay Blondie a visit. She had liked him he thought. Yes, that's what he would do; show her what a real man was like.

Blondie was now drinking a coke, and smoking a cigarette. Her legs had not been tied at all, just made to look as if they had. She was unharmed, but she thought Bill had put the tape around her mouth too tightly. She had hardly been able to breathe. She sat on the sofa feeling exhausted. She thought that the man had done a good job and he looked a bit tasty. She kind of liked it when he touched her breast. *Different circumstances.* she thought, *who knows. I must remember to thank the Governor for getting rid of that piece of shit.* She laughed.

'The fucker will never come back now.' she said out loud. Now the tears she shed were ones of laughter. *Maybe when she thanked the Governor she might ask him the guy's name,* she thought. She put out her cigarette, got up and went for a shower.

Bill got to his car, pleased with his evening's work. Now he had to go to the hardware store. He had a lot of stuff to get for his road trip. Then he'd kip in his car. As he got into his car, the phone beeped. It was a message which read 'Don't hurt her, Dad I will do whatever you ask.'
Got him, he thought to himself, and drove away grinning like a Cheshire cat

Chapter 19

It was 9.30 by the time Daniel got over to see Chief Inspector Simon Goldstone. The police station is on the High Street of Newport, The public entrance is off a side street, which Daniel took. He walked through the two glass doors. The officer on the desk recognised Daniel and, after a phone call, told him to go up to the inspector's office. He walked up the one flight of stairs to the right of the reception area. The police station was unusually quiet, although he could hear someone shouting in the distance. *Probably from the cells* he thought. At the top of the stairs, to the right, was Simon Goldstone's office, which wasn't as flamboyantly furnished as he might have expected. A few filing cabinets, an old oak desk with a swivel chair that the inspector was now sitting in, a coffee table against the wall with nothing on it, a computer desk in the corner with an iMac on it. There were photographs on the wall that Daniel presumed were of Simon's kids and wife. The walls were painted cream, and the chair on which he sat was uncomfortable. He shuffled in his seat, feeling slightly nervous. The Chief Inspector was also concerned. Daniel had sounded desperate on the phone. He hoped it didn't have anything to do with his investments because that wouldn't be good. That wouldn't be good at all.

He pulled out a bottle of scotch and two glasses, poured two fingers into each, offering one to Daniel. They both took a sip, immediately feeling the warmth as the scotch hit their insides. The Inspector put his glass down and sat back in his chair, the feeling and the warmth relaxing him a little.

'Now then, Daniel, what's up?' he asked.

Daniel shuffled again in his chair. *Might just as well come straight out with it* he thought.

He looks nervous, which is unlike Daniel. Simon thought. It seemed like there was some kind of confession about to be made.

'I need a favour. I need you to find out where my father lives. I need to go and see him.' He leaned back in his chair, sighed, took a sip of the whiskey and waited for the answer.

Simon Goldstone leaned forward, clasping his hands together on the desk and raising his eyebrows. He hadn't been expecting this,

'Now why would you want to go and see that son of a bitch?' He sat back in his seat, curious.

Daniel didn't know what the reaction would be, but he wasn't prepared for that simple question, why? He had presumed the Inspector would just do as he asked. After all, he was making him a mint.

'It's a family thing. I just need to talk to him.'

The Inspector again leaned forward, this time taking another sip of the scotch. 'Wouldn't be anything to do with Wendy Cross, would it?'

Another question Daniel hadn't expected. 'How do you know about that?'

'It's my patch, Daniel. I know everything. How are things going with that? Have you found her?'

'Sort of. Anyway, can you do this for me?'

'Tell me why.'

'It's private.'

The inspector stood up, leaned across the desk and put his hand on Daniel's shoulder, as a father would to a son. With his hand still on Daniel's shoulder, he said

'If you tell me, I will help you, you know that, but I can't grant your favour without knowing why.' He sat down. 'If he has anything to do with Wendy Cross going missing, you have to tell me.'

'Of course it isn't. Wendy's just gone night-clubbing, or something, like your sergeant said.'

The inspector raised his eyebrows. Daniel dropped his shoulders.

'I can't tell you. Please, just do this favour for me.'

'Daniel, let me help you. Let the police help you. If you know where Wendy is, and your shit of a father has anything to do with it, for Wendy's sake,' he paused, 'and for your sake, tell me.'

He started pacing the room. Daniel watched him.

'I can't.'

'Then I can't help you.' He now stood beside Daniel, with both hands on the desk.

Daniel stood up, holding out his hand. 'Okay, Simon,' he said, 'be seeing you.' He turned to leave.

'Sit down.' the Inspector said. Daniel sat, thinking his move to leave may have worked. He knew the Inspector was now interested. The Inspector sat down. He paused, scratched his neck, loosened his tie, took another swig of scotch, and licked his lips. Daniel did the same.

'I know it's out of my jurisdiction, but I'll get some of their boys to call on him, and I'll let you know what they find. Will that do you?'

Daniel thought this was better than nothing. He knew he wasn't going to get anything else out of Simon.

'Sure,' he said. 'Thanks.' getting up to leave.

They shook hands, and just as Daniel was about to leave, the Inspector called him back. Daniel turned around to face him, the door half open.

'You said you'd like to speak to him. Is there any message you would like to give him?'

'No message.' Daniel said, and closed the door behind him as he left.

Daniel stood outside the office door wishing he hadn't bothered. He should have known Simon would have asked questions. He understood that Simon was looking after him. A feeling came over him that he had just made things worse. He knocked, and opened the office door again. Simon was sitting at his desk.

'Just forget I ever came, okay.' Simon raised his eyebrows as if to say I can't do that.

'Well if you don't, you and I are going to fall out. Keep out of it, Goldstone.'

He turned around and left once more.

As soon as the door was closed, Simon Goldstone got on the phone. He reached Sergeant Bates.

'Yes sir?'

'I need Daniel Fenton watched around the clock. I need to know everything he does, and everywhere he goes. If his brother leaves the house, follow him too. Don't let either of them out of your sight. Any overtime needed its authorised. Keep me informed. And as soon as you find Wendy Cross, I need to be the first to know.' He put the phone down. *A good man or not,* he thought *no one threatens me.*

Tracy was in her element. *I'd better do some overtime tonight* she thought. *What better job could you have then legally stalking Daniel Fenton?* She sung a Springsteen song in her head. *You can look but you better not touch* She smiled. *Work to do.*

Daniel stood out in the street. It seemed busier than it had been twenty minutes earlier. He needed to think how to get out of this mess. Seeing Goldstone was a mistake. He should have known better. Goldstone may fiddle his taxes but he was a good cop. Daniel wished he had gone to Tracy Bates instead. Now he would have to do it on his own. As he walked to his car, he knew he had to take his father down.

Chapter 20

Mickey Bolan had been stirring for the last thirty minutes. Now he was almost fully conscious. He sat, propped up against a wall, near a pile of clothes with blood stains on them. He wasn't sure what had happened, but remembered that Bill had hit him. He couldn't remember hitting the floor. He couldn't remember anything after that blow. His head hurt like buggery, his jaw hurt, his mouth and nose had been bleeding. There seemed to have been a lot of blood, but it had stopped now. That was good. He thought his head might explode. It was the worst headache he could ever remember having, far worse than any hangover he had ever had.

As he focussed, he could see that the flat was empty. They had all gone, and that bitch, Kate, she had just left him there. For all she cared, he could be dead. There was blood on him, and there was blood on the clothes that lay beside him. Who else had Bill hurt? Then he recognised the clothes as being the ones worn by the bitch that they had kidnapped. *I hope Bill hasn't killed her* he thought, *I need some me time with her*. He wished it was Katy who had died for leaving him there. Both the bitches would get it. He would make sure of that.

He managed to get into the kitchen, where he turned on the tap, and put his mouth under it. That felt good. He let the water run over his face. It hurt to begin with, then it felt good. He didn't think anything was broken. He worked his jaw, it hurt, but seemed to function okay. *Won't be eating steak for a while* he thought. Then he tried to remember the last time he ate steak. He couldn't. He tried to remember the last time he ate, realising it was that morning. He looked around for some dope or cigarettes. He only found a small amount of vodka. He poured it into a glass, and sat on the sofa. His head still hurt.

He was hoping the Vodka might relieve it, but he knew he would need much more than half a glass full.

Mickey Bolan had a family no more than eighteen miles away, south of where he lived. His parents lived in a three-bed semi, with his sister, Jude. He had left home when he was sixteen. He was now twenty four. He had been fed up with the house rules and his father's strictness. His father should have realised that these days everyone was into pot and crack. When his father had found the crack in his room, a big argument started. His father told him that he had to leave if he didn't sort his act out. That had been eight years ago. He had only seen his parents twice since then, and both times they had tried to persuade him to come home. Living rough was okay. He didn't have to work and he was soon given a flat in St. Paul's. *Mind you, there were plenty available* he thought. Most people just broke in, and took possession, but he was there legitimately. The rent was paid by the benefits agency. It was his home and he could do what the fuck he liked, and he did. He took drugs, and moved Katy in. She was okay. He liked her, and she gave him sex whenever he wanted it. All she wanted was some dope, the stupid bitch. He really had to think now. He was fed up of being treated like shit.
Katy, Bill, even that Becky they had kidnapped. They all treated him like shit. He was fed up of it. He would sit here for a while, until he felt better, then he would begin his revenge. He took a half-smoked butt out of the ashtray and lit it. It felt good, and that's just what Mickey Bolan did, thought about his revenge. Battered, bruised, but not beaten. Fed up of always being the punch bag, he sat and planned his revenge.

An hour later he got up and left. Still battered, still bruised, but feeling a whole lot happier with himself.

114

Chapter 21

They were sitting on the sofa now. Both girls feeling cleaner, less hungry, and drinking their second cans of lager. It was a strange feeling for Wendy, like something from a TV reality show. She was still scared. She wasn't sure what would happen next. Her stomach ached. She was confused. Jezz had been a perfect gentleman. He sat in the armchair, watching some documentary on the telly. Wendy held the can of lager with both hands, wondering what was coming next. A few hours ago she had almost been raped. The girl who helped to kidnap her, had saved her from that ordeal. Then she was with a violent man, who she thought had, in all probability, killed the other kidnapper. She could now be a witness to murder. Then, suddenly, things had changed. She's showered, fed, given clean clothes, and the kidnapper who she was sitting next to, had now become a victim like her. While she hated Kate for the part she had played, Wendy had to admit she had grown to like the girl. It seemed that she had had a hard life, and certainly gave off a hard exterior but Wendy felt, deep down, there was a heart in there. Perhaps she just needed a break. Whatever predicament she was in, and whatever was in store for her,   she knew, for sure, that Todd and his brother would be looking for them, and she needed Kate, just as much as Kate needed her. Jezz fumbled in a drawer next to where he sat, pulled out some tobacco and a large Rizla. He filled the Rizla with strands of Golden Virginia, and then sprinkled the contents of a little bag full of green stuff.

'Bush.' he said, 'Good stuff.'

He rolled the cigarette, screwed up the end, and lit it with his lighter. He puffed out large plumes of smoke and inhaled deeply. The room seemed to fill with smoke. He sat back, contented. He offered the girls a drag. Both refused.

Katy thought if he had enough of that stuff maybe he would fall asleep, and they could make their escape. She had seen Jezz put the keys in his right hand pocket. They could be difficult to get out.

Wendy broke the contented silence. She sipped her lager, and sat forward.

'Jezz.' she said.

'Yes, babe.' he said, blowing out another large plume of smoke, his big eyes looked at hers,

'What's going to happen to us?'

He leaned forward, stubbed out his roach, and Katy thought that perhaps she would have to think of another plan.

'I don't know, man. I'm just the babysitter. Bill will be back. I think he's going on a road trip with you. But you'll be okay. If he wanted to hurt you, he would have by now.' he switched his gaze back to the television. His words had given them no comfort.

'Why don't you just let us go?' Katy asked.

'No can do.'

Neither girl pursued that option. Katy sighed, wiped her mouth with her hand, wishing she had never run away from home at fifteen. Maybe she would be with her mum now, but she knew that was unlikely. Her father's dislike for her would never have changed. Always getting on at her. She thought of Mickey. He didn't deserve what happened to him.

'I think he's killed Mickey.'

Jezz showed no emotional reaction. 'Hey man, that's tough. Guess he deserved it.'

'He's in the flat, dead.' A tear came to Katy's eye.

116

'Please, Jezz,' Wendy pleaded, 'just go check on him. You can lock us in. We won't scream or anything. Just make sure he's okay.'

Jezz thought for a moment. He liked Katy and Wendy. They had been good company, and offered him no hassle or resistance. What harm could it do?

'I suppose.'

He got up, took the keys out of his pocket, and unlocked the door.

'I'll go look.' he said.

He opened the door, and locked it behind him. He had walked down two of the three flights of stairs, when he heard talking. *Could be anyone* he thought, but he took the last flight carefully. It seemed the voices were on the floor where he was heading. When he got to the bottom of the stairs, he was still hidden from view of the passage with the flat entrance. He could see the flat where Mickey lay, Bill's flat, and the door was open. He could make out a figure of a policeman. He heard the radio crackle. He tried to make out the conversation. He needed to get closer, but he was sure he would be seen. He picked up words like 'clothes' and 'sure'. The word 'blood' was said, but the words that struck him the most, were the ones the policeman spoke, 'murder inquiry'

He went back upstairs into his own flat. The girls were true to their word. They had not moved, not that there was anywhere to go. Jezz felt a bit nervous with coppers there, three floors below. He told the girls that Mickey was dead. They both cried as they sat on the settee. Jezz got his phone and called Bill. Bill answered straight away.

'Get the girls out,' he told Jezz, 'before the place is swarming with police.'

He told him to take the girls to the old pizza place, the one that had been shut down and boarded up. He would meet them there at the back.

Slowly but surely, the three of them walked down thirteen flights of stairs and into Jezz's car. They pulled away just as two police cars with the blues and twos flashing, arrived.

Meanwhile, the alleged dead person, Mickey Bolan, sat in the car that he had stolen, three hundred yards from the flat. He had seen the police arrive. He had seen Jezz take the girls, but he had not seen Bill. He guessed that Jezz was taking them to Bill. He started the stolen Focus and followed Jezz. The police arriving in the squad cars paid no attention.   'Time to party.' Mickey said.

Back in Ashbourne, less than twelve hours after Wendy had gone missing, Sergeant Tracy Bates was informed that the Missing Person inquiry had now been upgraded to a possible murder inquiry. She was ordered to inform the Fenton's. Another sergeant was on his way to inform Mrs Cross, Wendy's mother.

Daniel, Todd, Becky and Carol were sitting, working out what to do, when there was a knock on the door. It was Chief Inspector Simon Goldstone and Sergeant Tracy Bates. They greeted Daniel as a friend, but Daniel wasn't interested in friendship at the time. He regarded the police officers as a nuisance. The four house occupants showed no emotional reaction, when they were told what had been found at the flat in Bristol. Todd and Daniel stared poker-faced, making no comment. Carol went into the kitchen and poured herself a glass of water. She did not offer the visitors a drink. Becky sat looking out of the window, as if it were just a normal day. She was, in fact, watching some kids playing football in the street. It was just a normal day in those children's lives. She wondered when their family would next have a normal day.

'Are you sure there's nothing you need to tell me?' the Inspector asked.

'We've told you all we know.' said Daniel.

Simon didn't believe him. He didn't believe any of them. Their reaction to it being upgraded to a murder inquiry was not right. It was as if he was telling them nothing new. There was no reaction, no questions as to how or why, no what happens next? Nothing. They didn't want them there. He could see that. He just didn't know why. Something wasn't right.

'I've upgraded it to a murder inquiry, Daniel, so that I can put my best men on it. We have no reason to believe Wendy has been murdered, though we have reason to believe she has been hurt. The lab tests will confirm that. I've fast tracked them, and we should know in hours.'

'You want a medal?' Todd asked.

The inspector ignored the question. 'There has to be a reason why he's taken her.' the inspector continued, 'if you hear from him, you must let us know immediately.'

'We will.' said Daniel.

He stood, as if to show them out. The officers ignored the hint.

Goldstone stood firm, his voice stronger, more urgent. 'He's a violent man. If there is anything you know, you must tell me.' 'How do you know it's him?' asked Carol. She had come back into the room and she was standing by the door.

'What do you mean?' the inspector said.

'Well, you've found some clothes in my ex-husband's flat. By all accounts, it was a drug den. Maybe it wasn't him. Maybe it was a number of people. Have you found out who took her?'

119

The Inspector, not liking her tone, said 'We have leads on that. We believe the people who took her were the same couple who were in the cafe. We have no confirmation of that and ...' Carol interrupted. 'Are you idiots. Of course they took her. So start looking for them.'

'I know you're upset . . .'

Again Carol interrupted, her voice growing louder, stronger, more confident.

'Don't you dare patronise me. Just get out.'
The officers started to leave.

'Keep us informed.' Goldstone said. 'Would you like me to leave Sergeant? Bates here?

'That will not be necessary.' Becky said immediately.

Daniel escorted them to the door. As they were just about to walk out, Goldstone turned round and looked at Daniel, while Bates walked to the car. Their eyes met. Goldstone's look was sincere and he could see in Daniel's eyes that he was hiding something. He held out his hand for Daniel to shake, Daniel's hand met his. The Inspector noticed it was sweaty.

'What are you hiding from me, son?' he said.

'Can you do me a favour?' Daniel asked.

'Anything.'

'Can you call the Sweeney off? You have gone way, way too far.' he looked at Simon solemnly.

'You know I can't do that. If you're holding information, that could make you an accessory. You know that, don't you?' 'Then I'll have to do your investments from a prison cell.' Daniel went inside the house and closed the door.

The Inspector called Bates over. 'Watch them 24/7.' he said. 'Will do sir' she said. 'Did you notice the reaction, or lack of it?

The inspector stared at the house.

'He wants me to call off the search. Said he could deal with it. Something's not right.' He turned looked at Tracy. She smiled a nervous smile.

'He's a good man. He wouldn't be involved in anything corrupt.'

Simon's thoughts went AWOL for a moment. *Not corrupt. No,* he thought, *just the finest tax dodger in the country.* 'Maybe not,' said Goldstone, 'but he's up to something, and I want to find out what.'

Daniel went back into the room. The others waited patiently.

'Time to move it up a stage, I think Todd.'

'The thought had crossed my mind.'

'What's the plan?' asked Carol.

Chapter 22

Todd was six, Daniel eleven. The young lad had grown big and strong and looked more like a fifteen year old. It was Cardiff. It was April, Easter Sunday. It was unusually warm for April. The sun shone, the temperature lifted to a warm sixty six degrees. The garden of the modest bungalow was vast, an array of trees, bushes, flower beds, a large green house to the side, a shed in the corner, two kidney-shaped lawns on one of which stood a children's play area that Vera and Doug had put in for the boys, when they visited, swings, a seesaw and a climbing frame.

Doug had tried to build a tree house, but his age had got to him, and he was unable to complete it. They loved having the grandchildren over, in their old age. It gave them comfort, and kept them feeling young and focussed. For a long time they had tried to persuade Carol to bring the boys to live near them, so they could spend more time with them and give Carol some more free time. Carol had refused, even when the offer came of free accommodation, as her parents had offered to pay the rent on a house nearby. She liked Ashbourne. The kids liked Ashbourne, bad memories and all.

The garden party was in full swing, the barbecue roaring. Burgers sizzled, sausages fried, and the beer flowed. There were six other couples there, with eleven other children whose ages ranged from two to nine. The others had been childhood friends of Carol's. She could only remember three of the six other women that were there, but everyone was in good spirits. Daniel was the oldest child there. It made him feel good, as if he was responsible. They climbed the frames, played on the swings, and kicked a ball into the mini goal that had been set up. A table full of soft drinks, beer and lager, kept needing to be restocked by Doug, as everyone tucked in to the goodies on offer.

A rather drunk man in his twenties called Mal Jones was there. Carol could remember him from school, a bully. Mal decided it was time to start the Easter egg hunt. A total of fourteen eggs had previously been hidden amongst the trees and the bushes by Doug. The children were given large wicker baskets to collect the eggs. These were far too big for the younger children to hold, but they didn't complain. They all stood in line until the ex-school bully said ' Go!' and the children ran in every direction, baskets in tow, excitement in the air, whilst Daniel stood and watched, laughing as the children shouted and screamed in joy. Yes it was a good day for the Fenton's.

The adults were all sitting on various kinds of garden furniture as well as six kitchen chairs that had been brought out. They drank beer and lager and chewed on chicken whilst the children searched for the hidden Easter eggs. It was only ten minutes later when they all saw Todd running towards them, his basket laden with eggs. Everyone looked surprised, as he counted out thirteen of the fourteen eggs that had been hidden.

'That Sally Grimshaw got the other one' he said, 'I found it, but she took it off me.'

Everyone looked on in amazement except Daniel, he smirked, and rolled his eyes.

'Todd,' Carol said, 'how did you find them so quickly?' Todd grinned.

'Bloody obvious!' said the school bully, 'He bloody knew where they were. You told him.' casting an accusing look at Carol.

'I did no such thing.'

'Whoa, whoa, whoa, whoa.' Doug forcibly said. 'It's just a game. We can hide some more, and let the other kids find them. Maybe Todd was watching when we hid them, and we didn't know.' He looked at Todd and gave him a 'cheeky bugger' smile.

Todd just shrugged his shoulders. 'Whatever.' he said. 'Must have a good memory.' a woman in her thirties said and laughed as she picked up another burger and took a bite. The drunken bully slumped in a chair and opened another can of Fosters. The kids came running back, some in tears, but the tears soon stopped when Todd gave each of them an egg. Off they went, running into the garden, all of them winners. The party was soon back in flow, no one taking any real notice of what had happened.

Except for Carol. Another strange event in the yet short life of Todd and Daniel Fenton. They never ceased to amaze her, never stopped making her proud. Daniel saw a little concern on his mother's face, and went over and kissed her. She smiled and hugged him. Todd came over, not wanting to miss out on the hugs. Carol hugged him too. She had both children held close to her.

'I told you not to find them all straight away.' Daniel said.

'Well, I told you I didn't want to play. It's a stupid game.'

Carol looked at both boys. 'Did you know where they were, Todd?'

Todd released himself from his mother's grip, and went running into the garden, saying 'Nah. I just felt where they were.'

Daniel gripped his mother's hand. She noticed the strong grip from a boy at such a young age.

'He's fine, mum. He's just good at finding things.'

124

The party flowed on, as Daniel walked over towards the drunken bully.

'Would you like another beer?' he asked the bully, slumped in his chair with a full can in his hand.

The bully said 'Yeah.'

Daniel touched the bully on his shoulder. The bully didn't like it, almost as if he had been gripped in a vice by his shoulder   Daniel bent down whispering in Mal's ear, 'He's good at finding things, and if I ask him to, he can find out where you live. Now you wouldn't want that, would you?' He released his shoulder and walked away.

The bully sat looking at Daniel as he walked on, not knowing what had just happened. He felt strange. There was a strange feeling burning up inside him. He didn't like it. It had happened when Daniel had touched him, he thought, and as he looked at Daniel walking away, without realising what he was doing, he took his can of lager, and poured the whole contents over his head. He just sat there in the chair looking liked a drowned rat. Everyone turned around to look. The bully sat, as if nothing had happened. He ate a burger that was covered in lager. 'Why are you all looking at me?' he asked.

People stopped staring, and went on partying.

Carol noticed Daniel, who stood by the fence, watching the drunken bully. He was laughing, laughing like a drain. She looked at the bully then back at Daniel. She frowned. How on earth had Daniel done that?

Chapter 23

Simon Goldstone sat in the briefing room. His eagerness to get to the bottom of Wendy's disappearance had more to do with his dodgy investments and overseas banking, than anything else. His feeling was that as long as Daniel was involved in this, he would not be focussed. So his priority was to find the girl, dead or alive. *She must be found and, perhaps,* he thought, *he might even be able to put that bastard Bill Fenton away forever.* It was eleven pm, late for a briefing, and the team show their anxiety. Tracy Banks was there, along with two detectives and two constables, a large team, considering it had only been a few hours since the girl went missing.

The grey room was stuffy and depressing in its looks. Three tables, each with four plastic chairs, where the team was sitting, spread out amongst the tables. At the front was a raised desk about twelve inches high. Notice boards and incident boards adorned the wall behind it. There was just one computer on the desk, and a telephone. Some of the boards held information from other cases.

Goldstone used the white board, on which were the names:

Wendy Cross - missing
Bill Fenton - suspect
Kate Harrison - suspect
Mickey Bolan - suspect
Daniel Fenton - ???
Todd Fenton - ?

'Here's what we know.' Goldstone said, 'She didn't return home from work today. He paused. 'Okay, okay, I know what you're all thinking, it's only been six hours, but we have good reason to believe she is in imminent danger.'

'From whom, sir?' asked detective Stuart Thomas, a slightly overweight man in his fifties, who was chewing on his pen and not looking really interested.

Goldstone waved his hand, as if to say I'm coming to that. 'Bill Fenton.' He paused, as if to let the name sink in. 'We believe he's kidnapped Wendy Cross as some form of revenge against his estranged wife and children. However, we do not think he acted alone. Kate Harrison and Mickey Bolan, we know are acquaintances of Fenton's. At this moment, we have been unable to contact either. We know these two had been observing Wendy Cross at the cafe where she worked. CCTV is available, and I suggest you all look at it before you leave tonight. Get yourselves familiar with their faces. I need to speak to these people.'

'Was the blood at the scene, Wendy's, sir?' asked a young constable, Dylan Williams, who had been on the force for three years and had shown real promise. He was one of Goldstone's favourites, and loathed by Tracy Bates.

'Yes. The blood results have been fast tracked, and they belong to Miss Cross, as do the clothes. The good news is that the loss of blood was low at the scene, and is very unlikely to have been life threatening. Our priority at this moment, is to find Harrison, Bolan and Fenton. They are the key to this. The Bristol police force will give you all the help they can.' There was a smirk from almost everyone.

Goldstone continued. 'Whilst it will lead us into their jurisdiction, this is our case and nothing happens without my say so.' He cleared his throat. 'We are working on the known associates of Fenton, but everyone seems to have gone to ground. No one's speaking.'

David Stuart, the rookie cop, who was one of the constables, raised his hand. Goldstone acknowledged it with a nod.

'Why are the sons on the board, sir? Daniel and Todd.'

'Good question.' Stuart sat back in his seat, looking smug. 'Truth is, I don't know. There's something they're not telling us. They are to be observed 24/7.'

He moved away from the desk. 'Wendy Cross may not have been kidnapped at all. The Fenton's seemed too laid back about it, yet Helen Cross, her mother, is distraught.'
'Why the high profile?' asked detective Thomas.

'Fenton's a dangerous man. He needs taking down.'

'Can't we just let the Bristol mob do it?' said Thomas. 'I've got lots to do and I ....'

'Detective Thomas, this is your current task. Keep me informed of any development, and I mean *any*.' he said angrily. 'Drop everything. Just bloody sort it.'

Everyone in the room noticed the anxiety on Goldstone's face, and they all knew there was something he wasn't telling them.

'Sure, sir.' The detective stood pointed to Stuart. 'I want to know everything about Harrison and Bolan. Dig where you have to. I want it on my desk by close of play tomorrow.'
'Yes, sir.' said Stuart, not looking so pleased with himself now.

Thomas turned to Tracy. 'Sergeant, how's the surveillance on the brothers going?'

She smiled one of her sexiest smiles. Thomas loved that. 'There are two officers there now, sir. I'm just about to relieve them for a couple hours, so they can eat, sir.'

'Good. Make sure you sleep. I need you fresh in the morning. The rest of you, go home. Nine on the dot in the morning.'

With that the room emptied except for Stuart, who was Googling the name Kate Harrison.

Sergeant Tracy Bates got into her car. She looked in the mirror, re-arranged her hair, took some Lipsol out of her pocket and applied it. *Oh what fun it is to be a policeman* she thought.

It was a chilly night, but the skies were clear. She could see the stars out of her windscreen; she thought how nice it would be to make love under those stars, maybe on a sandy beach, or a field laden with soft grass. She closed her eyes, and sighed a little as she imagined how nice that would be. She hadn't been in a relationship for seven months now, and that one had ended dreadfully. He had turned out to be a bully, and tight as a duck's ass, as Tracy had put it. There had been no one since then, despite almost everyone on the force thinking she had screwed her way to sergeant, but the truth was she loved her job. She thought of the last time she had sex, but put it out of her thoughts quickly. No one had interested her since, not until now. She started the engine, put the car in gear. *Daniel, here I come* she said to herself and drove towards Ashbourne.

Chapter 24

The Pizza place was just on the outskirts of St. Paul's just before the exit to the M5. It had been boarded up and derelict for years, originally vandalised, but now generally left to rot. The roof was still intact, and the windows and doors had been boarded up. Throughout those years, people had found ways in.

Today Frankie's Perfect Pizza was empty, well it had been until Jezz had brought the girls there to meet Bill. He had parked the car behind the restaurant, so as not to be noticed from the road. Jezz was feeling a bit anxious now. He didn't mind looking after the girls at his flat. In fact he had enjoyed it. Now was a different kettle of fish. He felt uncomfortable, and at one time, he was going to let the girls go, telling Bill they had escaped. But he knew how angry Bill would get, and Jezz thought he might probably pay with his life. He was a match for Bill, he thought, but that man just would not give up. It seemed there was nothing Bill wouldn't do. The girls remained terrified throughout the short car journey. The solitude and security of Jezz's flat was now gone, and they were due to meet the man who terrified them most.

Bill was waiting inside, as Jess pulled back a flap of boarding to gain entrance. Bill was sitting on a chair, leaning on a table which had surprisingly been left undamaged.   'Good man.' he said to Jezz, once they were inside.

The girls stood and looked at their new home. It smelt of damp and sweat. The high ceilings seemed to eat up the sound. Every crack and hole appeared to hide the darkest of secrets. They could hear the skittering of mice. Katy just hoped it was only mice. The feeling of not wanting to be there overtook

Wendy's body and mind. Not wanting to be there, especially with him.

It was surprisingly hot and, as Jezz closed the flap behind him, it was stuffy. The main counter was still there, vandalised, but still there. It seemed to look eerie, as if ghostly figures would suddenly emerge holding pizzas. Behind the counter, you could see the ovens where the pizzas were once cooked. The walls were full of graffiti and the floors were strewn with rubbish, mainly broken bits of furniture, and glass from broken windows, and with her brain playing tricks, Wendy almost felt like ordering a pizza.

Bill thanked Jezz and told him to leave. As he left, Jezz looked at the girls solemnly. Deep down, he felt like he was betraying them. The thought of him leaving, frightened the girls even more, they didn't want to be left with this monster. The girls looked at him, almost pleading, to free them from this ordeal.

'It will be okay.' Jezz simply said, and left, hoping beyond all hope, that it wouldn't be the last time he saw the girls.

As he drove away he didn't notice Mickey Bolan, hiding in the nearby bushes. Mickey had followed Jezz and the two girls to the Pizza place. He didn't see Bill, or anyone else, there and, with all the windows boarded up and in the dark of the night, it was impossible to see inside no matter how close he could get. He was surprised to see Jezz leave. He could only presume that the girls had been delivered. That had to be the case, or the girls would have left. He knew he couldn't tackle Bill on a one to one basis. Bill would surely kill him if he tried. He had never had a plan, wasn't even sure why he was there, but there were three things on his mind. They kept going round and round in his head: one, he would kill Bill, two, he would give Katie a slapping for leaving him, and three, *oh yes, especially three,* he thought, the bitch he helped kidnap was going to get a good shagging.

Bill sat at the table, smoking a cigarette, looking dirty, smelly, and as mad as ever. He threw his cigarette on the floor. For a moment Wendy hoped it would catch, and set the building alight. They would all be in panic as they fled the building, and they could make an escape, but it was just her mind playing tricks.

He told Wendy and Katy to sit, pointing to the floor. They sat next to each other, as close as they could get, having checked the floor and kicking away any rubbish first. A mouse ran out from behind the rubbish they had kicked. Katy let out a silent scream. That was when they noticed the holdall on the floor besides Bill. Wendy hoped beyond hope there weren't instruments of torture in there. Her mind was shot at the moment, playing all kinds of tricks with her. Katy clutched Wendy's hand with her own. They both held tightly. There was silence, a real uncomfortable silence, as Bill just sat smoking, looking at the girls. It felt as if he was judging them, deciding who to hurt first, deciding who to kill first. His look made both girls shudder. Katy stared at the floor. Wendy looked at him, eye to eye, her heart raced. She had to get her head clear. 'So what's your plan?' she asked. She tried to smile, but it came out more of a grimace.

She wasn't sure if she wanted to know the plan, if there was one, especially if the plan involved pain or death. But just sitting, waiting, not knowing what would happen next, she could not bear. In the last eight hours, this was the third place to which she had been taken. She just needed to know. She just had to ask the question, and hoped she could cope with the answer.

Bill didn't answer at first, he just stared at Wendy. His mind drifted to his son, Daniel, thinking how lucky his son was. He thought of Todd, the son he had never really known, and wondered what sort of boy he had turned out to be. They had never visited him in prison, where he could have seen them. He had wanted to see them. They never came. They had deserted him. He stood up, still not speaking. He walked over to the serving counter, bent down and grabbed the metal foot rest and pulled it as hard as he could. It held firm. The girls just watched. He stood, went to his holdall. He lifted it, put it on the table and unzipped it. The girls' eyes never left his movements, Katy had thought about running while he was pulling on the foot bar, but she knew that by the time she got the flap open, he would have got her. Even if she had got through he was too fast. There was no getting away, at least not yet. He pulled out a blanket, and laid it in front of the footrest on the floor. He motioned for the girls to sit on the blanket. They both got up and did so. It felt better than the floor, not much, but better. No one said a word. As they sat on the blanket with their backs against the counter, they watched as Bill took two sets of handcuffs out of the holdall. He handcuffed Wendy's right arm to the foot bar, and Katy's left. The girls held hands with their free hands.

Bill sat at the table, and pulled out a pistol from the bag. For one terrifying moment the girls thought that this was where they were going to die. They gripped each other's hand as tightly as they could. They thought about the goodbyes they would never get to say, as they watched Bill lay the gun on the table and put the holdall on the floor. He leant back in his chair, and put his feet on the table.

'This is the plan.' he said. 'Get some sleep. You're going to need it.'

133

With that he closed his eyes. With their arms handcuffed to the foot bar, Wendy and Katy lay down, got themselves as comfortable as they could, and huddled each other, as they both drifted in and out of sleep. Meanwhile, outside in the bushes, Mickey Bolan slept like a baby.

It was now one am. Jezz was sitting in his flat. The place wasn't quiet. Three floors down the police were still there. Most of the neighbours, at least in the flats that were occupied, were awake. Many of them were in the corridors, nattering to each other. Incidents in the flats weren't uncommon and the police seemed to be there as often as some of the residents. They liked winding the police up, and Jezz could hear a lot of name-calling by his neighbours. It made him smile, but he wasn't happy. The information which Jezz found out on returning home, was that there had been no body found at the flat, just a pile of clothes with blood on. There were officers from the South Wales Police who were looking for a missing girl, who was believed to have been staying at the flat after being kidnapped.

He sat in his chair, pulling at a roach. There were three things he could do: go down, talk to the police, and tell them everything; make a phone call to the police anonymously, telling them to look in the Pizza Place; or he could do nothing. He pulled on his roach, thought about how much he liked the girls, and how much he would really like to help them. Then he thought about Bill, even if he were put away, he had contacts. The Governor would see that Jezz paid. As he was thinking, there was a knock on the door. He had been expecting it. He opened the door and there stood two policemen.

'We are making enquiries regarding a missing person.' one of them said.

Jezz invited them in. In the five minutes he spent with the police, Jezz Dwayne told them nothing.

He made a coffee, lit a cigarette, he was missing the girls. Even though he knew they were there under duress, he felt let down, he felt used. Bill Fenton had used him again, all for a few fucking quid. He stood up, kicked over the table. His coffee was on it, and spilled on the carpet. He stood looking at the empty mug and the stain growing on the carpet. He knew he wouldn't sleep, too much going on in his head. His head monsters wouldn't let him go to sleep tonight. 'Fucking Fenton,' he said. 'Fuck him!'

Part Two

Chapter 25

Family Get Together

As Wendy and Katy drifted into an uncomfortable sleep, Carol Fenton, Becky Fenton, Daniel Fenton and Todd Fenton sat in the living room of the Fenton's family home. Sleep was far from their minds. It had been a tough day, as tough as it gets. Their estranged father had kidnapped the only girl Todd had ever loved, believing it to be the wife of his older brother, Daniel. They knew that the police had messed up big time. By making it public they had put Wendy's life in danger, and Bill Fenton must never know he'd got the wrong girl. Now there was only one thing they could try. One thing they had never ever tried before.

'We can't go looking for her. The cops outside will just follow us.' said Daniel. He sat in the armchair, looking at his mother who was sitting between Todd and Becky on the sofa. 'So me and Todd's got an idea.'

Daniel nervously played with his ear, Carol noticed his nervousness. From the time Daniel was old enough to realise it, about the same time he tried to catch a plane home, because he knew his mother was going to have his brother, he knew he was different from other boys. He could feel things. Things that he wasn't meant to feel, things that were impossible to feel. It was like his mind would go into a spasm, and a sixth sense would take over his body and give him information. Daniel tried to hide it as much as he could. He certainly controlled it. As he grew older, he found out that if he thought hard enough, and the recipient of those thoughts had a mind that Daniel could get into, a mind that was open to exploitation, he could get people to do things. It frightened him.

As he grew more mature, he stopped it. He now knew that if the authorities knew his power, they would exploit him and want to use it in their so-called research or development. So he controlled it, and the longer he controlled it and laid it to rest, the harder it was to get it to resurface. Today Daniel was almost a normal regular guy. Almost.

His kid brother, however was different. He could find things, which, in everyday normal life was a good thing, and Todd had used it many times to find lost keys, etc. When Daniel asked him how he did it, he had no real explanation, other than telling him that he had a feeling that he knew where the lost things could be found.

Todd was an enigma. He had an enormous range of gifts which people, if they knew, would describe as super powers. Astral projection was one of them, where he could put himself in two places at once. He had done it once when he was a kid. Both boys had been sleeping in the same room. They were about seven and twelve. Daniel woke up to see his brother floating above him in the bedroom. His brother also lay in bed soundly asleep. Daniel chatted to his floating brother whilst he also lay asleep in his bed.

The next morning, they were terrified and swore never to tell a soul. Daniel made Todd promise that he would never do it again. People would treat him like a freak show.

Todd's laid-back personality was not ideal for a man of his ability. He didn't understand. Didn't care to understand it, and certainly didn't understand what would happen if the consequences got out. When Todd was nine, a school report stated that Todd showed unusual behaviour in class, and sometimes frightened other pupils with his behaviour. This behaviour had been playing tricks, moving things. Some of Todd's behaviour, gift, power, call it what you will, seemed to be generated by trauma, and could occur at unpredictable times. That was what made Todd vulnerable. That was why Daniel was always close, to protect Todd from these occult practices, which society might label astral projection or paranormal behaviour. The Bible suggests it opens up the individual to demonic possession. Years ago he would have been burnt at the stake. Until now they had hidden this. Until now.

'Just tell us.' Carol said.

Daniel shifted in his chair 'Well, you know how Todd used to find things.' Carol nodded, Becky sort of knew, as Daniel had told her bits.

'Well,' Daniel rolled his tongue around his mouth, licked his lips, shifting again in his chair. He didn't like this, 'Well' he continued 'He's going to try to find Wendy.'

Everyone's eyes looked towards Todd. Todd sat forward.

'When I was young I used to sit in my wardrobe. It was massive then.' he said. 'It used to sort of make contact with me.' He licked his lips

'Make contact. How?' Carol asked.

'Not speak. It was just like there was a presence, and it made me see things. Later on I found out I no longer needed the wardrobe. I think the wardrobe was my sanctuary. It was a place for me to hide. It made me feel safe.' He shifted in his chair. He crossed his legs, then immediately uncrossed them.

'Why can't you see her now, Todd?' asked Carol.

Todd held his mother's hand with both of his eyes looking straight at her.

'Whenever I've seen or felt anything, it's not because I wanted to see it, or chose to see it. It just happened, and I really only realised it had happened after the event has passed. Then it would scare me. It was like I was evil. As I grew up, I knew it wasn't evil. It just happened. Daniel has it, but perhaps to a lesser extent'

They all looked at Daniel. He nodded. He wanted to tell them that he had controlled it. He was a stronger man. Todd was weak in that way. But he couldn't tell them that. He daren't.

Carol knew. *My two boys, my wonderful boys, with that curse, or blessing, resting on their shoulders,* she thought. At that moment she was as proud of them as she ever could be. She didn't know that she would soon become even more proud.

'I don't understand, sweetheart.' said Carol.

Todd stood. Daniel stood beside him.

'I need to go upstairs and try to summon whatever it is that I feel, and try to find Wendy.'

'Oh, Todd.' Carol said, a tear coming to her eye.

'Will it be safe?' asked Becky.

'I don't know.' and as Todd said that, Becky burst into tears, as the emotion had built up inside until all she could do was let it out. Daniel immediately put his arms around her, as he sat beside her. He hugged her close tightly, stroking the back of her head

'It's all my fault,' she said between the tears, 'it should be me out there, and now Todd has to do whatever it is, when it should be me.'

'Becky.' Todd said, raising his voice a little. She drew her head from Daniel's shoulder looked at him, mascara trickling down her face.

'It's not your fault. It's the bastard who took her, and if it was you out there, I would still be doing it.'

She wiped her eyes, trying to smile. It made her feel better, just a little.

'It might not even work.' he added.

He kissed the girls, hugged his brother. 'I'll probably be down in five minutes and you'll all call me an idiot.' He laughed nervously.

'I'll be right here Todd.' Daniel was always there, Todd knew that.

Todd went up the stairs and stood in front of his wardrobe. The monstrosity of it seemed to fill the room. The two doors were ajar, his clothes hanging there, and the floor of the wardrobe empty, always empty. His heart raced. He was anxious. He felt alone, even though the people he loved, the people he would die for, were just downstairs. He needed to see now. He wasn't sure how it was going to work, or even if it would work. He had to try. *Did he have any power?*, he asked himself. *Were all those incidents in the past just coincidences?* If he had some sort of power, some sort of sixth sense, then why was Wendy kidnapped? How badly had he failed her? He stood and thought.

Perhaps he was cursed, his father killing someone not long after he was born, his mother having to bring up two strange kids on her own. If Wendy dies, there will be nothing left. His mind drifted to Wendy. What did she see in a five quid a time window cleaner?

He almost left the room, doubting his own ability. They would think of something else. Daniel would sort it. Daniel always sorted it. But deep down, he now knew. Daniel couldn't sort it. For once in his life it was up to him.

'Time to find out whether this is a blessing or a curse.' he said aloud.

The doors of the wardrobe were ajar, his clothes were no longer there, Todd had noticed, but that didn't seem to bother him, as if it were expected. He looked deep into the wardrobe. It looked bigger It looked deeper. It looked darker. He could make out the back wall of the wardrobe. It seemed to be beating, beating like a heart. The wardrobe was alive. He knew that. He had always known that. The whole wardrobe now seemed to be pulsating like a giant heartbeat. As he looked, the back wall seemed to turn into a face, a face he didn't know. A face he didn't recognise. Not a scary face. It did not scare Todd. It was the face of someone you would like to meet. Someone you would like to get to know, have a chat to, and, perhaps, the face would tell him where Wendy was. *That's it,* he thought, *the face will tell me.* The face was inviting him in, taunting him.

He rubbed his eyes to refocus. As he opened them again, the face had gone, the wardrobe was gone. All that was there was a door, an open door and as he looked in the distance, a distance that really shouldn't be there at all, what he could see was a light, a white, bright light, that seemed to be alive, that seemed to be inviting him in. Without any hesitation, his mind purely focussed towards the light. Todd walked into his wardrobe towards the light.

When he got inside the light disappeared, and now he was in his wardrobe again. He pulled both doors shut, and sat, with his knees raised and, as he closed his eyes, something happened that had never happened before.

It was as if he was now outside his wardrobe, outside his body. He was looking for a miracle. He was looking at the silly young man sitting in the bottom of his wardrobe, knees up, eyes closed, wishing for a miracle. *But miracles never happen,* he thought.

Then it did. The wardrobe began to shake, just a little at first, then more violently. Todd drifted into a place he had never been before.

Daniel, Becky and Carol were standing in the kitchen. Fresh coffee made it smell good. They were all full of anxiety, scared of the unknown, even Daniel was now wishing he hadn't sent his brother to do what he should be doing. But did Daniel have the power. He somehow doubted it. They heard a small bang at first, then what appeared to be a rattling upstairs, which got louder and louder. Then it seemed to get closer and closer. The coffee cups on the table shook, and the liquid in them seeped over the sides of the mugs. Then one cup tipped over, spilling its contents, and went crashing to the floor and smashing. As pieces of china splattered around the floor, the other mugs followed. For a moment they all just stood and looked at each other for what seemed like an age, but it was probably no more than two seconds.

Carol screamed, and headed for the stairs. Daniel held her back. There were tears in Carol's eyes. Daniel held her and his wife.

'Let him be. Let him do It.' he said.

A "kitchen is closed" sign fell to the floor. All the cupboard doors flew open, as if there was a poltergeist in the room. Plates and other china fell to the floor smashing as they did so. The trio simply stood there. Knives started to fly from the rack where they had been hanging, one narrowly missing Becky. Daniel quickly got the two women out of the house.

'Wait across the road.' he said. Carol and Becky both protested.

'You'll get killed in there.' Becky screamed. Daniel kissed her.

'Todd would never hurt me.' he shouted above the noise. Daniel ignored their protests and closed the door.

'My boys.' Carol cried.

The movements in the kitchen had stopped, but the house seemed to be trembling, shaking. Daniel went to the stairs. He wanted to get Todd. He had to end this. He had to end it now, but he couldn't. He stood at the bottom of the stairs and, although there was no voice, no human form, he knew that the bright light at the bottom of the stairs would prevent him. The light was like a face, and the face seemed to be daring him, challenging him to make that move, Daniel, later on, would really wish he had made that move.

Carol and Becky stood outside, on the opposite side of the road, looking at the house which seemed to be trembling. It reminded both of them of something out of a horror movie. The last house on the left, the Amityville horror.

Tracy Bates who was still outside, trying to catch a glimpse of Daniel, before the commotion began, she saw the house shaking, and the bright lights coming from inside, Sergeant Tracy Bates screamed at Carol and Becky.

'Daniel's in there!' and she ran towards the house. Becky went to run after her, not to prevent Bates getting into any danger, but her mind was focussed and trained to keep Bates from Daniel. Carol grabbed her arm, stopping her.

'Let the silly cow go.' she said.

Neighbours' lights started to go on. They had been awakened by the noise. There were faces at the windows, looking over towards the Fenton's house, not believing what they were seeing. There were flashes of lightning, and the roaring sound of thunder. Yet the skies were clear, the stars and moon shone through, brightening up the streets. The storm seemed to be coming from the Fenton's house.

143

In the distance, no one noticed the two men in black, a military uniform, but with no insignia. One was on his mobile, the other held his hand firmly on the gun in its holster, as they watched, hidden, out of sight.

Tracy Bates struggled to open the door. She pulled the handle which released the latch, but it wouldn't open. The door was unlocked but it just would not open. She pushed and pushed, her shoulder against it, until her shoulder began to hurt. She could feel the sweat pouring from her hands which felt warm and sticky, and she pushed on the handle. Suddenly the handle started to glow an orange colour that grew brighter and brighter. Tracy yelled out a scream, as she pulled her hand away looking at her blistered palm where the door handle had burnt her.

She ran back towards Carol and Becky shouting 'The house is on fire. Dial 999.'

The door handle no longer glowed. It was no longer hot. By this time, some of the neighbours had come out onto their porches, watching the events happening in their street. Some, still in their pyjamas, not really believing what they were seeing. There were now about twenty in all, and they were slowly starting to gather around the two women and the policewoman.

'No one call the police!' shouted Carol.

No one had. No one had thought of it. No one cared to. Then suddenly, as if out of some comedy movie, whilst the house was shaking with a storm inside and two boys trapped, a man came out with a crate of two dozen cans of Fosters and started handing them out. What was more amazing, Carol thought, was that she took one. Then another guy came out with eight cans of John Smiths saying, 'It's all I've got.' as if apologising to the Fenton's for not being properly prepared for this evening.   Carol told him that it was fine and eight cans was more than enough. Becky just stared at her as if to say what are you doing, Carol shrugged her shoulders. She had no idea.

Then everyone seemed to be going inside their houses, bringing out whatever alcohol they had inside, a woman and a man were carrying out their kitchen table, followed by the chairs. Other people cottoned on, and did the same. One couple even brought out their two-seater sofa. More chairs and tables followed, crates of beer, bottles of wine and vodka.

'I've got whisky!' someone shouted, holding up an unopened litre of Bell's. Music blared from a house two doors away. It was Mumford and Sons, their windows were opened, so everyone could hear the fifty watts speakers belting out. Carol looked around at what was happening all around her. She saw a lady with sausage rolls, and ten metres away from her, three guys were doing a barbecue.

My house is falling down and they're having a fucking street party, she thought, *that's fucking crazy.* She felt hungry as she sipped her can of lager.

A couple started dancing, and more and more started to join the party from other streets. Tracy Bates showed Carol her hand, explaining that the house had burnt her. Carol looked at it, and told her that it was superficial, and she shouldn't be such a baby.

Tracey Bates took her mobile out of her pocket. It was time she took control of this, after all she was the law.

'What are you doing?' Carol asked.

'Phoning the police, ambulance, anyone that will come. Everyone back inside!' she shouted at the revellers. No one heard her, or if they did, took no notice. They didn't care much for coppers, and certainly weren't going to listen to one lonely female cop.

145

The lightning struck the house, the thunder roared, as over two hundred people danced and sang in the street.

'Put your phone down.' Carol said.

'Are you fucking crazy?' asked Tracey, who was now standing right in front of Carol and Becky, trying to look authoritative. Carol noticed how desperate she looked and felt a bit sorry for her. Tracey started to dial, but before she could reach the second digit, Becky clenched her fist and thrust it into Sergeant Tracy Bates face as hard as she could. The sergeant fell to the floor, dropping the phone as she tumbled. It didn't break, but Becky's foot dealt with that.

Carol looked on in amazement. 'You've hit a copper.'
'I know and it felt fucking good.' The crowd cheered at the floored copper, and then there was a louder cheer as everyone turned to look, as coming up the street at 1.30 am was an ice cream van with its chimes playing.

'I have chocolate ice cream and Vanilla flavoured with Vodka.' he shouted. Within minutes his van was swamped, as people dug into their pockets for cash.

'Fucking great party!' someone shouted. Everyone seemed to agree.

Every house in the street was lit up now, and with the bright moon and the light from the houses shining onto the street, and the thunderstorm that raged over one house, Carol thought it was the most surreal thing she would ever see. There was only one person responsible. That was her son, Todd Fenton.   Of all the lights shining, the brightest light came from the Fenton's comfy council-house home. A neighbour from across the street passed with a crate full of Stella with their tops already taken off. He offered them one. Carol took three. She gave one to Becky, and one to Bates, who was now getting up,

146

wiping a trickle of blood from her mouth. Bates took a swig, then spoke.

'Becky, I'm arresting you for assaulting a ......'

'Shut the fuck up!" Carol said.

Bates did. She looked at her phone on the floor, then picked it up.

'You've broken my fucking phone!' she exclaimed then drank the remains of her Stella. 'Where did all these people come from?'

'Drinking on duty.' Becky said, and both she and Carol laughed until they cried.

Two guys, who knew Carol, came over to ask her if everything was okay, obviously referring to the copper. 'It's fine,' said Carol, 'but if she plays up again, can you lock her in the shed?'

'It will be a pleasure." the taller guy said. 'Great party, Mrs F.' he added.

'Yes it is.' said Becky, who was standing with a burger in one hand and a can in the other. Her hand hurt, but she thought it was well worth it. Tracey slumped her shoulders this time, admitting defeat.

'Great right hook, Becky.' the other lad said as they walked away.

The tears came again, tears of laughter, and as she laughed and cried, Carol looked around at the swelling group. 'This is crazy.' she said.

The party stood at over seven hundred. The storm still raged. Tracy Bates just stood beside the two girls, staring at the house that seemed to be alive. *No one had told her about this sort of thing in training,* she thought. *If you can't beat them, join them.*

She went looking for another Stella. Someone offered her a hotdog. She took it, found her Stella, and went to join the others.

Chapter 26

Daniel was standing at the bottom of the stairs. The noise upstairs had grown, but now stayed at a constant level. It sounded like a thunderstorm but he guessed it was something that Todd had created. Daniel's thoughts were confused. Perhaps he should have just let the police deal with it. What had made him think that they could deal with this? Why had he allowed his kid brother to go through with it?

He's up there now, going through God knows what, and all because I had told him to. The feeling was one of immense guilt. He simply wanted to get his mum, Becky and Todd out of the house. *Oh Wendy,* he thought for a split second. He was disgusted by his thoughts. Wendy never came into it. All he was thinking about was his family, not about the girl Todd doted on. Daniel's head whirled, and he felt a tightness in his chest. He determined to go up and get Todd, end this, and let the police deal with it.

He took one step towards the stairs, the light which was about half way up, grew brighter as he moved towards the stairs. It made Daniel take a step back.

'I just want to get Todd.' he said out loud, not really realising he was talking to a light on the stairs. He walked up two steps, and the light grew bigger and brighter, and it roared like a hyena, high pitched, yet at the same time deep. The light now filled the stairs, seeming to form a shape on the stairs, like a giant head, with arms coming out from where his ears should be. Daniel would have sworn that he could see the eyes, but the shape was constantly changing. Then he saw inside the shape, what he thought was a baby in a crib. He looked closer. Yes, it was definitely a baby. He stayed where he was on the stairs, trying to look into the light that had somewhat dimmed.

It was showing him a picture. It was clear now, though the baby was only about six months old. Daniel could see who it was. The features were clear, and there were the same photographs all over the house. The baby in the crib was Todd, and the light was telling Daniel to keep away.

Todd hovered above himself, looking at himself in the wardrobe. *How can I be here, and there?,* he thought, yet it felt so real. He wondered if the Todd in the wardrobe could feel it. He looked real. It was him. *It is me,* he thought, *then why am I floating around the room looking at myself?* He remembered that he had done this before, some years ago, when he and Daniel had shared a bedroom. They swore they would never do that again. *So why was this happening now?* This wasn't supposed to happen. All he had wanted was a vision, to be able to find things like he had done in the past. Just be given a vision, so that he could tell Daniel, who would sort it, because Daniel always sorted it. It was as simple as that. He would tell him where Wendy was, and then Daniel would go and get her. He heard a roar from the stairs, a shrieking noise like some wild animal. He hoped and prayed that his family downstairs were okay. He didn't want to be here. He felt lost. He felt lonely, but most of all he was scared.

The boy in the wardrobe remained still. Todd knew that he was resting in the wardrobe and that this out-of-body experience he was now having was the special Todd, the Todd who could find things. The boy in the air spun and spun like a whirlwind. Then there was the loudest crack of thunder he had ever heard. The room shook. The house shook, and then by some miracle he flew through the roof and into the night skies. As the light on the stairs faded, and the storm calmed, he could see below that there was a massive street party taking place.

Chapter 27

The party was in full swing, and growing by the minute. Tracy Bates, Becky and Carol were still standing on the opposite side of the street looking at the house. They had seen the lights grow brighter and heard the roar of some wild animal. The two coppers, who had been relieved by Tracy to get some food, were back. They had to walk back, as the roads were blocked by people carrying chairs, barbecues, boxes of food, and crates of beer.

'It's manic out there.' they told their sergeant. 'The roads are blocked. There's thousands of people.'

The older copper looked at Tracy. 'What happened to your lip?'

Tracy looked at Carol and Becky, the two girls looked back. No expressions. Neither a look of remorse nor a look of satisfaction.

'Nothing.' said Tracy. 'Now go and get a beer, and if anyone calls for back-up they will have me to deal with.'

Carol looked around. 'With all this racket, I don't think it will be too long before they get here.'

Tracy nodded, then looked at the house. *And what the fuck do I tell them?,* she thought.

As the light grew brighter inside the house, in the upstairs bedroom of Todd Fenton, there was a flash of lightning and an enormous sound of thunder which made everyone look round towards the house. There were sounds of 'oooh's' and 'ah's' and gasps of amazement as, in the roof of the house, a hole appeared. Roof tiles were falling into the garden. Through the hole came the light, now about the size of a football, until it got into the sky, then it seemed to grow over the whole extent of the street, lighting up the area. The crowd roared in amazement, because, following the light into the bright sky was a silhouette of Todd Fenton. He floated in the skies, away from Ashbourne with the grace of an eagle. It appeared that Todd Fenton had learned how to fly, and the crowd thought it was a great spectacle for a party.

'Todd.' Carol simply said. Becky just put her hand to her mouth.

'Oh my God' Tracy said

The fields surrounding the south side of Ashbourne which separated Ashbourne and the smaller village of Ringway, and the one road that joined the two towns appeared to be alive, moving. In fact the roads and fields from Ringway to Ashbourne were full of people, carrying food and beer to a party.

No one had told them to go. No one had heard about the party but still they came. The two villages had at one time been rivals and there would often have been street fights when they visited their neighbouring town. Tonight the two villages were united and the long-time rivalry seemed to be a thing of the past.

The population of Ashbourne was just over twenty two thousand. The people on the streets were fourteen thousand, six hundred and twenty five from Ashbourne. The only ones not there were either too old, too young or too sick. As Todd soared into the sky, he was watched by nearly twenty thousand partygoers. By now the news of the party had gone viral. News reporters were on their way and the reporters already there were commenting on a violent storm approaching. People were taking to the streets in the County of Newport marching towards the town of Ashbourne, blocking the roads. The reporters were pleading with them to return home, to allow the emergency services to get through, though no one heard. They were on their way to a party.

The BBC and Sky News were putting two helicopters in the sky. If they had been ten minutes earlier they might have seen Todd Fenton fly past.

Back inside the house, the other Todd lay in his wardrobe. He seemed to be dreaming, as his eyes entered the REM stage. On the stairs, about half way up, was a light, not bright, not really glowing, more like one of those solar lights which people put in their gardens. It was the size of a golf ball. As Daniel stared at it, he knew it was there either to protect Todd, or to prevent Daniel from reaching him. He just hoped and prayed that it was the former.

He went into the kitchen. Things were quiet now. Strewn on the kitchen floor were broken plates and mugs, and various kitchen implements. It looked as though someone had trashed it. He found a Superhero plastic mug that lay unbroken on the floor. He smiled as he picked it up. It was Todd's favourite mug. When he was at home, he wouldn't drink out of anything else. Daniel switched the kettle on, which remained intact, put sugar, milk, and coffee in the mug. He picked up the kitchen chairs, and put them back in their rightful places. He looked around at the mess, took a black sack from under the sink and started clearing the mess away.

When the kettle boiled, He poured his coffee then went to the living room where the damage was very much less. From the drinks cupboard, he grabbed the whisky, and went back into the kitchen, and poured a little into his coffee. He took a sip. It tasted good. He had heard the loud thunder crack as the bedroom ceiling exploded, and although he hadn't seen it, he knew Todd had entered the skies. He sat at the table, took another sip of his whisky-laden coffee, picked up the black sack and continued to clean up. He knew he couldn't leave the house. The orange glow of the handles on all the doors and windows told him so.

The Newport Police station, where Simon Goldstone sat at his desk, had been inundated with calls about a street party in Ashbourne that had simply gone out of control. He was unable to get hold of Tracy Bates, who he knew was in Ashbourne, watching the Fenton's. Neither could he get hold of the two other officers who were assigned to the case. He was annoyed at first, getting angry as his officers failed to respond. Then he grew concerned about them.

What he didn't know was that all his officers were fine, and that they were simply enjoying the festivities that were happening in Ashbourne, and the crowd had simply taken their phones and radio's from them. He had received reports from the officers he could get in touch with, that the streets were grid locked. The BBC, Sky News, and now Fox, from the USA, had been on the phone to him. He had taken their calls, telling them that there were officers at the scene now. He tried to play it down as a street party that had got out of control.

He was horrified to learn that two news stations had put their own helicopters into the air. He knew if they could not get access, he too would have to put his own chopper in the air. There were reports of a thunder storm but he had checked with the Met. Office and the forecast was of a clear calm evening. Facebook and Twitter were full of the event, and now You Tube had put up a video of a storm, showing lightning and you could easily hear the sound of thunder. As he browsed more, even more videos were streaming on all platforms. Some of the storm and others showing the house that appeared to be glowing and shaking. Most of them were of the party goers, people dancing and singing, an ice cream man selling ice

154

creams. Everyone seemed in good spirits. This somewhat reassured him. He made some calls; got all the available men he could, telling them to go on foot if they had to. He also got the chopper airborne. It would be over Ashbourne within thirty minutes.

He flicked the news channel to Sky. They were reporting the incident, saying their 'copter would be there within ten minutes. They showed airborne pictures of crowds of people filling the roads and adjoining fields, walking towards Ashbourne. There were reports that One Direction were making an impromptu concert, and that was the reason people were gathering, but Goldstone had checked this and found it not to be true. But he would rather they believe that.

He knew this had something to do with the Fenton's. He guessed it was a distraction, so they could get up to whatever it was they were planning, but how could he explain the storm? How could anyone explain the storm? He leaned back in his chair, just as the phone rang. His secretary told him Sky News was on the line again. He told her to tell them he was busy. *What was happening here?,* he thought to himself. He tried Bates' phone again. The line was unobtainable. *How can one family organise so many people?,* he asked himself.

He clicked to the next video on You Tube. It was a video of party goers and as the camera panned, he put his hands to his head and shouted 'Fuck!' as the camera panned on to Carol Fenton, Becky Fenton and Tracy Bates. They all seemed fit and well, and Tracy Bates was holding a bottle of Stella. In the distance he could see one of his officers in a paddling pool stripped to the waist. He speed dialled his secretary who answered immediately.

'Get me a driver. I need to get to Ashbourne.'

Within ten minutes, his driver was pulling out of the police station car park for the twelve mile journey. Seven miles down the road the traffic was at a standstill. They could neither go forward nor backwards. It was no good trying to manoeuvre the traffic with the blues and twos, as there was simply nowhere to go. He looked to the left, across to the fields that led to Ashbourne. It was probably a three mile walk. He was fit, and that would be no problem to him. The problem was much clearer. How would he fit in with the thousands of people who were descending on Ashbourne? He got out of his car told his driver to try to continue the journey. As he moved away from the car, and climbed the fence on to the field, he heard the sound in the sky. Though the night was dark, the moon was bright. He could clearly see the lettering on the side of the chopper reading SKY NEWS.

'Fuck it,' he said, and joined the thousands in their walk. It was still a mild evening and as he walked, how he wished he hadn't been in uniform. People were glancing at him, pointing in his direction. He wondered how many of these people he might have helped put away. How many would seek retribution and take out there revenge? *It would be easy to die out here* he thought, *easy for someone to kill him and probably never get caught.*

He grew scared. Whilst he had always been opposed to arming the police force, he had served his time as an armed officer for four years and he never had to use his firearm, but how he wished he had a gun now. He was afraid now, and as he walked his worst fears came to the forefront, as a group of about five lads walked over to him. They were in their twenties, and to Simon they seemed intent on mischief. Each of the lads was carrying a bottle of something.

The leading lad spoke first as he approached, 'Yo man, you on your own?'

'No. I have some officers behind.' He thought this was a good reply.

The lads just dropped in beside him and didn't bother to look and find out if there were any officers behind him.

'We'll walk with you, bro, till they catch up.'

The lads seemed friendly enough, and in the moonlight, Simon didn't recognise them, which he thought was a good thing. It was a strange, eerie feeling. He was with all these people, how many he didn't really know, yet they were all walking peacefully towards the light on Ashbourne Hill where a party was in full swing. There weren't any arguments, fights, raised voices, indeed all the videos and reports he had seen and heard, not one of them reported or showed any violence. Even his own officers appeared to be joining in. That was something he would not leave alone. He would get to the bottom of it later. But now he had to close this party down. The Fenton's had a lot of explaining to do.

As he walked into the night towards Ashbourne, a relatively calm feeling overpowered him. He felt content. He felt happy. All the worries he had earlier had were clearly gone. In fact, he felt in the mood for a party.

One of the lads lit up a spliff and started smoking it. He passed it round the other four. The Chief Inspector ignored it, thinking that one spliff wouldn't hurt. The banter was good. The company seemed reassuring and as he walked, a lad offered him his spliff, and, without realising it, Simon Goldstone took the spliff, took a deep drag, held it for a moment and as he exhaled, he let out a loud 'Ah.' He passed the spliff back, as if it was the most natural thing in the world. No one seemed to notice the Chief Inspector smoking a spliff

157

with a gang of youths, as he was walking across some fields to go to the biggest street party his force had ever come across. If anyone had noticed him, then they just didn't care. Another spliff went round. Simon joined in. One lad passed him his bottle of Vodka, Simon took a sip. Jokes were flying around; some of them were not of the political correctness type, Simon laughed.

Twenty minutes earlier, he had walked across the field wishing he was armed. Now he was getting stoned and drunk with a gang of youths he really liked. *It's been a strange day.* he thought.

He would not realise why he had done it until later, much later. The same could be said of the partygoers that had hit the streets and walked miles to get to, what some might say, was a calling. Others would say it was just a good idea. Some would even say they were following a light, as it called them. Yet others would try to deny ever being there. Even a few would openly boast about being there. Everyone would have an opinion as to why it happened. Only a few would really know.

With Todd flying over rooftops, the party went on and on. There was music blaring from every street in Ashbourne. Almost every house light was on, barbecues were everywhere and all you could smell was the odour of cooked meat. The news stations were amongst the crowd now, getting interviews and exclusive shots that were being beamed live across the world. Yet, when they tried to get near to the Fenton's residence they were stopped. The reporters would protest at first, but later they could also be seen eating hot dogs, and drinking lager, and wondering what all the fuss was about. Whatever it was being spread around Ashbourne and its neighbouring village, no one knew but it sure felt good. In fact

158

the only people who were not getting into the swing of things, were the two military style men, dressed in black, hidden in the background in Ashbourne. They were trained for this, but now it had got out of hand. Their organisation would have to act soon, before it got too late.

Chapter 28

Bill Fenton smoked a cigarette. He seemed to be smoking one after another. He leaned back in his chair with his feet on the table. He couldn't sleep. His mind kept racing back to the past, back to things that he didn't want to remember. His father's 'visits' after his mother had left him, *and who could really blame her* he thought, but *why oh why didn't she take me with her*. If she had, maybe things would have been better. He wondered what she looked like now. Was she still alive? What sort of life had she had after she left? Did his father haunt her, as he does him? He hoped so. She deserved the same torment. He blamed her. He blamed his father. He blamed everyone really. *None of this was my fault* he told himself.

Only two people in his life had been special to him, Carol and Daniel. How he loved that girl was beyond comprehension. But they had both deserted him. They both loathed him, and now they would have to pay. *They didn't understand* he said to himself *and they should have*. They had made him like this, and it was them who would have to pay. Payback time was going to be oh so sweet.

The already stuffy room was full of smoke, as Bill lit one cigarette after another. It wasn't cold, despite it being the early hours of the morning. He had a plan, well, not a plan as such. He had places to go. The next few weeks were going to be very busy, starting with a holiday tomorrow. He laughed to himself. He looked at the girls, who were cuddled up, sleeping. But he could tell their sleep wasn't a peaceful one. They had been shuffling a lot, and, at one time, Katy had started mumbling in her sleep. He had tried to listen, but it was all mumbo jumbo. Katy had become a problem. She wasn't part of his original plan. He had considered killing her, but the thought hadn't lasted that long. She had been loyal to him, done everything that he asked and, perhaps, she could become useful on this venture. *If not useful,* he thought, *well, she could always be there for sex.* He reached into his holdall, pulled out a bottle of water. It was warm as he swallowed. He lit another cigarette. He would have to wake the girls up soon. It was time to go on their first trip. He was hungry. He had a few chocolate energy bars in his holdall. There was a twenty four hour garage and store open about a quarter of a mile away. They sold coffee. How he needed a coffee. He would have to get some. Coffee and sandwiches sounded good.

He walked towards where the two girls were chained, shook them. They both awoke immediately as their sleep wasn't deep. They looked at their kidnapper, as he leaned over and checked the handcuffs. He was happy they were secure.   'I'm going to get us some breakfast.' he said and turned away.

He removed the panel, and left the pizza hut, securing the panel behind him. It was dark, but the moon was bright tonight. He knew this area well, and could reach the garage without really having to walk on the main road. There were plenty of cut-through's he could take. It would be the long way round but it would ensure he would not be seen. He walked into the bushes just past where Mickey Bolan slept. Bill did not see Mickey, and as Mickey slept, he did not hear Bill.

Once they were sure Bill was out of earshot, both girls started to try and get the foot rail from the counter. They pulled and pulled, turned themselves round and kicked at it with their feet, but it was no good. The foot rail stood firm. They decided to shout for help, but that didn't last long. Katy knew where they were. She knew the area, and unless someone was going to the deserted pizza place, there was no reason for anyone to pass, especially in the early hours of the morning. If anyone was there, they would probably be up to no good.

They both slumped back against the counter, with their hands still securely cuffed to the bar. Their hands were hurting. Where they had pulled, red marks could be clearly seen, they were exhausted, both physically and mentally, and both girls wanted to pee.

'What do you think he's going to do?' Wendy asked.

'I don't know.'

'You're a part of this. You're why I'm here. I don't believe you don't know.'

'I brought you here, because he just wanted to meet his daughter-in-law. The deal was that you'd get to go back.' She looked at Wendy. Wendy met her eyes, and she believed her.

'Do you think he planned all of this?' she asked.

'I really don't know. He's planned something, and somehow I don't think I was part of it.'

'Maybe you're here to help him do whatever it is he's going to do.'

A tear came to Katy's eye.

'I've had e fucking nuff of doing what he says. See these?' She opened her mouth, revealing her two missing front teeth. 'He did that. Hit the shit out of me.'

'Why?'

Katy sighed. More tears came. 'Because he could. I thought that when I left home, things would be better.'

'Why don't you go back?'

Amid the tears, Katy sniggered. 'My dad wouldn't have me, and my mum's too pissed to bother.'

Wendy took her hand and held it tight. Katy responded by putting her head on Wendy's shoulder.

'Why are you so nice to me?' she asked.

Wendy pondered the question but chose not to answer.

'You can get your teeth done, you know.'

'That wasn't the question'

'Well, I guess you need a break and, besides, I need you.' Wendy kissed the top of Katy's head. 'And I like you.'

'I like you too.' said Katy, and both girls snuggled close together.

'I wonder what he's getting us for breakfast.' Wendy said. They lay in silence for a minute, both enjoying the comfort, warmth and security of each other's body. Wendy broke the silence.

'I'm not Becky, you know.' Now she had put her complete trust in Katy. If Bill found out, she dreaded to think what would happen.

Katy sat up, put a finger to Wendy's lip.

'Shh' she said. She took her finger away and sat back.

'I know you're not, but please don't tell me your name. Not until this is all over. If I don't know your name, then I can't call you by it.'

'I hope I get the chance to tell you.'

'You will.'

'I need a pee.'

'Me too.'

Bill easily got to the garage unseen. He picked up three Tuna and cucumber sandwiches, and made three take-away coffees from the machine, stuffing his pockets with milk and sugar that was available. The cashier ignored it. Bill paid for the stuff, along with forty Embassy.

'Where's that? he asked, pointing to the telly on the wall behind the cashier. Sky News was on. It was showing what appeared to be a rave.

163

'Just over the bridge. Ashbourne or somewhere.'

Bill looked closer. He recognised the place. The sound was low. He couldn't really hear it, but the station panned to a reporter and in the news bar going across the bottom of the screen he was reporting that a girl had been kidnapped from Ashbourne, and the girl's name was believed to be Wendy Cross. There were also reports of a mystery storm, and although the Sky reporters were unable to get to the street, due to the sheer volume of people, it was also reported that a house had seemingly burst into light.

'Wendy fucking Cross!' Bill said out loud.

The cashier looked at him strangely. 'You what?'

'Nothing.' Bill said, and he took his goods, and walked out of the door. The cashier thought nothing more of the strange man.

As Bill walked out, he noticed the security cameras.

'Fuck it! What was I thinking.' he muttered to himself. He had to rethink. He had the wrong girl. They had brought him the wrong girl, and what was all that about a party? It had all been a fuck up.

He walked back the way he came, unseen by anybody, although there were very few people or cars on the road at this time of night. As he walked, he decided to play the game. This Wendy was obviously known to Daniel. Maybe she was his bit on the side, he thought. He would have to think this out before acting. Things had changed, but he could still use it to his advantage. Yes, Daniel had to pay. Someone close to him would have to die, so he would know what it felt like to lose everything. It may not be his wife, but it was still going to cost him a fortune to get her back. Only the money wouldn't be well spent. Oh yes, he would get her back. He would get back a dead body.

Ten minutes later, as the girls chatted, they heard the panel being pulled back and Bill entered. Both girls noticed the new anxiety on his face. Something had happened. Something had bothered him. He put the coffees and sandwiches down on the table, chucked the girls a sandwich each and brought over the two coffees which he handed to them. Both girls took them. 'It's still warm. It's in them thermo-cup things. Keeps it hot for ages.'

As each had one hand still handcuffed, they both turned so that they would be able to take each other's lid off. Katy bit her sandwich packet open and took a bite. Bill's eyes did not stop watching the girls. The coffee was good. The sandwich was needed. The atmosphere was tense. Something had happened when he went to get the coffee, something not good.

'I need a wee.' said Wendy.

'Me too.' said Katy.

Bill got his keys out, uncuffed Katy, and pointed to the corner of the room where she should pee. She didn't argue. She didn't care if he was watching as she went over to the corner, pulled her trousers down and wee'd. When she had finished she sat back down. Bill cuffed her again, and uncuffed Wendy. He pointed with his head to where Katy had just been. Bill didn't take his eyes off her as she undid her clothes, and did her business. His eyes were firmly on hers as he cuffed her to the railing. Both girls were now cuffed again.   'Right. Which one of you can I fuck?' he said.

The girls shivered in horror, this was something they weren't expecting.

Wendy looked him in the eye. 'I'll tell you one thing,' she said, 'if you're going to have me, you're going to have to fight for it.'

Katy spoke. 'You've fucked me for the last time, Bill.'

Both girls wondered where their braveness came from. Maybe it was their new found friendship, a bond. Now they were in this together.

Bill laughed, a little too loudly. It sounded eerie. 'Katy,' he said, 'you're mine, whenever I want you. That's what you're here for. You're my little slut.'

'Was.' she said defiantly.

Bill grabbed her by the throat, applying no real pressure, Katy's heart leapt into her mouth. She knew what this man could do. Her eyes were wide, scared. Her bottom lip quivered. Bill let go and sat at his table, drank his coffee, and ate his sandwich, never taking his eyes off them. He finished his coffee and threw the empty carton at Katy. It missed. He went over to her again, knelt beside her, drew back his hand and slapped her in the mouth. Her head moved sideways from the shock, her mouth instantly started bleeding. Wendy, thinking she was next, kicked out at Bill. He easily caught her leg as she lay on the floor. He dug his fingers into her ankle and she let out a cry of pain. He let her leg go and returned to the table.

'Feisty fuckers, ain't you.' he said.

'What the fuck was that for?' cried Katy, holding her face with her free hand.

Bill lit a cigarette, blew out the smoke. 'For bringing me the wrong girl.' he said.

He sat down at the table, leaned forward with both elbows on the table, the cigarette in one hand. 'Now, who the fuck is Wendy Cross?'

Both girls shivered as they huddled closer to each other. He had found out who she was. Katy looked at Wendy and smiled. 'Wendy?' she asked. Wendy just gave a frightened smile she shivered.

166

'It's going to be okay, Wendy.' Katy whispered.
Both girls knew that was very unlikely.

Chapter 29

After the police had gone from his flat, Jezz sat there. He had done some bad things in his life, but nothing he had previously done had bothered him in the least. He had fought tough men, and lost, and bore the scars to prove it. He had fought tough men, and won, and they bore the scars. He'd stolen, he had lied, he had dealt drugs, and he had hurt people and was sure he probably had destroyed lives as he had done it. But none of it had bothered him. It was what he had to do to survive. He had never felt remorse until now, leading those two girls into a situation he knew nothing about. Yet as unsure as he was, he was sure that it would be their final destination. He hadn't slept. Every time he closed his eyes he could see the look of horror on their faces as he left them in the pizza hut with Bill. He knew it was right not to inform the police. That's not what his type did, because he knew if he had done, then his life wouldn't be a long one. *Not in this world* he thought. *In my world the pigs are scum, you want something, you just take it, you want something done then you do it.*

His head was swimming. He asked himself the same question, time and time again. *Can I live with it, if those two girls die?* Each time he was wishing for a different answer, but it was always the same. It was always *No.*

He went into his bedroom, put on a jacket, lifted the mattress, and pocketed the gun that was under it. He took a packet of cigarettes and a lighter which were on the table, grabbed his keys and walked out of his flat door. He wasn't sure how he was going to do it, or whether he could do it, but he knew he must try to get those kids back.

He had grown up in this area, in a town where people blatantly littered and jaywalked. Prostitutes on every corner, violence on every street. His father had been an addicted gambler, and his mother was on the game to fund her drug habit. They had both died. His father had been found dead on a piece of waste ground, when Jezz was twelve. He had been stabbed, probably because of a gambling debt. His mother had died from an overdose, when he was eighteen.

He still lived in the same flat. He had sworn he would never be like them. His flat was spotless, but he couldn't turn away from the life that haunted all of his kind, the people left behind, the ones on the street, or on the scrap heap. He was black. He didn't fit in this white world. That's why they were put in the slums of England.

He was now a self-proclaimed gangster. He had seen things and done things that would frighten other people to death. He had no brothers or sisters, which he thought was a good thing. He hadn't been abused as a child, but his awful memories were longer-lasting and more damaging. They were harder to deal with. He knew justice would never be delivered. His life had not been as bad as others, but worse than most. It gave him a bit of perspective, which helped him deal with reality over the years. Now he only did the things he did for money. That was the only way he could live, hurting people for money.

He had never bargained at all on it being two young girls, who were just kids. He had no technique for surviving, and it wasn't until he was twenty, that he realised he had a mind of his own. He could make his own decisions. That was when he realised he was a big strong man and people were scared of him. It was then he used that to his advantage. An animal that does not trust its own instincts, will almost certainly perish. Today Jezz had to trust his own instincts.

Chapter 30

'I'm Todd's girlfriend.' Wendy told him.

She felt scared now that the truth was out. Would he kill her? She didn't know. Her life seemed to flash through her mind. She wondered if this really was the time for her death. In spite of Katy being beside her she felt so alone.

'My mother will have called the police, not Todd or Daniel.' she added.

'This changes things.' He shifted in his chair. He looked angry. The girls could tell he was trying to think things through.

'Why should it? You still have me. Daniel will do whatever you ask. I'm his little brother's girl. He will do anything for Todd. I think I'm more of a prize than Becky ever was.' That made sense to Bill. Wendy was quite clever in putting that thought in his head. Maybe having his brother's girl would work out okay. Maybe it would work out better. Daniel's little brother's girlfriend gets killed, and it's all his fault. How would that affect their kinship? He smiled at that. This was good.

'What's he like?' For probably the first time in years, Bill thought of the son he had never really got to know. He wondered if he had grown up like Daniel, big and strong. He hoped so. The Fenton's were tough. He wanted two sons to carry on that tradition.

'Who?' asked Wendy.

'Todd, my son. I don't know him.'

Wendy smiled. 'He's wonderful. He's so clever. He writes poetry and songs, and he has a lovely voice. I put his words to music and we sing them all the time. I love him, Bill. You can be very proud of both your sons. They are wonderful people.'

I must win him over. Wendy thought, *I must befriend him.*
Bill just shrugged his shoulders. 'Proud?' he said. 'Nothing to
do with me. I was inside. I haven't seen Todd for seventeen
years.'

'Prison must have been hard.'

Katy held Wendy's hand again and squeezed. Her mouth had
stopped bleeding, but it hurt like hell.

'It was hard.' he said, 'But life out here is a lot harder.'

'How come?'

'In prison you're safe. Yeah, okay, you got to put up with a
lot of crap at first, be prepared to be raped, and beaten. But
once you've made your mark and you've earned respect, it's
easier. I was top dog in prison, you know.' he added proudly.

'Oh my God! That sounds terrible.'

'In there I *was* something. Out here, I am no one. I will go
back one day and get back what is rightly mine. People in
there, owe me.'

He thought back to his time in prison, and realised that the
last time he was happy had been when he was behind bars.
There was something about prison life which had made him
feel safe. He had everything in there, even power.
He missed some of the people, and that felt strange to him,
never really knowing what it was like to miss someone. He
thought of Carol, his only love. Yes, he missed her.

'I like you, Wendy.' he said. 'That may even keep you alive.'
'I hope so, Bill, because I would like you to meet Todd, get to
know your son, and I know he feels the same. It doesn't have
to be like this, you know. We can work something out.'

Bill didn't answer. Wendy didn't follow it up. Bill uncuffed
them. 'We're leaving.' he said. 'I've booked us in at the dirtiest
place you can imagine.'

It was nearly three am when they pulled out of the pizza place. The two girls were handcuffed together in the back seat, Bill driving, and as he approached the Severn Bridge he burst into song. 'We're all going on a summer holiday.' He felt sad and wished he was someplace else.

Chapter 31

'What the fuck!' said Mickey Bolan, who had just been woken up with a kick in the ribs, He rubbed his side, looked up, but he didn't know where he was for a moment. He recognised the man.

'Jezz. What the fuck did you kick me for?'

Jezz had made his way to the pizza place and had literally stumbled across Mickey sleeping in the bushes.

'What are you doing here, Mickey?'

Mickey sat up. 'They're in there. I was watching, but I must have fallen asleep. I think that beating Bill gave me, took it out of me. My fucking head hurts.'

Jezz laughed. He knelt beside Mickey, looking at the pizza place. The night was still and quiet. The silhouette of the pizza place looked eerie against the sky. Mickey shivered. He didn't know if he was scared or cold.

'He thinks you're dead. So do the girls.' Jezz said.

'Why do they think that?'

'Long story, but I told him you were.' His eyes stared at the abandoned pizza hut. Mickey looked at Jezz. He began to shake, struggling to get his words out.

'You ain't going to hurt me, are you, Jezz?' Jezz grinned, thinking how he had come to be like this. He was here to help, and all Mickey could think of was that he was going to hurt him. How had he become like this? What had he become? 'No, my friend, you're gonna help me get those girls back.'

'How're we gonna do that?'

'We're gonna grab some of that scrap metal over yonder, get in and hit the fuck out of that bastard.'

'I don't like the sound of that.'

Jezz laughed. 'You,' he said, 'you go round to the side and make some noise. Bang on the boards on the windows. Let him know you're there. Ask him outside for a fight. Tell him you're gonna kick his ass.'

Mickey panicked. 'You must be joking. He'll kill me.'

Jezz pulled out the gun he had tucked into his waist band. 'He won't have a chance, because as soon as he comes out, he gets a bullet in the head.'

'What if you miss?'

'I never miss. Now go do it. I'll get closer so I can get a good shot.'

Mickey stood up. 'Okay.' he said, 'Just make sure you hit the bastard.'

'I will, and Mickey,' he looked at Jezz, 'you let me down and do a runner and you get the bullet.'

'I won't let you down, Jezz.' and Mickey meant that. He wanted Bill Fenton dead, and he wanted those girls. Especially Wendy, oh that cute Wendy.

Mickey walked slowly and quietly to the pizza hut and reached the side of the building with the boarded up windows. He watched Jezz position himself just outside the flap, where Bill would come out, but unseen from any point in the pizza hut. Jezz nodded, and Mickey started banging the boarding, shouting obscenities.

'Come on out, you fucker. I'm gonna beat your brains in.' he shouted. He was frightened, but at the same time the adrenalin had kicked in. He started to jump up and down, kicking the side of the boarding. This went on for about a minute, the excitement building up in Mickey, the bravado. For at that moment he really believed he could beat Bill Fenton. He was the king of his particular jungle. Jezz moved from his stance, lowered the gun to his side, and motioned for Mickey to stop.

Jezz walked cautiously to the flap where they would get in and out. He noticed that it was open, and hadn't been put back. Cautiously and slowly, he looked inside. It was empty. At least the main dining area and kitchen were empty. There were a few other smaller rooms in there but he wasn't going to bother looking in them. In any case, if Bill had been in there, he would have done something by now, just to shut Mickey up.

After seeing that it was safe, Mickey walked over.

'It's empty.' said Mickey.

Jezz turned around, grabbed Mickey by the collar lifted him a full six inches off the floor.

'You stupid bastard!' He threw Mickey on the floor, where he cracked his elbow on the ground. Jezz paced back and forth, 'You're useless. You spend all night spying on them, and the building's fucking empty. They went, and you were fast asleep.'

'I'm sorry, Jezz.'

Jezz didn't answer. *Well, he tried,* he thought. *At least he tried.* Now, if anything happens to those girls, it would not be on his conscience. He looked at the pathetic figure lying on the floor, his faced bruised, looking like he hadn't slept or eaten in weeks.

'Why were you out here, anyway?' he asked.

'I wanted to try and save them. Katy's my girl, and he's got Her. I gotta try and get her back Jezz.'

'So what were you gonna do?'

'I dunno, really. '

'Get up.' He helped Mickey to his feet. 'You look awful.'

Mickey just shrugged his shoulders

'You hungry?' Jezz asked

'Sure.'

'You smell, man.'

'Sorry Jezz.'

Jezz looked at the beaten boy standing in front of him, a remnant of all that was shit in this society. A boy left out on the streets, who was neither big enough, nor strong enough to cope. Life was full of users and abusers. Mickey was one of those who got used, and abused, time and time again, and the idiot was still out here, taking on the likes of Bill Fenton. Jezz felt a sudden admiration for Mickey. Then he felt sorry for him. He has accepted this kind of life, being bullied and beaten, and all Mickey got out of it was a bit of pot, and the occasional tab. *It's a fucked-up world*, he thought, *full of fucked up people.*

'You're gonna get yourself killed, man.' Mickey shrugged again.

'Come on, let's get you to my place, have some food, and we'll think of a plan.'

They got into Jezz's car, leaving the stolen Focus behind. He had to find out where Bill had gone. Now was his time to make some amends, to do some good. It was time to move on. To move his life on. Just one more piece of scum to remove from this crappy world. He smiled as he drove. His life was going to change from here on in, for the worse or better.

Chapter 32

Once over the Severn Bridge and into Wales, Bill could see the carnage on the roads ahead. The signs ahead, warning of long delays on the A48, which was the road leading to Newport and Cardiff, and two junctions which took you off to Ashbourne and Newport on the M4 were closed. Bill wasn't concerned about that. He knew some back roads to where he was going, and that was neither Newport nor Ashbourne. They can fuck their party. He was going to have a party of his own, and only a select few were invited.

The two girls, sitting in the back of the car, were again wondering where they were going. As they reached the tolls on the Severn Bridge, it made Wendy feel better, knowing she was closer to home. She had thought about shouting out, just taking the chance. Maybe the toll man would take down their number. *They're bound to have cameras on the tolls,* she thought, *so if she screamed and shouted that would alert them.* The number would be noted, and soon the police would be round. She thought about the roads being blocked, but the police would find a way through. She was sure of that. They had to.

As they crossed the bridge, and approached the tolls, she noticed that a series of tolls were unmanned. That's where Bill Fenton drove, dropped his cash into the bin, and drove through the tolls. Just an ordinary driver, on an ordinary night. *There will be a chance* she thought *there has to be.* Katy had sensed her idea, and when she realised what had happened, she put her head on Wendy's shoulder.

'It will be okay.' she whispered.

Wendy wasn't too sure. It was dark. They had no idea where they were going. One thing was sure. They weren't going to like it.

Bill took a detour through Chepstow and Caldicot, two towns just on the border of Wales. Wendy knew these areas, but became lost again when Bill drove into back roads which were deserted and dark, and void of other traffic. A perfect place to commit murder and leave a body. Both girls thought there would be nothing as simple as that. Somehow they were expecting a lot worse. They drove for about thirty minutes through the lanes and back roads. No other cars were seen, until they got onto a dual carriageway. There was hardly any traffic here. Wendy had seen this area before but she couldn't remember where she was, until she saw the signs saying 'Wentwood Forest, the largest ancient woodlands in Wales', where it was rumoured that a resident from Ashbourne, back in the 1970's which was at that time a much smaller village, had killed his wife and buried her in Wentwood forest. Her body had never been found.

It was soon clear where they were going, as they turned down a lane that was signposted Wentwood Forest two miles. Wentwood was famous for many things, not just the illegal rave that took place in 2007 with over three thousand people attending. The area contains Bronze Age burial mounds, and was the scene of riots in 1678 regarding the ownership of the land. It is now a forested area of hills which rise well over a thousand feet. Some areas are dense, and rumours have it if you go deep into the forest you are unlikely ever to come out. It is virtually an unbroken band of dense woodlands stretching between the rivers Usk and Wye, a perfect place to kill and hide a body.

They pulled up to a picnic area just outside the forest. Wendy remembered the time she and Todd had come up here with Daniel and Becky, and had a barbecue. It had been a lovely summer evening, and they had explored the woods together. The pairs had split up from each other. She remembered that Todd had made love to her, deep in the woods, whilst Daniel and Becky were probably doing the same. She remembered when they had met up again and how red her face went. She was sure the others realised what they had been up to. Todd was the only man she had ever been with. How she longed, at this moment, to feel his naked body next to hers. Just one more time. Then they could make love forever.

This was where the roads stopped. They would be driving no further. Bill got out of the car, opened the boot, and took out his rucksack and what was clearly a shot gun. He opened the rear door to speak to the handcuffed girls.

'Get out!' he said.

The girls shuffled out of the car and stood beside it, still cuffed together, their vacant faces just staring into the abyss. Bill liked this kind of power. He thrived on it. It made him grow stronger. It made him more evil. He could do anything he wanted. No one could stop him. They were his, under his control. Bill uncuffed them, raised his gun into the air, and warned them not to run, not to make a move. After some thought, he cuffed their hands separately.

'Just for now.' he laughed.

Wendy looked around. It was dark, but moonlight shone. She could smell the composting leaves, and could hear the crackling of branches as she stared into the forest. It seemed deep and alive, with its ancient glory untouched and overgrown. Its groaning trees seemed to be beckoning, and the hostile screeches from some animal sounded chilling, as they walked into the forest. Katy thought about her past, and the life she had led. She hoped that for one more time she could feel happiness, whatever that feeling felt like. It had been such a long time. They walked deep into the forest, to an unknown destination. To a future of uncertainty and probable death.

Chapter 33

Todd had no idea what was happening, or where he was going. Not the Todd in the wardrobe, who lay still and looking somewhat comatose. That Todd was just the body which housed the Todd who now flew in the skies. The Todd who had somehow taken to the skies, and was now flying over the United Kingdom. He had no control over where he was going. There was no fear, no sense of anxiety, and no natural wonderment as he flew the skies. The only sense he had, was one of a purpose. He was sure that purpose would become known soon. This was no natural journey. Things seemed dark and demonic, a timeless journey of suspense. Sometimes he hovered, sometimes he sped, most of the time he just flew gracefully through the darkened skies. He had no idea which route he was taking. He had no idea what was holding him up in the skies. He wasn't flapping his hands like a bird's wings. There was no engine attached. No motors to keep him going. He wondered if someone could actually float with enough helium balloons. He had already decided that when this was all over, he and Wendy would try it. Then he thought of Wendy and let the determination overwhelm him.

There was no sense of time as he drifted through the air. He had no knowledge what day it was, what year it was, whether he had been up there for an hour, a minute, a day, or a week. He could see roads and houses, forests and fields, towns and cities. Maybe he was flying in a circle, and he would spend his days just going round and round in an everlasting circle, until he could fly no more. Then he would descend to the ground in a final moment before his death.

He wasn't scared. He wasn't anything. He was just some human form flying through the skies, alone amid the stars and the clouds, the breezes and the winds. But he wasn't alone. He was never alone. There was always the light with him, not bright, but constant. He knew that the light was leading the way. The light would save him. The light would lead him to his, and Wendy's, destiny.

He could see the sea now. He now knew where he was. He was on the west coast of England, about a five hour drive from where he lived. Had his journey taken five hours? He doubted it. Maybe five minutes, maybe five days but somehow, he thought, never five hours. He flew past the tower of Blackpool. He loved Blackpool. Then Blackpool had gone, and he hovered like a kestrel over Lytham St. Anne's. He was hovering in the air, studying the ground below, as if scanning for something or someone. He felt like a predator, searching for prey, searching for food, searching for answers. He drifted closer to the ground, still hovering gracefully. The house below seemed large with lush, beautiful gardens. Was this where he was meant to be? Was this where he has to go? Was this where Wendy was?

Then the light grew bright, and Todd's thoughts no longer seemed to be there. Now he was just like that kestrel hovering over his prey as the storm came in and started raging all around him. He embraced the storm. This was how it was meant to be.

The elderly lady was asleep. Her sleep wasn't natural. Very rarely was it these days. There were always dreams, regular nightmares and her brain just never switched off. It was always thinking, always awake, while her body wanted to sleep. Tossing and turning would be regular, a look at the clock every fifteen minutes, hoping that hours had passed since she last looked, and she had actually fallen into a deep sleep. But that never happened. She couldn't remember the last time she slept, really slept. Sometimes the dreams were pleasant. She would dream about her grandsons, playing football in a field laden with daffodils and daises, and a murder of crows flying through the air, as the football her grandsons had kicked, disturbed them into flight. The two boys chasing the wild rabbits, which sped into their burrows. A secret world of wonderment, where she and her grandsons played, but those dreams never lasted long.

They had never happened. Dreams had never come true for Marie Rose.

But the nightmares. Oh those nightmares. Those were just re-enactments of her life. The beatings that she had taken from her first husband, and the raping's she had taken from him, as he battered and bruised her. She could see her own son's face in those fearful dreams, as he would watch his father beat her to within an inch of her life, with the smile of a demon on his face. They had happened so many years ago.

She had made herself a good life, a gifted fortune-teller who knew how to say the right things. Numerous television appearances which had raked in a fortune, and the insurance pay out when her second husband fell to his death.

The home that was laden with the riches of her misspent life. She looked at the clock again. Surely some hours had passed. It was 2.32 am. The last time she had looked it was 2.11. She sat up in bed, the moonlight shining through the open drapes. Her bedroom looked onto her vast garden, and she always had the curtains open, because she loved to look out into the night, at the moon and the stars. She got out of her bed, took her gown off the hook on the back of the door, and wrapped it round her. She put her feet into her white fluffy slippers. Although they were over ten years old, she loved the feel of them on her feet.

183

She walked to the window and looked at the skies. The moon was bright, the stars were in abundance tonight. As she scoured the skies, she noticed a dim light in the distance, hovering. She watched its movement. *It didn't look like a plane* she thought. She gave it no further thought, as she went downstairs to make a pot of tea, and have a cigarette. She didn't want to try and sleep anymore tonight. The nightmares had been deeply bad. There had been no dreams of fields and rabbits, of footballs and crows, and the gleaming faces of her grandsons. They had not come tonight. *Would they ever come again* she had thought as she went down the stairs.

She sat on her sofa, with a cigarette in one hand, and a Famous Grouse in the other, after deciding that whisky would give her more comfort then any pot of tea. She knew she drank too much, but what else was there to do at her time of life. She was now seventy one and in remarkably good condition, looking twenty years younger than her age, despite her heavy indulgence in cigarettes and whisky. The large clock above the fire place, which had butterflies as numbers, showed it was 2.47. She quickly drank the whisky, and stubbed out her cigarette in the ashtray.

'Maybe I should move.' she said out loud.

She didn't read fortunes now. She had retired from that ten years ago. It had been an eventful career, a rewarding career, but she had grown so bored by it. She had been hoping that she would meet another Carol, a raven haired beauty who bore the signs of an angel, who bore angelic sons. Of course, something beautiful in life is always preceded by horror. Carol's horror was the man she had married. The man that Marie Rose would only ever to refer to as the demon. Not the son of an angel, more like the son of Satan himself.

Marie Rose always thought of her grandsons, whom she had never met. She was sure that one day there would be a calling, and she would spend the rest of her days tending to them as a grandmother should.

She lived in the same house in Lytham St. Anne's, with the extravagant gardens, which she paid to have tended, and a cleaner came in twice a week to clean the home in which she lived. She had often thought of moving, after her second husband died, but she never did. She knew she never would. She had got to know her neighbours a bit now, and sometimes they would pop in to each other's houses for coffee and a chat. Her neighbours were in their late fifties and extremely wealthy, as most people around here were. She never got too friendly. She needed her own space, for her thoughts and wishes. Her own company, at times, was the best company she could wish for. She walked a lot of the time, though she had never been into Blackpool since the last day of her fortune telling. She didn't want to. She hated the hustle and bustle of it. The drunken people from down south, on some stag or hen weekend drove her mad. Her home was more serene, filled with areas to walk amongst natural beauty, and enjoy the sea air, without the fousty smell of beer, vomit, and sewage, which she associated with Blackpool.

Life for her was okay, sometimes lonely, and even at the age of seventy one she still sometimes longed to be held by the strong arms of a male companion. She debated whether or not to have another Grouse, and decided she would. *The wind was coming up outside* she thought, as she lit another cigarette. *That had come up quickly*. She walked towards the windows which looked out over her gardens. She leaned on the large oak cabinet underneath the window, putting her drink on the lace doily on the cabinet. The wind was now growing really strong.

185

She could hear it howling. *Where did that come from?,* she thought. She loved the storms, when she was tucked up warm in her home. As she looked out of the window, she felt an enormous sense of loneliness. All the money in the world could not rid her of this feeling. When the calling came she would be ready. If it never came, then she would die as lonely as she now felt. She looked out, noticing that the trees were still, but she could still hear the wind. Not just hear it, she could feel it. Her long hair which was hanging loose, blew across her eyes. The wind was in the house. *My God,* she thought, *it's in my house.*

She turned, looking across her large oak-furnished living room. The curtains were moving. How was that possible? A feeling came over her, one that she had never felt before. Something inside her told her to embrace it, adorn it, follow it, breathe it, and let it take her. Marie Rose knew this was what she had been waiting for, for more than twenty years. This was her time, her calling. They had come for her, and she wasn't going to let them down. The howling was louder and stronger, as the storm took hold of her living room. Paintings started shaking, and one fell to the floor, shattering the glass of the frame into a thousand pieces. The room started to shake, building up to a violent paranormal activity. Ornaments started moving, and soon flew across the room. An ornamental figure of a young child reading a book, caught her a glancing blow on her head, drawing blood. She wiped her head with her hand and looked at the blood on her finger. *This is my time,* she thought *The Lord is calling.* Maybe this is how it is meant to end, caught up in a storm and dying alone, all alone. 'It's not my calling,' she said to the storm, 'It's my ending!' Then she thought about the boys in her dreams. How she had never

186

met them, never seen them. They would be grown up now, but she had always been sure she would see them. It couldn't end like this. She wouldn't let it.

There was a streak of lightning followed by a sound of thunder, as the storm grew stronger, and took hold. She had never ever heard a sound like it. The whole house shook. Through the thunder came what sounded like voices. She heard the voices telling her to go, telling her to get out. The wind was forceful now. She tried to move, having to fight against the wind, as she inched her way towards the door. Was the wind trying to keep her back, or was it trying to guide her? She wasn't sure. She had to get out. She had to. She wanted to see her boys, just once, then the good Lord could take her. There were now too many voices to comprehend, and, as the rain came, she screamed!

The wind had now eased but the rain came, her heavy dressing gown was already sodden, feeling heavy on her body, weighing her down, her nightdress clung to her skin, and as she wiped the rain from her eyes more just came, turning to hail which hit her violently, stinging her face. The lights flashed and went out, sparks came from the sockets in the wall, then hailstones the size of golf balls rained down on her. The frozen balls battered her as she crawled along the floor towards the door. Pain racked her head. She felt as though her hands were broken as she crawled into the hallway. She could see the front door now, the keys still in it. Maybe she would get out. Maybe this was just a warning. She crawled towards the door, as a table flew across the hallway narrowly missing her. The umbrella stand flew into the air, and three umbrellas hovered above her like something out of a Harry Potter movie. She felt sure that one was going to stab her as they descended to the ground, yet it missed her by inches. She stood up when she was just six feet from the door, but the golf ball hail rained down on her, knocking her to her knees again. Her whole body hurt. She wasn't going to make it. Tonight she would die. Then the locked solid oak door opened wide. She could see outside now. Shading her eyes with her hands, she raised her head to look. The door was open, but all she could see was a light. She had no idea what it was, but she knew she had to reach it, so she crawled on her hands and knees as the hailstones rained down on her battered body, into the light. Into the light that called her.

Chapter 34

Madison's hair was a rich shade of mahogany, flowing in waves of silk that adorned her glowing, porcelain-like skin. Her eyes, framed by long lashes that naturally curled, were a deep emerald green that seemed to want to brighten the world. With full lips, and a perfectly formed nose that complemented her high cheek bones, this young sixteen year old girl seemed to be a picture of perfection. A natural beauty that thousands of women would pay millions to have, and hundreds had, without achieving such perfection. When she smiled, it made people around her feel contented. When she laughed it made people want to laugh with her. She was funny and articulate, stubborn and proud. When she cried, it was as if the whole world would want to comfort her.

Madison never chose to look this way. She never realised her beauty. She was modest but fiery, determined yet vulnerable. She merely wanted adventures. After all, she had only just turned sixteen.

Sue, her mother, was a wonderful mum, only thirty eight herself. It was clear that Madison got her good looks from her mother, who had done everything a mum could do for a daughter. They were friends, as well as being mother and daughter, Sue had never regretted having Madison for one moment. That night, seventeen years ago, after a drunken one night stand with a Welsh hunk, when she had been visiting Cardiff.

On a night out with friends, she had been ashamed when she woke up, lying next to that man the following morning, in some sleazy hotel. It had made her feel dirty, but nine months later when she had given birth to a beautiful daughter she considered it to be the best thing that had happened to her. She had never thought to look for her one-night stand to tell him. Why should she? Why would she? She had met Morgan, when Madison was three and married him three years later. He had a good job working for the M.O.D., although no one really knew what he did. It was a consultancy role which took him away from home quite often. He always wore a shirt and tie, even when not at work.

Madison knew that Morgan wasn't her real father, but she called him Dad and loved him as if he were. He loved her, and she always teased him about having two surnames and no Christian name. Their life was good, bright and happy, but . . . There was always a *but*. Madison knew there was something else, something deeply hidden, somewhere in her world that would not reveal what was to be her destiny. There were people in her life that she hadn't yet met. People who were special. She knew that, as an only child, as a bright student, she was going to grow up to be someone special. To her parents she already was special. Madison Hughes, a sixteen year old, like any other sixteen year old, wanted her life to be an adventure. Yet she hadn't bargained on the life that was about to come her way.

Madison Hughes wasn't your regular sixteen year old. She seemed to have a gift, not one she had chosen, not one she could really control, but every now and again she could hear people's thoughts.

She had never told her parents about her gift, but her father was aware of it. In fact, her gift was the reason he had met her mother. He hadn't bargained on falling in love and marrying Sue. That hadn't been the plan but he couldn't help who he fell in love with, and it had worked out okay up to now. Madison didn't really know how to read people's thoughts or what it was about her. It hadn't started until she was thirteen, or at

190

least that was when she could remember it starting. Yet people were aware of her gift when she was a three year old. At that age, the young mind fails to comprehend these things, and treats them as normal. Between the ages of three to six, Madison had been able to read minds, until Morgan had almost successfully taken it from her.

It still happened, but now it was of no great concern. Her first real memory of it was when she was in class sitting at her desk. A teacher, whose name now eluded her, was sitting at his desk, with another thirteen year old pupil standing beside him. The child was being chastised for poor work in front of all the class who could see and hear everything. Every pupil was watching and thinking how inappropriate it was.

Suddenly Madison could hear the teacher's thoughts. At first she wasn't sure where it was coming from, so she felt somewhat confused. She looked around and realised that no one else could hear these thoughts. The other pupils were still watching the poor girl who was almost in tears. Mr. whatever his-name-was, was having lewd thoughts about how he would like to punish this girl. At that moment Madison said nothing, and the class continued as normal. What had happened frightened her a little bit, but nothing had ever been clearer. She had heard his thoughts. She was sure of that. When the bell rang, and the pupils were leaving the classroom, Madison, who was quite sure what she had heard could not let it go. She made sure that she was the last pupil to leave, and before she left, she repeated his exact words back to the teacher, and left the class. That teacher never came back to teach. Madison had never seen him again. She had never told anyone about this as it frightened her a little.

It had happened three other times. Once, when she was in a shopping mall, she heard the thoughts of a young boy who was plotting to steal a handbag from an elderly woman. She had warned the elderly lady, and saved her from that ordeal. The other two occasions were when girls to whom she was talking were mentally slagging her off. In each case Madison had answered them, as if they had spoken the thoughts out loud, both amazing and frightening the girls at the same time. For a while they had called her Mystic Mad, but the name never stuck. Truth be told, some girls weren't just in awe of her, they were a little bit scared.

Today was a good day. Her best friend, Chantelle, was staying over for the first time since they had met, as Madison's parents were having a weekend away together. This was the first time they had left Madison alone overnight. After warning her against any wild parties off they went. After two pints of cider each, and two flick chick movies, and a whole host of crisps and goodies, the two girls had gone to bed at two am. Chantelle slept soundly in Madison's bed, whilst Madison herself was curled up in her parents' king size divan. She loved that bed. She clearly remembered that when she was younger she would sneak in with her mother, when her father was working away. The bed had seemed huge in those days, when she and her mother would snuggle up all night. She loved those memories. The simple things were always the best.

Todd wasn't sure what had happened. He remembered hovering over a large house just on the outskirts of Blackpool. Then a violent storm had erupted. He seemed to be at the centre of the storm, yet he felt no danger. Not only was he at the centre of it, Todd was sure that he had caused the storm. How long it had gone on for, he wasn't sure, as he still had no sense of measuring time. He remembered seeing a lady run out of the house, screaming as she ran from the storm. He wasn't sure what was happening, why he was there, or who the lady was. He had never seen her before, and saw no significance in his being there. He just wanted to go home now, and find Wendy to tell her how much he loved her. He hoped the old lady wasn't hurt. She didn't look too good. Todd Fenton didn't like this. He didn't like this at all.

He now found himself in Manchester, above a nice private housing estate, He couldn't remember leaving Blackpool and flying to Manchester. All he could remember was flying over Old Trafford, the home of his favourite football team, and seeing the statue of Sir Matt Busby. He wondered if there was any significance in that. Why take him that way? Why bring him here at all? He was hovering like the graceful bird which he became when the light that guided him would once again glow bright, and the storm would rage all around him, while the skies remained clear, and the moon lit up the streets of Manchester.

It was the sound of the wind which awoke her first. She didn't think she had been in bed that long. Her throat was dry. *Probably too much cider* she thought. She got out of bed to go downstairs to the kitchen to get a drink. She grabbed her dressing gown. As she passed her own bedroom, she noticed Chantelle was sound asleep. She could hear her snores. She smiled at that, as it reminded her of her mum who always snored. It seemed strange not having her parents' home. The king size bed seemed way too big for one person. She put some squash in a glass and went to the sink to top it up with water. As she turned the tap, the sky lit up with a flash of lightning, and the window pane burst, showering her with broken glass. Her instinct forced her to the floor. For a moment she just sat there in shock. She checked to see if she had been cut, and was pleased to see that she hadn't. She could feel the force of the wind now blowing through the smashed window. She needed to get out of the kitchen and up to Chantelle. *Could the wind break a window like that?,* she thought, *or did someone break it? Was someone trying to get in? Someone who knew her parents were away and had decided to break in?* She wanted to scream, but couldn't. Then something crazy happened. She heard a voice in the same way that she had heard other people's thoughts, but this time she could hear a dream. Chantelle's dream. She was dreaming about nice things. No storms raged, just dreams.

Madison managed to stand. She looked at the broken window. She wondered what her mother and father were going to say. Was the voice telling her that Chantelle was safe? She hoped so. Her hair blew across her face, and through the window she could see a bright light which was spinning faster and faster, getting nearer and nearer like a spinning top, or a hurricane that you see in the movies. The drawers were opening in the kitchen now. Cupboard doors slammed open and closed. She stood by the window. Surely the noise would wake Chantelle up, and she would come down, but what could she do. At least she wouldn't be alone. The voice she had heard hadn't happened again for a while. She cowered down, wishing she had her phone.

The lights in the house were flashing now, and the noise was awful. *How could a storm be in my house?,* she thought. She had to get out. She stood up, and looked out of the window, not believing what she saw. There seemed to be someone in the sky, at the centre of the storm, and he was calling her, beckoning her to join him. Then the light grew nearer, and Madison felt an overwhelming sense of wanting to reach out and touch the light, and that's what she did. The next thing she felt was her feet lifting off the ground, and in one swift movement the force of the hurricane lifted her out through the window. Madison could swear that she could see someone in the sky, waving to her as he flew away, Madison would not remember anything about how she landed. At sixteen years of age Madison's beautiful adventure was about to begin.   Her best friend, Chantelle, slept soundly, snoring in Madison's bed. The storm would not wake her. She would not realise her best friend had gone missing, until she woke in the morning.

Chapter 35

Things weren't actually becoming clear to Todd now. In fact, he was more confused than ever, but, as crazy as all this was, he guessed there must be some significance in it. The elderly lady, and the young girl, a stunning young girl, that he had literally pulled from her house, and into the storm must mean something. Even though he could not see them now, he somehow knew he would see them again. The storm had calmed. He was sure the women were not hurt. They certainly would have nothing to do with Wendy's disappearance, because he knew who was responsible for that. What had all this to do with his father? Or is this strange trip merely to keep him away? Keep him from saving Wendy?

He thought he was going home now, as he had been floating in the sky at speed since leaving Manchester. But no, here he was hovering above a bungalow in Smethwick, West Midlands. He hovered, expecting a storm, and he wasn't disappointed.

Doctor James McCarthy finally left his surgery at eight pm. The days were getting longer and longer, and he was feeling too old for the job now. This grey-haired man, whose eyes seemed to be constantly tired, was very weary. He seemed to be constantly exhausted. At six feet two inches and weighing two hundred and fifty pounds, it felt like all his muscular body ached. Tonight he wouldn't be on duty at the hospital. He was going home for pie and chips with mushy peas, oh, and whisky. Don't forget the whisky. He thought about his job whilst he drove home, a route he had taken thousands of times. It was all right for the government to introduce longer surgery times. It was all right for them to allow patients to see their doctor on a Saturday, but the targets were killing him. How are you supposed to guarantee that a patient would see a doctor within two days? There were only so many hours in each day. Question Time was on tonight, and that was one of the topics. He would watch it with interest. He thought *let's see what those government arseholes have got to say.* It was all about managing now, skills and knowledge performance charts, communication, partnership and teamwork. All the words he hated. He simply wanted to treat patients. It took nine days, on average for patients to get an appointment at his surgery. *Nine fucking days* he thought, *you could die in nine days.*

He had been a GP at Smethwick surgery for over thirty years, a job he had once loved, yet which he now hated. His thirty seven years of marriage had ended when his wife had died two years ago at the age of fifty five. Young lovers. First and only lovers. He still missed her, always would. They had no children. They just wanted to enjoy life, and when the time was right, they might have kids. But they kept on enjoying life, and that time never came.

Then the cancer took in. He knew she had it. James McCarthy could smell death. That was his curse. Not a gift, definitely a curse. He smelt the cancer in his wife in the same way he could smell it when a patient came into his surgery. Without speaking, if any patient were at death's door, he could smell it.

In many cases, he could prolong life, as his curse always gave him early diagnosis, which enabled earlier treatment. Yet death still came, as it had with his beloved wife, Elsie. Cancer was unforgiving.

He had a lot of time for those people, a caring doctor with empathy, yet he had no time for the hundreds who visited him with no illness at all. *He hated them, and that was the problem* he thought.

Today's surgery had been no different. He had seen thirty patients, knowing that ten of them could have just taken an aspirin and gone to bed. Two he had referred to hospital for tests. He was concerned about them. There was no smell of death, yet he was worried enough to refer them. He still loved doctoring. The ability to help people and cure their ailments gave him the most amazing feeling of satisfaction, but it was the red tape he hated. It had left him saddened by it all. There was a lack of respect. Doctors had been regarded as gods when he was young. Now he felt like a lap dog.

It wasn't a particularly warm evening. He had his chips, and sat with a whisky. He got up from his cream sofa, and turned the gas fire on low, just to take the chill off. He sat down and watched the TV, but he was not really taking it in. The whisky was making his head fuzzy and, as Question Time came on, James had fallen into a deep sleep on his sofa. He dreamt of all his patients, the good and the bad. He dreamt of his wife as he always did. Those were nice dreams.

It was the heat that woke him in the early hours. He had slept well, but he woke up feeling intense heat. His body was soaked with sweat. *The fire* he thought *I've left the fire on.* He focussed his eyes, the gas fire was still alight, but the flames were now above the mantelpiece, scorching the wallpaper. He could see the wooden letter-rack on the mantel burning. He tried to understand the situation. He tried to get to the gas fire to turn it off, but the heat was too intense. As the flames now spread, being fanned by the wind. The wind which was now in his home. He looked around, the curtains were burning, the sofa on which he sat was burning, and the whole room was alight. The windows smashed with the heat, the door was ablaze.

There was no exit that way. Panic set in. He didn't want to die. For a second he wondered if he could sense his own death. He couldn't. That reassured him for a moment, but how was he going to get out. The house was burning. There was no way out, He cried as he waited for death. For a moment, he thought about his wife. He would soon be joining her and everything seemed all right, because he was no longer in a burning room. There were no flames, no fire, no smoke. He thought that he had died and been taken to wherever it was when your death took over your body.

The cousin of Marie Rose, Dr James McCarthy, had been taken by a light which lifted him through the ceiling of his room, through the roof. He hoped he was going to heaven, but he somehow knew that wasn't the case. Elsie would have to wait. He knew he had other patients to see. Patients he had yet to meet. How he hoped that they would not smell of death.

Todd watched the home burning. He thought for one moment that the man inside was going to die. Todd wanted to help him but he couldn't. All he could do was watch, helplessly, as he saw the man struggle. He didn't want to be a part of this, not killing someone. He thought of the lady and young girl. Maybe they had died too, and that scared Todd.

This whole thing was so fucked up he wanted to scream, and stop this stupid flying. He wanted to go home. He had killed people, or at least hurt them. He now hated his gift. He should have left it where it was hidden. His father had made it return. He was responsible, just as he had been with all the bad things in their lives. Only one man was responsible. He was now sure that all this was his father's doing. His father had sent him up here, so that he couldn't save Wendy. Then he saw the storm close in and douse the flames in the house, and somehow lift the man from the carnage. As with the other two, Todd didn't seem to know this man. He was glad that he looked okay. Now, as with the other two, the man had gone, disappeared, lifted from the fire into the storm and gone. As before, the storm calmed, having done what it had been sent out for. As he made his way home, Todd could see the thousands of people walking to Ashbourne. As everything else was going crazy today, Todd hoped he hadn't missed the party.

Chapter 36

The girls had been walking for almost an hour now. Neither Wendy nor Katy were dressed for a terrain such as this. They were cold in their thin jumpers, their jeans felt damp against their skins. Their shoes were not made for walking through damp, dense forest, and were now cutting into their feet as they walked, causing their feet to blister. Their cuffed hands were making it difficult to get into a stride. Their wrists were hurting, where the metal cuffs were chafing. The voices of the night, and the screams of wild animals, chilled them to the core. They shivered from fright, they cried through fear. For tonight they were going to die.

Bill, who was dressed in a thick hoodie, and walking boots, still looked strong as he walked. The heavy rucksack didn't seem to be a burden to him. Every now and again, as the girls lagged behind, he would grab their hands and drag them, cutting their bodies on the roughness of the forest floor. On one occasion he had dragged Katy by her hair, and her screams should have been heard miles away. No one heard, except the night of the forest, and maybe the wild animals busy looking for their own prey. The forest took no prisoners, made no allowances. It was unforgiving in its brutality. Bill had changed since they got into the forest. He had only spoken when telling the girls to get a move on. He looked different. He looked evil. He looked mad. They needed to rest.

The skeleton-like trees had got thicker and there was no longer a trail to follow. It was misty, and Wendy wondered how many mysterious creatures would be lurking in the woods, waiting to attack, viewing them as another meal. She hoped Bill was a good shot. The girls walked closely together. Bill was always two yards in front, never more than two yards,

In spite of it being summer the ground was now boggy. The moonlight was barely shining through the trees, and where it did, it gave an eerie glow. The trees were whispering now, calling their names, calling them deep into the forest, to meet their fate. Both girls feeling emotionless, as if their death loomed as they walked deeper and deeper into the primeval forest.

They walked for another fifteen minutes. The trees did not seem so dense now. They needed to rest. The girls sat on a log now. They had to rest. Bill could do as he wished. They could walk no further.

'Move!' he shouted at them, pointing with his shot gun.

'We can't. We need to rest.' cried Katy.

Bill sat beside them on the tree stump. He took his torch from his rucksack, turned it on and shone it in the faces of the two girls back and forth, then he shone it on their bodies. The girls didn't care now. They were too done in.

'What the fuck happened to you two?' he asked as he looked at the cut up bodies of the girls.

'It's where you dragged us.' said Katy, and she just burst into tears. Bill went to his rucksack, took out some water and a sandwich, handing them to the girls.

'You should have said. We will rest here now, while you eat and drink to build up your strength.'

The girls took the water and food. Although it was welcome, the Jekyll and Hyde character of Bill made it scarier. They huddled together, cold and shaking, wet and hurting, as Bill Fenton lit a cigarette and climbed onto a branch of a tree, and looked down at the girls.

'You rest, build your strength up, because you're going to need it.' Then he laughed, long and loudly, like a hyena in the dead of the night. He sat in the tree, as the girls rested, watching them, always watching.

They rested for a couple of hours, with Bill watching from the tree all the time. He didn't need sleep, it was too big a day to sleep. It wasn't long before he got them up and going again. The girls' bodies were still aching from the beatings they had taken. The terrain became rocky in its nature, with hidden caves, dark and uninviting in the mountainsides. They could hear the sound of running water. They could now see the hills against the sky. As the trees seemed to thin out, the moonlight lit the ground.

'We're here.' was all that Bill said.

The girls didn't know where 'here' was, but they felt somewhat relieved, hoping that they could rest up properly, hoping they might see the nice side of Bill. They could now see what 'here' was, as the trees parted to show a clearing. As they walked towards the wooden cabin, which was hidden deep in the woods, in a small, picturesque clearing.

Both girls realised that the trek they had just been on was deliberate. Bill Fenton had known exactly where he was going. As they walked closer, the cabin became clearer. They didn't know what was in store for them. They had survived this long, and the longer they survived, the more determined they grew to get through it. They just needed one chance, one opportunity to make their escape. Surely Bill Fenton would soon let his guard down. He hadn't slept, he would lose his focus. They felt that it was their only chance. Nobody was coming to rescue them.

Chapter 37

With the kidnap of a young girl from their own estate, no one really knew why there was a need to party. Ashbourne Estate was awash with partygoers. Carol, Becky, and Tracy were joined by the blurry-eyed Simon Goldstone on the opposite side of the street from Carol's house. The thousands of people were now shouting Wendy Cross' name, as if she was some superstar rather than a lost, frightened girl. Every street was full of people. The news reporters were conducting numerous live interviews from the estate and also from the people who were still walking towards Ashbourne, and yet the crowd would not let the reporters anywhere near the street where the Fenton's lived. That was out of bounds. Simon Goldstone only got through, because Carol had allowed it. The whole country was watching, maybe even the whole world. The two men dressed in black still watched, just waiting for their orders.

Simon Goldstone stared at the hole in the roof, and the glow coming from it, it was one of the most eerie things he had ever seen. His walk across the fields had given him new faith in the youth of today. He had enjoyed the walk, enjoyed the company. Maybe he would have a different outlook after this. He wished he hadn't enjoyed the vodka and the dope as much. 'You say it was lightning?' he said Carol stared at him.

'There's no storm.'

'Simon, why are you here?' she asked

He looked at her, then at the house, then at the people still partying in the streets, shouting for Wendy Cross.

'I've no idea.' he said.

'Then just shut up.'

The four of them just turned to stare again at their house with a hole in its roof. Partygoers from the other estates were setting up tents in people's gardens. Camping stoves were being set up. Ashbourne Estate was being turned into a holiday resort. As the cafe opened up for food in the middle of the night, Phil Collins' 'Something in the Air Tonight.' played. Simon Goldstone stood and looked, thinking that there had never been a more apt song.

Todd returned home in the same way that he had left, through the roof.

Everyone saw the light coming towards them, growing brighter and brighter, until it disappeared through the hole in the roof, with a crash of thunder. No one seemed surprised. It was as if they were expecting it. There was a big cheer, and then, as if the landlord had called time, people started packing their stuff away. Those who lived nearby went home whilst those who had travelled for miles packed up their tents which they had only just pitched. The cafe closed without serving a single burger. Sofas, chairs and dining tables were taken back in. People went to bed, and the visitors started their long walk back. The news reporters were packing away their gear, reporting that the rave had now ended, and everyone was going home, adding that they would try to interview some people in the morning, as no one seemed interested in talking now.

There was no light in the Fenton's house, no storm raged, the hole in the roof was barely visible, as the moonlight seemed to fade, and the lights from the houses went out as people went to their beds.

Daniel heard the thunder. He heard Todd coming back. The light on the stairs was no longer there. He stood hesitantly at the foot of the stairs. He could hear movement from Todd's room. He heard the wardrobe doors close, and Todd opened his bedroom door. Standing at the top of the stairs he looked at his brother.

'Who put that hole in the fucking roof?' he asked, and both brothers laughed nervously.

'I'm sorry, Todd,' said Daniel, 'I was supposed to protect you. Protect us. I shouldn't have let you do it.' Todd walked down the stairs, and hugged his brother.

'It's done now. No going back.'

As Daniel hugged his brother, he knew he had made probably the biggest mistake of his life. Carol hugged Todd, as if she was never going to let him go again. It had been the worst couple of hours of her life. Becky and Tracy stood in anticipation, wanting to hear what had happened. They had somehow expected Todd to return with Wendy. On this extraordinary night, that seemed the most natural thing. Yet they could tell from Todd's face that was far from what had happened. Carol was just happy to have her son back. Simon Goldstone looked on, wondering what he was going to report. He had no idea, as he didn't know what had just happened.

He and Tracy left, as they had been told, in no uncertain terms, that they were not wanted. They had no choice. No crime had been committed, even in the rave that went on, there had been no reports of wrongdoing, just a street party. They would have reports to write, interviews to give, and, somehow, an explanation as to why a sergeant was seen on national TV drinking whilst on duty. Goldstone hoped and prayed that no one had seen him smoking.

The family were sitting in the living room. Todd was trying to explain as much as he could remember about his trip. He told them that he had hovered like a bird, and then the storms came over three properties, forcing the occupants out and that he thought at one point that he must have killed them, and that he was still not sure what had happened to them.

'Blackpool, Manchester and Birmingham.' Carol said, 'Do you know where?'

'Smethwick in Birmingham. That was the old man.' he said, 'not sure in Manchester, but it was close to Old Trafford. A nice private estate. That was the young girl, she looked hot.' He stared, embarrassed, at his mother when he realised what he had just said. He felt a pang of guilt, as he thought about Wendy.

'She was very pretty.' he continued. 'The old lady was in Lytham St. Anne's. A big, posh house.'

'Are you sure it was Lytham St. Anne's?' asked Carol. Todd nodded.

Carol stood up, looking out of the window. The streets were quiet now, though strewn with rubbish. It would be getting light soon. There would have to be a massive clear up. She turned and looked at her two sons and Becky.

'There's only one old lady that I know from Lytham St. Anne's, and I think she's the reason why you were born.'
'Who is she?' Daniel asked.

Carol sat down. She looked exhausted.

'Your father called her a wicked witch. I called her a miracle maker.'

She told them about that first trip to Blackpool, where Marie Rose told her she was pregnant, and then on the second visit, when she knew Daniel's name, and told her she was going to have another son. She continued, telling how their father had grown angry at the second visit and that was when she first realised that he wasn't the man she thought he was. The three listened intently as she spoke, neither interrupting nor

207

commenting. When she finished they all sat in silence for a moment.

Todd was the first to speak. 'Do you think what I did was some sort of punishment?'

Carol thought about that. 'Why would you punish her? I have two wonderful sons.'

'Maybe,' Daniel paused, gave it some more thought, 'maybe she could tell us where Wendy is.'

'Maybe,' Carol said, not sounding too confident.

Becky shuffled in her seat. She hadn't said a word since they got back in the house. It was all a bit too surreal for her. 'What's all this got to do with Wendy?'

'I don't know.' Todd said. 'I just hope it has, or I've been wasting my time flying around the country.'

Carol stood. 'It will be daylight soon. It looks as if sleep is out of the question. I'll cook some breakfast. Then we can decide what we're going to do. As she moved towards the kitchen, the doorbell rang.

Chapter 38

Ten Years Earlier

The school playground was bustling. It was a glorious May Day, one of those freak days of weather that the United Kingdom occasionally provides. It was eighty degrees, and the forecast was that it would stay hot until the weekend, when there would be thunderstorms, and it would be significantly cooler. A typical British forecast. The field playgrounds were large, with a small group of trees in the corner. They had not yet been sold off for development. The school was trying to hang onto them for as long as possible, but there had been a policy to sell off school playing fields throughout Britain, and they knew it wouldn't be long before they had to succumb to the authority's wishes. The fields would soon be replaced by a much smaller concrete hard standing, and a shopping centre would soon be built.

Ashbourne Estate was growing all the time. The residents didn't like it, and protested vehemently, with posters splattered everywhere, proclaiming that their village was being destroyed, and the community along with it. Their concerns were understandable. They had seen communities completely destroyed when the Conservative government shut all the pits. Yet not only would Ashbourne survive, it would thrive. Some communities just couldn't be broken.

The primary and secondary schools shared the same grounds. Todd was up to his usual tricks, being the centre of attention. His friends were hiding things in the woods, and he would go and find them. As a seven year old, he didn't really understand his ability, nor did the children around him. The school authorities were getting concerned, and Daniel was worried big time. He had told his brother to stop it, because people would regard him as a freak. He would tell him it was just fun, it was entertaining, besides which he liked being the centre of attention. He wasn't yet the reserved person he would eventually become. Daniel used to watch over him at every break time. Todd was his kid brother. It was his responsibility. Daniel was by far the biggest pupil in both his year and the year above him. He had natural muscle and strength, and an amazing ability with numbers. He loved maths and sport. Nothing else in school interested him. If he could have had maths every lesson he would. He would miss other lessons, and get in trouble over it, but he didn't care. Give him numbers or a ball and he was happy.

Todd finished school at three pm, and walked the short distance home. Daniel's school day went on for thirty minutes longer and, as the bell went, Daniel walked out of the school for the ten minute walk home. Most of the pupils lived on the estate, so there was no real big school run, particularly on a hot day like today. Very few cars were there, waiting for the children. Pupils scattered in different directions as they walked home. Daniel waved goodbye to some friends and began to walk home. He hadn't got far when he saw a young girl of about twelve. Daniel had never seen her before, but she was distressed and crying. He crossed the road to her, and asked her what was wrong. She told him that her dog had fallen into the brook which ran alongside the village, and she couldn't get him out. Daniel asked her to show him where, and they both ran together towards the brook. After about five minutes, the girl stopped. They were approaching the brook which ran at the bottom of a tree laden field.

'He's just over there.' she pointed, 'just behind the trees.' Daniel ran on thinking the girl was behind him, but her job

was done. All she had to do was wait where she had been told to, and her father would pick her up. Daniel reached the brook, and turned to the girl to ask where, and then he realised she was gone. There was no girl behind him, just two men dressed in black. They looked like soldiers, but were unlike any soldiers Daniel had ever seen. He noticed one was on his radio. Daniel hoped they did not have guns, though he suspected that they did. Who was that girl? Why had she set him up? The first soldier raised his hands in a gesture that said they were not going to hurt him. Daniel stepped back. He had nowhere to run. The brook was behind him. He would have to fight.

'We are not going to hurt you Daniel. We are here to protect you. We are on your side.'

The two soldiers made no attempt to grab Daniel. They knew he had nowhere to run.

'What you on about? What side?'

'It's about your brother. We need to talk to you. You have to get him to stop.'

Chapter 39

As Carol got up to answer the door, Daniel thought back to ten years ago, where, as a thirteen year old boy, he had been told that his brother was in great danger if he continued to use his powers. The men had told him that there were people out there, who would use Todd, use his powers. At that time, Daniel didn't fully understand it. Now he knew that those powers he and his brother held could be used for other purposes. A new weapon. A new research and development programme. If the brothers continued to use their powers, then their only protection would be isolation. There were people out there who would be watching them. He had been told that once they stopped using their powers, then eventually they would disappear, or become harder to use and develop them. It was called 'parking', and if you parked them, just like an old car left to rot, they would rust and no longer work. He had been told that he didn't need to know any more.

He did what was asked, explaining to Todd as much as he was able to someone so young, and he had been successful. His power, or gift, had all but gone. Todd's had been more difficult to park, no matter how hard they had tried. Both brothers felt like they had unleashed a new chemical weapon on the Town of Ashbourne. They were frightened, not only for trying to get Wendy back. They were frightened of the consequences, the hornet's nest that they opened would change their lives forever.

Chapter 40

Marie Rose woke in a field, shivering and wet. For one moment she thought it had all been a dream, but she could remember it vividly. She could feel the grass beneath her. It was wet. Her clothes were wet. She thought she was in her garden, but, as her eyes grew accustomed to the dark, she could see she was in a field.

She stood up, more to get out of the damp grass than anything else. She had no idea how she had got here. She remembered being taken away by a storm, but that was it. Nothing more. Just waking up in a damp field. She had no idea where she was, but she guessed it wasn't anywhere near home, because if it was, it must have been a strange way to get her wherever she was. She had a feeling, deep inside, which she couldn't quite explain, yet it felt like this was the moment she had been waiting for. She had a feeling that she was going to meet her grandsons. After all, weren't they the ones who had brought her here?

She could see some lights on, not many, but just over the field she could see there was a housing estate. She brushed herself down, and although it had appeared that she had been through one hell of a night, despite being cold and damp, she felt good. She found herself walking. She couldn't really remember putting her feet in gear, yet she knew where they were taking her. She had to find the house, but there was so many. *This one will stand out from the rest* she thought *or what would be the point*. Ten minutes later, she stood outside a council house which appeared to have a big hole in the roof. It also looked as if there had been one hell of a party in the street. She just stared at the front door, from the top of the path. She was scared, although she didn't really know why. Being scared was not normally part of her make-up. *I should be rejoicing* she thought, but she had a feeling it wasn't going to be all fun. She hoped it would be what she wanted to see in the house, but she wasn't sure. Nothing made sense about today.

She doubted herself, her reasons for being here. She wanted to turn round and just go. She wasn't cut out for this anymore. Her hand shook as she rang the doorbell without realising she had done so. It was as if something or someone else was operating her hand. Her heart was in her mouth. Through the glass, she could see a figure she hoped she would recognise, coming to the door. She shivered and wanted to cry, as the door was opened. She wanted to hug the woman standing there.

'I thought it might be you. Come on in.' said Carol, as she saw Marie Rose standing on the threshold.

They hugged, holding on as if they had just found a long-lost loved one, for the first time in many years. To Marie Rose that's exactly how it felt. Then a feeling came over both of them, engulfing them in a moment of solidarity. That was when they both realised why they were together. Carol led her to the living room where Daniel, Todd and Becky were sitting wondering who was calling. Carol opened the door with Marie Rose beside her. She will never understand why or how she said what she did.

'It's time you met your Grandmother.' she said to the boys. It was only at that precise moment when the lounge door was opened that Marie Rose realised that Bill Fenton was her evil son, who used to laugh at her, while her husband beat her. Why she hadn't realised that before she had no idea. She thought back to the time in Blackpool when Carol was brought to her by the man she was with, the man she did not like. The man who put fear in her bones was her son. There was a bond after all. She had come to meet her grandchildren.

Everyone spoke at once for a moment, then the two boys looked in astonishment at the lady. When the chaos had calmed down Marie Rose sat and told them how it was. She told them about her life from the beatings given by her husband, the son who seemed to enjoy watching them. How she had escaped one night, and never went back. How she regretted leaving her son, although they were two of a kind, she told them, evil to the core.

'They would have killed me. I had to leave.'

She told them about her second husband and how he died. She told them how she saw his death, and did nothing to stop it, because she couldn't stop it. How it had hurt her. She explained about her gift, a gift which only rarely happened, and how she used to con those that visited her. She went into great detail about her life, the beatings, the husbands, the son that she loathed. As they all sat and listened, no one spoke. They just listened, taking it all in, just another part of a crazy day. She told them how she had met Carol, and the visions she had, and how real it had all seemed. How all her life since that time, she had thought about the boys, She knew they were special, how she now realised why. They were her own flesh and blood. She had missed out on their lives, which was her biggest, and probably only regret. She told them she wanted to know all about them, their lives, their choices, their likes and dislikes. She needed the missing years filling in, and hoped they would accept her as their grandmother. She would try to be the grandmother she had always wanted to be, but that would have to wait, as they had work to do. The sun was rising, but the skies were grey and spitting with rain, blocking out any glare which the sun could have given. The conversation was still flowing, when there was a knock on the door.

216

James McCarthy couldn't remember driving there. He wasn't sure he really had, as there was no way he could have got there in such a short time. At this moment he was sitting in his seven-seater SUV, outside a house with a hole in the roof. Rain was spitting outside. Everything was very confusing. He should have had a surgery this morning, but he was hundreds of miles away. He would have to phone in sick. Until this moment, strangely, he had been feeling very tired, the hours really getting to him. He had felt drained, but, as he sat in his car, he felt rejuvenated, felt like a new man. He thought about what had happened a few hours ago. How he had thought he was about to die, and how good that had felt, because he thought he was about to meet his Elsie and that had felt good. He would never again be scared of dying. In fact, he would embrace it. He told his wife that he loved her, then he got out of his car and knocked on the door with no reason to be there, except that it felt right. It was where he needed to be, and he was feeling good. Perhaps when this was over, he could just rest in peace with Elsie by his side. Oh yes he felt good, he felt really good.

'Did anyone call a doctor?' he said as a beautiful woman in her early forties answered the door.

They looked at each other. There was no recognition there. Was this the right house? Was this all a mistake?

'No, but you'd better come in anyway.' said Carol.

As she had done with Marie Rose she took him to the others in the living room. The others were more expectant this time, and weren't surprised to see the large man walk through the door.

It had been fifty eight years since Marie Rose had seen her cousin. To be honest, she didn't know if he was still alive, but childhood memories came flooding back as she hugged him. James gave them the story of the storm dousing the fire in his house, and lifting him to safety, a story which Todd knew only too well.

James spoke for ten minutes about his life, about how he sensed death. No one interrupted. Then Carol told James about Wendy Cross, and how Todd had gone flying through the roof.

'So you are related?' Todd asked

'I suppose I am.'

'Fucking hell! A Grandmother and her cousin. I wonder what's next.'

He looked at his mother, by way of an apology for the language. She waved it away as if to say it didn't matter, and it didn't. *There's going to be a lot more than bad language before we're finished* she thought.

'Why am I here? What part do I play in this?'

Daniel stood, and gave James McCarthy a hug. 'You're a doctor, and you have a gift. That's why you're here.' and Daniel explained about Wendy Cross.

'It seems as though my family is cursed with gifts.' said Daniel.

He didn't like what was happening.

'We should just call the police, before we get ourselves killed.'

He was thinking about the two men ten years ago. The ones who had told them that if they showed their gifts they could be in great danger.

'If you think I've just done all that, so you can call the police, Daniel,' said Todd, 'you have got another think coming. You know more than anyone what we have just done.'

'And what is it you have actually done?' cried Carol who was now in tears.

'We have become accessible, Mum, that's all.' The two boys hugged their mother. They knew it was too late to go back.

'So what happens now?' the doctor asked, after listening attentively to Daniel's explanation. They were all sitting now. Becky and Daniel sat on the floor. Daniel had told them all about what had happened, when the two men had talked to him down by the brook, how people would be looking at them, taking advantage if they could, and how the men were there to warn them, and protect them, but ultimately it was up to them. The boys explained that Daniel had trained himself to 'park' his gift, but that Todd couldn't.

'It was like it couldn't be parked' Todd told them, 'and tonight we used it and we shouldn't have.'   'So we wait for a knock on the door.' said Carol.

Madison was pissed off, really pissed off. It was the first time she had been left alone, which she thought at sixteen was a bit ridiculous, and her parents should have trusted her more. She was pissed off because she had not had wild parties, only one friend over, as agreed. But now the house was wrecked. Her friend would wake up alone, not knowing where she had gone, and now she was hundreds of miles away from home, walking down a council estate that looked awful. There were beer cans everywhere, burnt out barbecues, bottles, and fast food packets. The place was a dump. She felt like she had let everyone down.

It was kind of eerily quiet, like an abandoned town on the Walking Dead films. She expected to see zombies coming around the corner. She remembered that if she had to kill them, to go for the head, go for the brain. She loved the Walking Dead, but she didn't want to become a zombie, not today anyway. She was in her thin dressing gown. There had been no time to dress before she was pulled through the window. She was cold and wet, and had no idea how she got here, wherever here was. She thought she might be in Wales.

To make matters worse, as she walked down the street, she could see a house with a bloody hole in the roof. In spite of the cold, in spite of the anger that raged inside her, in spite of wondering what the hell she was going to say to her parents, or Chantelle, for that matter, she felt good. She looked around as she approached the house with the hole. The streets were deserted. *Must have been one hell of a party,* she thought. She couldn't remember all that had happened. She knew a young boy had been responsible for it, had caused the storm which had grabbed her and taken her to this dump. She really hoped Chantelle was okay. God only knew what she would think in the morning. She felt in her dressing gown pocket, somehow she had her phone. She would ring Chantelle later, when she could think of something to tell her. As for her parents, well, they were another thing. Maybe she could get home in time, and clean up before they got back. *The kitchen was wrecked* she thought, *the bastard wrecked my kitchen.*

She wrapped the sodden dressing gown around her as tightly as she could. She walked down the path, feeling determined, feeling angry. A rage was building up inside her, and that wasn't good, wasn't good at all. She rang the bell. *This had better be good.'* she thought.

The sound of the bell was no surprise to those who sat inside the house. As on the previous two occasions, Carol got up to answer the door. The others sat and waited. An air of expectancy hovered around the room. You could almost cut the atmosphere with a knife, taste it. They were all expecting a pretty young girl, they were not disappointed.

They both looked at each other for a second or two. Carol looking at this beautiful young girl that Todd had called hot.

Madison, looking at this lady and thinking that she was the most beautiful woman she had ever seen. Neither had a clue who the other one was, both knowing that they would soon find out.

'Can I come in? I'm bloody soaking.'

'Of course you can.' She opened the door wide, and Madison stepped in.

Carol told her to wait there, and ran up the stairs to fetch a thick, warm dressing gown. Madison accepted it gracefully, and quickly changed, Carol took her into the living room where the others were waiting. The first thing everyone noticed, despite the unkempt look of wet hair, no make-up, and wrapped in an old, towelling dressing gown, was how beautiful this girl was. She was truly stunning.

Madison looked around the room, catching everyone's eye. She caught Todd's. 'You!' she exclaimed. 'I hope you're going to fix my house.'

Hot tea and biscuits were served, as Todd gave up his seat to Madison and sat on the floor next to Daniel and Becky. It was Madison's turn to tell her story. It didn't take as long as her predecessors. Her life was many years shorter. She told them about her mother, and the one-night stand, her adoptive father, and how much she loved Morgan.

'Morgan Hughes,' she said 'I call him the man with no second name' She paused for a laugh. No one did. 'Oh, never mind. You're all Welsh, aren't you?' she said.

They laughed. She told them about her school, her friends, and that Chantelle was there at home, probably scared. She talked about things she liked, that their estate looked awful. She had a gracefulness about her, although her story was less interesting to her audience, she had an aura about her that made everyone just sit and listen. None more so then Daniel *She is hot* he said to himself.

As she was about to wind up her story, Madison stopped, looked at Daniel.

Their eyes met.

'Oh,' she said, 'and every now and again I hear people's thoughts.' she smiled. Daniel took his eyes away.

'Do you really?' said Carol, quite astonished about this revelation.

'Only occasionally, like just now.' She looked at Daniel. They both smiled.

'I don't get it.' said Todd, 'I grabbed my grandmother, because it was she who brought us into the world, James because he's my grandmothers cousin and he's a doctor, we all have gifts, we are all related.'

He looked sullen, as he spoke almost apologetically, 'Could I have got the wrong girl?'

Carol stood, there was a tear in her eye. She understood, she understood everything. She beckoned Madison over. Madison moved to her. As the two hugged each other, with tears in their eyes, they both knew. Everyone just stared. The two parted, held hands, looked at the others. Looked at Todd and Daniel. 'Meet your sister.' Carol said.

As the three siblings hugged, there wasn't a dry eye. Now they understood.

Bill Fenton had been that one-night stand, the result was the beautiful girl that stood among them. The evil father of three remarkable siring's, three of the finest young persons you could meet. The hugging stopped. The eyes dried.   Madison took Carol's hand. 'I'm sorry.' she said.

Carol kissed her cheek. 'You have nothing to be sorry for,' she said, 'we are just pleased that you're here.' There were more hugs.

'So you're my grandmother.' Madison said to Marie Rose 'Indeed I am, and very proud to be so.' More hugs. The crazy day just got a little crazier.

'What happens now?' Daniel asked and as he spoke, his phone rang. It was a message. He flipped open his iPhone, which showed a picture message.

'It's from him.' he said.

Chapter 41

The cabin's contents consisted of an old wheelchair, a wood burning stove that looked heavy and ancient, a table, a wooden bench and what appeared to be a bed comprising slats of wood, but no mattress. On the floor there was a cupboard, which at one time would have been attached to the wall. The cabin looked like an old hunting lodge, that hadn't been used for years, possibly a gamekeeper's place to stay. Whatever it was, there was nobody around. It was obvious that nobody had used this place in years. The door, also of logs, was off its hinges, and was placed closed, leaning against the frame. Both girls noticed this and realised it would make an easy means of escape when they had the chance. But where would they run to? They had no idea where they were, and no way would they be able to find their way back. Still, out there alone, would be better than being in here with the devil himself.

The girls sat on the wooden bench, which seemed sturdy enough, even if it was rather hard and uncomfortable. Their legs ached, and their bodies were covered with cuts and bruises which had been made by branches and falls. They felt as though they had been bitten all over. The rest was welcome. The venue was not as welcome. The unnerving actions of Bill were very unwelcome.

He sat in the wheelchair, and took out his iPhone, which he had fully charged on the car journey. He also had Wendy's and Katy's phones. Wendy's was also an iPhone, while Katy's was an old Nokia. The two girls looked battered and bruised.

Dawn was breaking, but it was raining, leaking in at places in the cabin. For the moment they were out of the rain. The girls sat close together, as they had done since arriving at the cabin.

They sat in fear, wondering what would happen next. Sitting there, still cuffed, they watched as Bill Fenton used his phone. He sent a picture message with the words written 'This is war I do now"

He closed his phone, and walked over to the girls. He uncuffed them, then sat back in the wheelchair, which creaked. It didn't look as if it would hold his weight. The girls rubbed their wrists. It felt good to be free of those restraints. They could hear the rain outside. It was falling more heavily.

'This used to belong to a man, who used it for hunting. He would stay up here for weeks, with his disabled son. They would both go hunting, his son in this wheelchair. He taught the boy to shoot. I knew him when I was a kid.'

He shuffled in his wheelchair, wiped his lips with his hands, and then spat on the floor.

'I became friends with his son, and his dad used to bring me along. I loved the shooting, the killing.'

He stopped talking, and looked out through the glassless window. The rain was coming in quite heavily through the window, wetting the already damp ground of the hut even further.

'What happened to them?' Wendy asked, feeling it was a question Bill wanted asking.

Bill wiped his lips again, then licked them. 'The old man died, the son not long after. I think he died of a broken heart. I don't think anyone's been up here much since then.'

He opened the rucksack, took out a bottle of water and two Mars bars. He gave them to the girls. They accepted readily, and gulped the water, then ate the chocolate. It felt good.

'We can stay up here for weeks.' he said. 'There's a fresh water stream. I can hunt. You don't always need a gun. We can set traps for rabbits. I have a pan, we have a stove. It will be an adventure. We will be free.' Both girls shivered.

'We can have sex, regularly.' His voice became excited, his words speeding up. 'It's a beautiful place. I'll show you around soon. You'll get to know the place, make yourselves at home.' The two girls just sat there, still shivering, wondering what was going on in the mind of this crazy man.

Bill looked at the girls, 'You need a bath.' he said. 'You both smell.' He laughed. 'Come on, I'll take you to the baths.'

The girls just sat there, their wrecked bodies too tired to move. A bath sounded good to Wendy, but she wanted a hot bath with loads of bubbles, and maybe Todd washing her back, telling her how beautiful she was. She thought about that, but it seemed a million miles away.

'Why?' she asked Katy, holding her hand, clasping it tightly, as if trying to protect her.

'Why what?'

'Why are you keeping us up here? What happens in a few days, weeks? What's it all about?'

'It's about payback time.' An evil smile lit up his face. His lips pulled back over his teeth. His eyes seemed deeper now, darker, just black holes in his head.

'I sense death.' he said. 'Death is what will happen.' He laughed. 'And it won't be mine. Now it's fucking bath time.' He gestured for the two girls to stand. They did, too frightened to do anything else. He nodded towards the door, which he had now removed. Katie and Wendy both moved out of the cabin.

As they stood outside in the damp rain, Wendy said 'You're going to have to kill me, before I have sex with you.' 'That can be arranged.' he said.

Her whole body shivered. If the situation wasn't so real, both Katy and Wendy would feel it was probably the most beautiful place they had ever seen, the waterfall cascading down the beautiful rock face, falling aggressively, then calmly spreading into the waters below. It was clear and beautiful, white as it hit the pool, then spreading into blues and greys as the fall merged with the pool, blissful and inviting. The perfect place to make love, and let all your inhibitions go. Maybe in another time, another world, another life, but not now. They didn't want it happening now. The girls, having been forced to strip naked, now bathed in the pool. Both were swimmers. They swam gracefully, as they felt the surprisingly warm water soothe their bodies, their aches and pains. It felt good and refreshing. The pool seemed to be alive and comforting them, inviting them in, as though it was their saviour, and some pool monster would rise from its depths, and take away that horrible man, who sat on the rocks with his iPhone taking pictures. But the monster never came. The water dragon, or whatever it was, remained asleep. The moment that could only be described as surreal, passed.

The girls were ordered to dress, putting on the damp clothes over their clean, damp bodies. As they dressed, the insane Bill Fenton threw rocks at them. The first one hit Katy on the shoulder. As she screamed in pain, the second one made a glancing blow on Wendy's head, causing blood to flow, which was rapidly diluted by the rain. Both girls screamed as the stones rained down on them. They huddled closely together, covering their heads, as their bodies were pelted and racked with pain.

Bill Fenton laughed as he threw more rocks.

'My father used to make me take hot showers, almost burning. Then he would turn it cold. I can't do that, so I throw rocks instead. It's kind of the same thing. Come on, let's get back to the cabin. I've got loads of pictures of you naked. I'll

show you them so you can tell me which ones you like best.'
The girls wiped the blood away, as much as they could, and
just cried.

Chapter 42

Daniel read the words 'This is war I do now.' He opened the picture message and looked away in disgust. His heart raced as he held his phone and turned it for everyone to see. It was a picture of a hand with a finger missing, blood pouring down, as if it had been freshly cut off.

'This is war I do now.' Daniel said, quoting the text.

'What!' Madison said. They all stared at her. 'This is *what* I do now' as in w,a,t,' she spelled out the letters, 'he misspelt it. It's an iPhone. It wouldn't pick up *war* as being misspelt.'

'Whose hand is it?' asked Marie Rose

'It's not Wendy's,' said Todd, 'It looks like a man's.'

Todd stood up, he was shaking, angry. *It is useless just sitting here,* he thought.

Daniel put an arm round Todd's shoulder 'We're going to get through this. I'm going to text him back, see if Wendy is safe.'

'Becky.' Carol reminded him.

Daniel texted 'I need to speak to Becky, or you get nothing.' They waited a while, and a text came back. Again it was a picture message of two naked girls, swimming in a pool. It looked as though it could have been taken on a holiday. The text read 'Then speak to her she's probably with you now. As u can see, Wendy's having a great time.'

'He knows it's Wendy.' he said, as he showed them the text.

Tears came to Todd's eyes. The others held theirs back. Madison grabbed the phone from Daniel, and fiddled a bit with it, pressing buttons. They all watched, hearing the phone beep as she pressed the digits.

'His first mistake.' she said as she handed the phone back to Daniel. The phone now showed a map. It was of Wentwood

Forest. 'That's where the photo was taken.'

She asked Todd if he had an iPhone. He said he did. She asked if Wendy had one. He nodded, handing his phone to her. She fiddled with the buttons.

'I don't know where Wendy is,' she said, 'but I can definitely tell you that her phone is in Wentwood forest.'

'You're brilliant. I think I'm going to like having you as a sister.' said Daniel.

'I know. And you will.' she replied. They all laughed. 'Okay then, who's coming to that forest?' asked Madison. They all stood.

Chapter 43

Simon Goldstone sat at the desk in his office, looking at the nameplate which sat on his desk: Simon Goldstone Chief Inspector Gwent Constabulary. The same wording that was emblazoned on his office door. He just sat staring at it, wondering how long it would be before that name changed. He had two unsolved murders, two armed robbery cases, and a kidnap, just in the last couple of weeks. It had been a very strange twenty four hours.

He didn't feel overworked, but things needed to be done. So why had he chosen to go to a rave, and smoke pot, and drink with people that it was his duty to arrest? However hard he tried he could not think of an explanation. His Boss was on his way over, and he would need answers. He looked at the pile of papers on his desk, the yellow stickers on his computer. *He had been a good cop,* he thought, *maybe one moment, one lapse would not totally ruin his career. Besides, who had seen him smoking? Who had seen him drinking? Only the lads he was with, as he walked across the fields. Why would they say anything?* he thought, *they were breaking the law.*

His mobile rang. It was a text from Daniel Fenton. 'Just what I need.' he muttered. He opened the message. There was a picture of two girls swimming, apparently naked. For a moment he thought Daniel had sent it to the wrong person. Why would he be sending lewd pictures to my phone. He read the accompanying text which said: 'As you can see, Wendy has decided to take a break with her friend.'

He studied the picture. He had seen pictures of Wendy Cross, and this certainly could be her. He texted back 'Okay I'll try to get to see you later.' He pressed send. *That will do for now,* he thought. He could now cool the search down, just park it.

There were lots of other things he could get on with, but Daniel would have a lot of explaining to do.

Goldstone couldn't get that evening from his mind. It felt like it was something out of a movie, and everyone was in a trance, walking to meet their fate. He knew it had something to do with the Fenton's, probably the younger son. But what could he arrest them for? Mass hypnotism? He had a feeling that this wasn't going to go away. He just hoped he would still be in charge to see it through. Before his boss came to see him, he had one thing he needed to do. Something he wasn't looking forward to, the person that he had nurtured, took under his wing. A fine officer whom he knew would go very far. The best sergeant he had ever had. He wasn't looking forward to the meeting.

There was a knock on his office door. He knew who it was as he told her to come in. He felt a sickness in his stomach.

'Sit down Tracy.' he said.

She did, shuffled her feet and put her hands in her lap. She had a feeling she knew what was coming. The Fenton's had probably ruined her.

'You look tired.' he said. He sounded as though he meant it. She replied, 'I've had no sleep yet, nor have you, sir, I guess.'

Simon nodded. He typed some things on his computer, a picture came up. He turned the screen to Tracy. She was expecting it. There she was in full uniform, with the Fenton's, at the biggest rave ever known in the United Kingdom's history, drinking a bottle of Stella. He showed her a few more pictures, all similar. She shuffled uneasily in her chair. She didn't know what to say. *He had been there,* she thought, *he knew what it was like. Why should she take the blame? Be the scapegoat?* She had butterflies in her stomach.   At that moment she wanted to tell him to stuff his job, her career, her pension all gone.

Finally, all she could think of saying was, 'It's not fair.'

Goldstone turned the pictures back, feeling sympathy for the sergeant for whom he had a lot of respect. 'You're a good copper,' he said, 'but it's all over the news, YouTube, everywhere. My phone hasn't stopped ringing.'

Again she shuffled. 'Sir, with all due respect, you were stoned out of your mind.' She didn't regret saying it, the inspector had certainly been stoned.

It was Goldstone's turn to look uncomfortable. He shuffled in his seat, let out a huge sigh, and massaged his temples as if he had a migraine. He looked really uncomfortable, and Tracy felt better for that.

'I was, and I can't explain It.' he paused 'but up to now, no pictures have emerged. I've no doubt they will. I know what happened, Tracy, I just don't know why.' He looked pensive. He fiddled with a pencil. Tracy knew what was coming. 'I have to suspend you, pending an investigation. You know that, don't you?'

Tracy did. 'I'll do everything I can to help you.'

'Thank you, sir.'

'One bit of good news.' he said, showing her the picture and text which Daniel had sent. 'It seems like she just went on holiday.'

'Looks cold there,' she said, 'but good news.'

To be honest, that was the last thing on her mind. She had no interest, whilst at least not at that moment.

'Hand in your card, Tracy, and get yourself off home, have a rest, and I'll do my upmost for you, if I still have a job.' Tracy stood.

'You're too good a copper to lose, Tracy.' His words, whilst comforting didn't really register.

She walked towards the door. Before leaving, she looked back at her boss sitting at his desk. He seemed to have aged in the past twenty four hours.

'Sir, what the hell happened?'

He leaned back in his chair. 'I have no fucking idea!' he said. Then his phone rang.

As she walked out of the station, after handing her card in she thought about the picture she had just seen. 'That was no fucking holiday.' she said out loud. The station was based in the centre of Newport, just at the top of Pill. She walked towards the transporter bridge which was used to ferry cars across the river. She needed coffee. Her modest flat on Cardiff Road could wait. She sat at her usual table, in her usual cafe, having paid for a coffee and a bacon sandwich. The bacon tasted good, the coffee was warming her body. She realised how hungry she was. She ate the sandwich, drank the coffee, and ordered another to take out. She could see the bridge now, and wondered why the Americans had tried to buy it, It looked old, and as if it was about to fall into the river. You could pay to cross the river without a car. In the summer, people would just sit on the bridge, and travel the three minute journey across the bridge, then back again, as they ate their lunch. She sat, listening to the creaking noises, as it slowly moved across the river, just one car on it. She wondered if it fell to the river, would she die. The banks of the river were of mud, dirty. The river was dirty. She thought about the picture that Simon had shown her. Her copper instincts had told her that it wasn't a holiday picture. The brief glimpse of it, didn't seem to be of a holiday resort or an idyllic spot somewhere, and it looked to be freezing cold. Why would Daniel just send a picture? Why wouldn't he have got Wendy to phone Goldstone to tell him she was okay? Something didn't fit. And what about that party. *Did she really see someone fly through the roof?,* she thought. She had forgotten about that. It was as though everyone had been in a trance at the rave. *This is too fucking weird,* she said to herself.

Fifteen minutes later, Tracy started her car's engine which was where she had left it, at the station. She put it into gear, and made her way towards Ashbourne Estate.

Chapter 44

Fed, showered, and with a full belly, Jezz and Mickey sat in Jezz's thirteenth storey flat. Jezz smoked a cigarette, blowing out long plumes of smoke. Mickey, feeling much better now, just wanted to go out and find the girls and make them pay for leaving him. He wanted Katy to know that she couldn't do that to him. She was his girl, she belonged to him, and that Wendy was going to get it big time. However, he didn't want Jezz to know that.

Sky News was on the Freeview box, reporting about the rave that had taken place, and a possible missing girl, called Wendy Cross, and how could people possibly party when a girl was missing? The breaking news banner flashed up that the missing girl was found. It cut to a Sky reporter who stated that, according to their sources, the missing girl had simply gone on holiday, without telling her friends or family. Next, it flashed back to Ashbourne Estate showing pictures of the after-effect of the rave, the streets strewn with rubbish. The camera zoomed in on a house with a hole in the roof. The reporter made some comment about further news and returned the camera to the studio, where a reporter told about freak isolated storms across Britain, which had caused significant damage to properties. The scene changed again. It was a reporter talking to a resident of Ashbourne.

Jezz watched closely. If Wendy Cross was found on holiday, then how the hell had she been in his flat less than twenty four hours ago? He had left her in a broken down pizza hut with that leg breaker. It didn't make sense to him. He still felt some responsibility towards the girls. He could have let them go. He knew he would never be really satisfied until he knew the girls were safe. For probably the first time in his life he had a conscience, and what was even more remarkable, he was going to do something about it.

'Come on. We're off.' he said to Mickey

Mickey quickly stood up. 'Where are we off to?'

Jezz gathered his keys and cigarettes, and stuffed them into his pocket.

'We are going to find Wendy Cross, and that girl of yours.' he said.

Mickey looked confused. 'But Wendy's on holiday.' he said. They walked the thirteen storeys down, not relying on a lift which seemed to spend more time out of order than running. As they walked, Jezz asked Mickey, 'Did you ever go to school?'

'Not much.' Mickey said, 'But I've broken in to a few.'

They got into the car. It was raining, the sky looming a thick mass of grey cloud, a dismal day. They made their way over the Severn Bridge to Ashbourne. Jezz Dwayne was on a mission. Throughout his life he felt he had bullied and let people down. Today he was going to change his life. Today he was going to make a difference. He had no idea what his plan was, no idea what he would do when he got to Ashbourne. Something had touched him today. Something he couldn't describe, but he certainly felt it. Even the mixed-up kid that was beside him, kind of inspired him. A street urchin, who had been taken advantage of all his life, and still, that kid wanted to find his girl. Jezz drove with a determination. He had to make this right, and when he did, he would change his life and the lives of those all around him. Just like those at the rave who had felt an enormous sense of loyalty. Jezz Dwayne felt that too, and this time he was going to do something about it. They reached the tolls. Now they were in Wales. He paid the toll.

'This is it!' he shouted, and drove the short distance to Ashbourne.

'This is what?' asked Mickey.

Chapter 45

Those in the Fenton house could see the Sky News cameras outside the house. They had knocked on the doors but nobody answered. Daniel, Todd, Becky, Carol, James, Madison and Marie Rose were gathering their thoughts. They had eaten. Carol had rustled up bacon and eggs, and made a load of sandwiches to take with them. Bottles of water were jammed into a rucksack. They checked their phones were charged, and the ones that weren't would simply have to do. Daniel was absolutely sure he had convinced Goldstone that it was all a misunderstanding. He knew Goldstone was smart, but he just hoped the Chief Inspector had enough on his plate at the moment.

They had all changed, getting into whatever clothes that Carol and Todd had been able to rustle together. Daniel and Marie Rose, as well as the doctor staying in the clothes which they were already in, as nothing else seemed to fit. Becky borrowed something of Carol's, while Madison wore a pair of Todd's jeans, holding them up with a belt, but they felt comfortable. Carol had given her some trainers, and she wore a sweatshirt and hoodie of Todd's. *Even in that get up, she still looked beautiful.* Carol thought.

There were seven seats in the SUV with plenty of boot room. As they were about to leave, Becky looked hesitant.
'I don't think I should go.' she said. They all looked at her
'Why on earth not?' asked Carol.
A tear came to Becky's eye, then the tears flowed as if all the pent up frustration had been released in one foul swoosh. 'I'm not gifted.' she said, amid the sobs 'It's all my fault.' and then the tears really flowed

Daniel hugged her as close as he could. He knew none of this was Becky's fault, but he could understand that she felt like this.

'You're the most gifted person I know.' he said.

'I'll be in the way.' she sobbed. 'I'll keep you informed if anything's happening here.'

'Are you sure?'

'Yes. Just let me know when you find her. Tell her I love her.'

Madison kissed the side of her cheek. 'Be back soon sister in-law. I want to hear all about my big brother.'

That cheered Becky up. She smiled. 'So much to tell.' she said.

'And I want to hear all about my grandson.' Marie Rose chipped in.

'Come along,' said the doctor, 'we have to go.'

They battled their way through the news reporters. As they got into the SUV, after loading up the boot, one reporter was particularly persistent, and Daniel threatened him on camera. That did the trick, and at that moment he didn't care who had seen it. They had things to do. The doctor drove, with Daniel beside him. Todd and his newly found sister, Madison, behind, Carol and Marie Rose behind them. Three generations on a journey to find a missing girl. They pulled out of Ashbourne Estate, as reporters flashed their cameras. Why? Nobody really knew.

If they had left two minutes later, they would have met up with Tracy Bates, and Jezz Dwayne along with Mickey Bolan, as their cars pulled into the street at the same time. Tracy, still in uniform, pulled up behind the other two. She tried to slip down in the seat so they wouldn't see her. She waited to see what they would do, watching as they both got out of the car, walked down the path of Daniel's mother's house and rang the doorbell. The reporters were gone for the moment, as they were still chasing the car holding the Fenton's.

Becky had dried her eyes and washed her face. The kettle was boiling as she stood in the kitchen, wondering if she had done the right thing. The doorbell rang. She assumed it was reporters and looked through the glass. What she saw appeared to be a large black man, with a smaller figure beside him. She ignored them. Then the bell rang constantly, as Jezz kept his finger on the buzzer. She still ignored it, but after a minute she opened the door. She saw a large black man and a smaller youth beside him. 'What?' she angrily said.

Jezz, in a perfect gentleman's voice said, 'I'm really sorry to bother you, but we're concerned about Wendy Cross.' 'You'd better come in.' she said.

The two followed her into the living room and sat down. Just as they did so, the doorbell rang again. Becky could see the police uniform. *Shit* she thought. She opened the door.

'Not fucking you.' she said.

Tracy Bates smiled. 'Just don't hit me.'

'What do you want?'

'I've been suspended,' Tracy said, 'but don't tell those two who just came in.'

'What do you want?' Becky repeated.

'I know Wendy isn't on holiday. This isn't official. I just want to help.'

Becky showed her into the living room. 'There's no one here.' she said, 'They've gone to get Wendy.'

'That's what I was afraid of. I really do want to help.' Tracy Bates walked into the living room.

'Oh fuck!' Mickey said

'Done any kidnapping recently?' asked Tracy Bates.

Chapter 46

Their battered bodies were huddled up on the floor of the cabin. Wendy now resembled Carrie from the film, as the blood had run down her face into her hair. She had managed to stop the bleeding by using her top to stem the blood. It seemed to have worked. She felt as though every part of her body hurt, and at one point she had wished that he would just finish it. Her fear had been overcome by exhaustion. The desire to escape had been quelled by the pain that racked her body. The thought of Todd rescuing her had gone. She just wanted to close her eyes and sleep, to make it all go away, and perhaps she would never wake again. Katy was very much the same. One rock had caught her on the ankle, she was sure from the agony, that it was broken. It came totally out of the blue. She could smell the aroma of death, it was all around her, inside her, inside him. No warning had been given. One minute they were bathing, the next the stones were hitting them. Their bodies bruised and battered, they huddled to each other, trying to stop the tears, trying to be some comfort to each other, in this horror of a day.

Bill was outside. They could hear him chopping wood with an axe. As he had taken it from his rucksack, both girls had looked on in horror, thinking that the axe was for them. Even through the desire of wanting to die, the adrenalin had kicked in when faced with it, but he had gone outside, and they could hear the sound of the logs being chopped. Both girls knew that the axe could still be used for other purposes. They were not cuffed, but they knew now, that even if they got away, they wouldn't get far. Their bodies still hurt. They huddled closer. 'He has to make a mistake.' Katy said. 'If he falls asleep, we could get the axe and kill him.'

Wendy tried to smile. The thought of burying the axe in his head, at that moment, appealed to her.

'Maybe. But I don't think I could even lift it, never mind swing it.'

Bill came into the cabin with some dry kindling and some logs. The girls remained huddled together, wondering what was next in store for them, wondering if this horrific day would ever end, and when it did end, would they walk away from it alive. A whole host of scenarios went through their heads, some too horrific to think about. That was when Wendy thought of her father. She had no idea why. Perhaps there was a subliminal message in her thoughts. She could barely remember him, which made it worse.

Bill chucked some kindle on the burner, and ignited it with his lighter. He had a cigarette in his mouth, giving the impression that it was just a normal day in his life. Within minutes the fire was going, and Bill put some larger pieces on the burner

'We'll soon be dry.' he said, as he turned to look at the girls. 'God, he certainly made a mess of you two. You look like death warmed up. You'll soon be nice and warm. I could make a cuppa. Do you want tea?'

'Why did you do it?' Wendy asked. Her lips were dry, in spite of her body and clothes being soaking wet. She tried to lick them. She had no moisture in her mouth. Katy buried her head in her hands, wishing Wendy hadn't asked. Katy began to cry. 'Because he can.' she sobbed.

Bill seemed surprised. He looked taken aback. 'Do what?' he asked.

'Throw stones at us.' said Wendy. 'You nearly killed us.'

243

He went back to tending to the burner which was now well alight. 'That wasn't me. That was my father' he said. 'He can be a right bastard at times.'

'Your father?' Wendy asked.

Bill carried on building the fire as he spoke. The girls could feel the heat now from where they sat, but it was of little comfort.

'Yes, he comes regular,' he continued, 'has done for years. I used to fight it because he would tell me to do bad things.' He held up a stick from the fire, its end glowing.

'This would be good for poking eyes out.' he casually said. Both the girls shivered.

'As I said I used to fight it. Now I don't. I like the bad things now.' He chucked the stick back on the fire.

'Is he here now?' asked Wendy.

He stood up straight, eyes wide, no pupils, just white. That was all the girls could see, the whites of his eyes.

'He wasn't,' he said, 'but he is now.'

The voice in his head was there again. It seemed that the source of all evil was in his brain, burning to his soul, controlling his mind. If there was such a thing as the devil, then this is what it would be like. *Do it,* the voice said, *Do it.* Both girls just stared, as he undressed and stood, naked, looking at them.

'Sex time!' he said, and he grabbed Katy by the arm, almost ripping it from its socket. She screamed at the pain in her arm, and the pains that racked through her body. 'No. No.' she screamed as he dragged her.

Instinctively, through adrenalin which overrode all the pain, Wendy jumped at Bill, jumped on his back, pulling his hair, and throwing feeble punches at wherever they would land. They were hurting her hands more than hurting Bill. He let go of Katy's hand, and landed a boot in her face as he did so. Her head rocked with the force, the fight all gone out of her. As she drifted into semi- consciousness, she could hear the noises of Wendy as she punched and screamed at the man whose back she clung to. In one swift and easy movement, Wendy was removed from Bill's back as he put both hands over his shoulders and lifted Wendy over his head and threw her through the air and up against the cabin wall where she slid down and landed on the floor on her back, where she moved no more.

The enraged Bill grabbed Katy by the arm, and through the daze that she was in, she wished that she was dead now, that he would kill her, take away all this pain, take her away from this life that she hated. She could feel the pain. She could feel the hurt as she drifted in and out of consciousness. She would wake up and her mammy would be there, and the mammy who never really loved her, would cuddle her and tell her it would be okay. But her mammy never came. She could feel the monster mauling at her now. Strangely she felt the warmth of the fire, and as Bill Fenton took from her, what she wasn't prepared to give, she thought of her mammy, and why she wasn't there to save her.

The SUV pulled out of Ashbourne Estate with its six occupants and their supplies, and if the circumstances had been different,

245

Chapter 47

You could swear that it was a family holiday just about to start. Carol though about this and hoped that maybe that would happen. She would get to know her new family and her family would get to know each other. She sighed, wondering what was ahead. She wondered whether her life was ever going to be the same again, although she knew that it never would be. The fear of what lay ahead was daunting. Doubt buried itself in her mind. Something was telling her this wasn't the right thing to do. Something was going to go terribly wrong. She thought of all the people to whom she had never said goodbye, her mum and dad, she could phone them but what would she say. She had taught her boys never to say goodbye, but always to say see you later. Goodbye was too final. It sounded as though you were never going to see that person again. She didn't want to say goodbye to her mum and dad. She hoped she would return, but something was nagging deep inside her and, no matter how positive she thought, that feeling would not go away.

'So, you can read minds then?' said Todd.

Madison gave him an annoying look. She had always guessed that having a brother would be annoying, and it seemed that she wasn't wrong.

'No I can't,' she said, 'I told you.'

Todd shut his eyes tightly. 'Right. Tell me what I'm thinking now.'

She nudged him with his elbow.

'Ouch!' Todd cried.

'I can't read minds!' she said. 'God. How could I get such a thick brother?'

Daniel and Carol laughed. Marie Rose and James smirked, both enjoying the conversation coming from their new found family.

Todd rubbed his ribs. 'That's what you said.'
'Todd, give over.' said Carol.

Madison looked out the car window. The estate had been left behind, they were out in the country, she could see mountains in the distance. She thought that they looked beautiful even through the rain.

'Four times!' she said. 'I told you. Just now was the fifth time. I don't choose to do it, Todd.'   'Did you read Daniel's mind?' he asked.

She looked at him, smiled secretly, enjoying the conversation with her brother who, twenty four hours ago, she didn't know existed.

She tutted, 'I heard what he thought. That's the difference.'
'What was he thinking, then?'
Daniel spoke. 'Todd, shut up, will you.'
'I'm only asking what he was thinking.' Todd insisted.
'If I tell you, will you shut up?'
'Sure.'
'His thought was *Todd was right. She is hot.* You wanted to know.'

Todd and Daniel turned to look at each other. They both laughed.

'That was before I knew you were my sister.' Todd said, defending himself.

Madison came straight back. 'So you don't think I am hot, then?'

They looked at each other and smiled, Madison took his hand.

'I think you're the hottest sister ever.' he said.

247

It was about thirty seconds before anyone spoke again. It was Todd who broke the silence. 'So how do you read minds, then?'

'Shut up!' said the other five voices in the vehicle.

Ten minutes later, the road ran out, and they pulled up behind Bill Fenton's car. They got out, and looked around. James spoke first. 'Although it's raining,' he said, 'these prints look fresh. I think they went that way.'

'Should we split up?' Madison asked.

'Not yet.' said Daniel, 'Let's see where this leads us.'

They took all they could carry from the car, and followed the trail that Bill and the girls had taken earlier. The woods were still eerie with ghostly branches reaching out for the walkers. As Daniel walked, he had the feeling of failure inside him. He knew that even if they all got out of this, there would still be consequences. Todd and Madison walked side by side. He tried to help Madison a couple of times, holding out his hand to help, but both times she shrugged him off, telling him she didn't need any help.

Todd was in dreamland. The way his mind was working, telling him that everything would be all right, and he couldn't wait for Wendy to meet his new sister. He was planning things which they could do together. He felt no fear. He was sure everything was going to be okay. Madison was a bit overwhelmed by it all, not quite believing where she actually was, finding out she had another family was enough of a shock, but being magically plucked from her home, to hunt down a convicted murderer was something else. She had wanted adventures but she had expected they would be less daunting then this. She had no idea where she was going or even why. She felt scared at that moment. She didn't really know the people she was with. *They're family* she told herself, *and family look out for each other.* She thought of her mum and dad. She knew they were going to go apeshit when they found out.

Carol walked beside Daniel. They didn't speak, but every now and again, Carol would look at Daniel. She could see the pain in his face, the determination in his eyes. He was hurting. She knew that, but she had no idea how to make it better. She really wanted to go back, turn around, take her sons home, and let the police deal with it all. She wished that her ex-husband had chosen her to get his revenge. Why choose his sons? What had they ever done to him? She wiped tears from her eyes as she walked, they were tears from a mother who had failed hers sons. When all this was over they would never forgive her, and that would hurt more than anything else.

Marie Rose and James trailed behind the others. James thinking about his beloved lost wife, and hoped that she would be proud of him. He so wanted everything to be okay with the girl who was kidnapped. That was all that mattered to him. For that he was prepared to give his life. He had had a good life, but without his wife it had become unbearable. Although suicide had never been in his thoughts, he sometimes wished that death would take him, and reunite them. That was why he wasn't scared of dying tonight, because the consequences of that, felt like they were just too good to miss.

Marie Rose, deep down, knew she had not been a good person, and she thought about that as she walked. She had run out on her son, as evil as he was. She should have stayed, and maybe he might not have turned out like he had. All this was her fault. Throughout her life she had been selfish. Even her second husband, a good man, she had let die. She could have tried to stop what happened, told him not to go to work on that fateful day. Would it have made any difference? She had no idea. She had chosen the easy route. Today she wanted to do some good, but as she walked, she knew that whatever happened next, she could never make up for her failures. Her selfishness had failed them all. She just hoped that there was still enough time left to try and make some amends.

Chapter 48

Tracy Bates sat next to Mickey on the sofa, after initially stopping Becky from strangling him, as it had been revealed that he was one of the kidnappers. Becky wanted him out of the house, but Tracy persuaded her that he might be useful.

'Tell me all you know.' ordered Tracy.

Mickey did tell them all he knew, and was ably assisted by Jezz. Mickey also added that Katy, one of the original kidnappers, had now been kidnapped by Bill Fenton. Jezz confirmed that, telling them about the time the girls had spent in his flat. Jezz looked sullen as he spoke. There was regret in his voice, but a determination in his manner. Tracy looked at this handsome West Indian, who spoke to her like a true gentleman. *He's handsome* she thought, *big, strong and handsome,* and she couldn't control the tingling that swept through her body, and she didn't want to. She wanted him at that moment, and Tracy seldom failed to get what she wanted.

'Why didn't you just call the cops?' asked Becky.

Jezz got up and walked to the window. He stared out at the rain.

'In my life, we don't call the cops.' he said, 'When I got back, I realised what I had done. Those poor girls stuck with that monster. I've come back to do what's right. I've come to get them back.' He turned looked at the three of them, one by one. 'If he has harmed them, I will kill him, then I'll hand myself in.'

Tracy stood, but before she could say anything, Jezz continued.

'My life has not been a good one. The only difference between me and Fenton, is that he doesn't care who he hurts. I was brought up to respect women. With those girls I crossed

251

the line. I have to live with, that but not before I try to make it better.' He stared at Tracy. 'If you're going to call the cops, miss, then I'm afraid I'll have to stop you. When I'm gone, you can do what you want, but I won't let you stop me. That's the way it is.'

'Tracy.'

Jezz looked confused. 'What?' he said.

'Call me Tracy, Jezz.'

'Okay, Tracy.' He smiled. He liked her

'I won't stop you. In fact I'll help you.'

It had been a crazy day. She was probably without a job. How much worse could it get?

'Fancy a trip to Wentwood?'

'Well, Tracy,' Jezz smiled, 'I was just about to ask you the same question.'

They both smiled. Their eyes met. They could both feel an instant attraction.

'I hate to break up this blossoming romance,' said Becky, 'but I'm going to be playing gooseberry.'

There were two reasons why Becky was not going to let them go on their own. The first was that she felt guilty for staying behind, and secondly there was no way she was going to let Tracy Bates anywhere near her Daniel, though it appeared to her that Tracy had now found other interests.

'And Me.' said Mickey.

The three looked at him.

'Not a hope in hell.' said Becky, and the other two nodded. Mickey slumped in the chair. *I have to get my girls* he thought. Becky got changed into jeans and trainers which she had left at Carol's. None of Carol's clothes would fit the buxom Tracy, but Becky did find her a coat which although a bit tight would do the job. She tried to make herself look more like a civilian rather than a copper, but the uniform still stood out. *It will have to do* she thought.

Jezz drove in Tracy's car, the gun still in his belt.

'Don't worry,' he told the two girls 'I'll look after you.'

Tracy liked that. She wanted to be looked after, and in what better way could she be looked after. Tracy wanted to sit next to this tall, handsome man. Becky was in the back, looking out through the back window of the car at Mickey Bolan, standing on the pavement where they had left him. *We will be back for you* she thought *you're going to pay.* She thought of what Daniel would do to him when he got hold of him. It gave her some comfort. She hoped it would be painful, lots of pain.

Whilst Mickey wasn't the brightest spark, he did have a gift. There weren't many cars he couldn't get into, and hotwire. Within minutes he was following in a Ford Fiesta, being sure to keep a safe distance behind. He didn't care who saw him. The news reporters probably filmed it, but that wasn't on his mind. After all, those girls owed him big time. Jezz had promised him that he would help him find Bill. Now he had just dumped him on an estate that he had never even heard of. How was he supposed to get home? That cop knew who he was now. He was in deep shit, but he would get his retribution. He knew where Wentwood was. *Everybody knew where Wentwood is* he thought *and its time those to bitches got what was coming.* He laughed as he drove to Wentwood Forest in the pouring rain. Mickey never had a plan, never planned anything in his life. He worked by instinct and his instincts weren't normally that good.

Chapter 49

The rain still came down as Tracy, Jezz and Becky drove to the forest, not knowing what they were going to find, or whatever was happening up there. Was it too late? They didn't know. They just had a feeling that they had better get there quickly. The rain still poured down as the Fenton family trawled through the forest, their bodies soaked and aching, their nerves on edge, their frustration boiling.

It still poured as Mickey Bolan thought about what he was going to do to those girls when he got them. *Sex will be involved, and slapping's* he thought.

It still rained as Katy lay on the floor of the cabin, every part of her body hurting, and she felt dirty. She felt dirty inside. Bill had taken something away from her today, and that something was choice. Today she had no choices. Bill Fenton had stolen them from her.

It was still raining as Wendy Cross lay there, still and motionless, caught up in a world that she didn't deserve. Caught up in a world that had no meaning for her, other than pain. Her teenage years, which were supposed to be the best of her life, spoiled simply because she had been mistaken for someone else.

The rain poured as Bill Fenton filled the kettle from a bottle of water he had brought, put it on the stove and said, 'I'll make us all a nice cuppa.' and, as he drank his tea he let the girls have their well-earned sleep.

'So much to do, so little time to do It.' he said.

Dr. James McCarthy sat on a log, his coat now soaked through. He was fit for his age, but he needed to rest. They had been walking for an hour and the terrain was tough, but the rain had destroyed the trail they were following. They were still sure they were on the right track, as it seemed to be the only available route. If they had gone off that route, then surely they would have seen some signs. Everyone was glad he had stopped. They all needed a rest. Sandwiches were passed around, and a hot drink from the flasks they had brought. It felt good. They had all found a place to sit, be it on a rock, or a log. They were all wet. They could sense an end to this. Madison was frustrated. She didn't want to stop too long. She wanted to get on, and meet her brother's girlfriend, from what Todd had been telling her about Wendy, as they walked. She knew she was going to like her, but Daniel had made her sit and eat, telling her that she needed to keep up her strength and Madison liked that. Her big, strong brother, looking out for her, caring what happened.

The terrain was getting rocky now, and it seemed that the trees were beginning to thin. No longer was there that thick density of wood which had sheltered them to an extent from the rain. Now it hammered through the trees as the ghostly forest spread. Marie Rose had kept up in spite of her age. She looked as fit as any of them. Carol wondered what was going on inside the older woman's head. After all, Bill was her son. Carol could see her face. How frightened it looked. How much of this could she take? Marie Rose had noticed this, sensed it maybe, and assured Carol that he wasn't her son but the son of Satan. Carol had kissed her then, hoping that one day they could spend some time together just doing normal things. She wondered if anything would ever seem normal again.

Bill's father seemed to have gone now, gone to bed, or gone away somewhere, wherever it was that he went, when he wasn't in Bill's head. He often wondered that, thought about where his dad went to, after he left his head. He wanted to find out and maybe when this was all over, he would ask his father where he went. Perhaps he could go to that place, as it might be a better place than this. He thought, *Yes I will ask him* but that didn't matter now. That could wait. Things had taken a bit of a turn. Had he really intended to hurt the girls? He didn't think so. It was his father who wanted them hurt, so he did it, as it was easier than not, and truth be told, he did get a kick out of it. But why was Katy hardly able to speak? And why wouldn't Wendy wake? His father had done this. Bill would always hide behind that. It was my father, not me, he would tell them.

He was expecting Daniel and Todd to turn up. He wasn't stupid. He had deliberately left Wendy's *find my iPhone app* on so they would find him, and they would be here soon. He had made sure there was a trail to follow. He hoped the rain had not done too much damage to it. His original plan had been to just get enough money out of Daniel, by kidnapping his wife, but that stupid Mickey had got the wrong girl. He knew Daniel had quite a bit of money and knew he would be able to get his hands on some more, if it was needed. He knew all about his son's dealings, and what a big player he was. Bill's father had put a stop to that. He had hurt them, he had raped and beaten the two girls, just like he had done to Bill. Just like the inmates did when he was inside. Those bastards who had held him down while the others raped him. But he had got them back, got them all back. They had all paid, either with their lives, or on occasions, even worse. Yet he thought that if he got them all back, then why was his father still fucking about with his head?

Of course, Bill still wanted to make his sons suffer, and the only way he could do that, was for them to watch someone close to them die, the same as everything close to him had died. He thought that Wendy girl may still be alive but she didn't look it. He tried to tidy her up a bit. He bathed her cuts, but she had not woken. She wasn't cold, which he thought was a good thing. He wanted her to wake. He wanted her to see what he had in store for her. He wanted her to feel it. As for Katy, *well, she was alive* Bill said to himself, *though he didn't think it would be long.* He had a good ending for her. Why did Katy have to turn against him? He would have let her go, if she had only played the game. Why had she forced him to take what she used to readily give? No, she had given up on him to protect Wendy, and Wendy didn't deserve to be protected. She deserved to die.

He looked at the semi-naked Katy. She sat in the wheelchair with her legs and arms taped to the chair, her mouth gagged, but her eyes were open now, open wide with a look of horror. He didn't want to blindfold her, he wanted her to see when he pushed her from the top of the cliff. He wanted her to feel it.
He made himself a drink. He knew this would end soon, and that he would try to get away. If he didn't, he didn't mind, because prison, or even death, wouldn't be so bad either. Any solution would be one he could welcome.

The cabin was warm, despite parts of it being open to the elements. He had kept the wood burner well stocked, but it still rained, just like a typical British summer. He had no idea what time it was. Time was of no significance. Even in prison, he never recognised time. Other inmates would count the months or years they had left, and when it came down to days, they would count them off. He never did. Time had no relevance for him.

He had bound Wendy's legs and arms lightly. He drank his tea, lit a cigarette, sitting, and looked at the motionless Wendy, as he blew out plumes of smoke. He checked his rucksack, took out a hammer and some cord. He would tie her up properly. She wouldn't last long, she was almost dead anyway. He picked up her frail body in his strong arms. Katy looked on as he held Wendy in his arms. She wanted to shout out, to tell him to leave Wendy, and take her instead. She had grown fond of the girl. She thought that for the first time in her life she had a friend, a real friend, but she couldn't shout, the gag prevented that. She wanted Bill to take her. She wanted that more than anything she had ever wanted in her life. She felt her whole body shiver, as he walked out of the cabin, carrying the girl she had grown to love in such a short time. It felt like an angel was being taken away to her final resting place. She realised that she would never see Wendy again.

The girl wasn't heavy, he could easily carry her. Her body was still warm. She was alive. He was sure that he could see her chest rising as she breathed, but he guessed death would come soon. He wouldn't need to hurt her anymore. It was almost done. 'Please wake up before you die.' he whispered to her. 'I want you to feel it.'

Twenty minutes later, she was staked to the ground. Her legs and arms were spread wide and tied to four stakes hammered into the ground. Bill stood and looked at his handiwork. He was proud of it. He thought it was a fitting end. It looked regal. It looked like a sacrifice, which was exactly what it was. A sacrifice. The rain poured down on her beaten body, washing the blood and dirt from her face. As Bill looked at her he thought how beautiful she looked. He bent down, and stroked her cheek.

'Goodbye sweetheart.' he said, and he would swear he saw her smile.

He wished he had got to know her better, before she died. But things didn't always go to plan. Soon she will be buried in mud falling from the mountain side, a fitting end to someone so pretty, Soon they would all die.

Katy, in the wheelchair, was now being pushed by Bill. The wheels were crooked, and it was with great difficulty that he pushed her up the side of the hill. Every bump in the chair, every rock that he hit, jarred through her body like a toothache. He would have a good view from the hill. He would be able to see them coming. He needed to rest. He still felt strong, still felt ready, but the hill was steep. The wheelchair was extremely hard to manoeuvre. He sat on a rock, lit a cigarette, and told Katy all about what he was going to do with her. Katy didn't care. She was ready to die, she just wished he would get on with it.

Madison was in front as they reached the clearing. No one knew where she got her energy from. She always seemed to be helping someone, asking if everyone was okay. They were all in awe of her, so pleased that they had met this wonderful girl, and she had chosen to go along their path. She screamed that she could see a cabin ahead. They all wondered where she got her strength from, as she jumped up and down, and flapped her hands. All six of them stood on the edge of the forest now, looking at the cabin ahead. They needed to be careful. If the three were in there, they didn't want to frighten Bill into doing anything.

Daniel had decided that he alone should approach the cabin, make himself known, because it was him his father wanted. They all argued. All volunteered, each having their reasons why it should be them. Reasons like 'I was married to him.', 'It's my girl he's got.', 'I'm his mother.', 'I'm the oldest. I should sacrifice.' Madison simply said 'Let me go. I can do this.'

'It's me.' said Daniel. 'I'm the one he wants.'

They sat on whatever they could find for a little while, staring at the cabin, looking to see if there was any sign of life, but it looked deserted. Madison stood, pacing. She wanted to get on. She wanted to do something.

Marie Rose and James sat together on the sodden ground, which didn't matter as their clothes were soaking anyway. James put his arm around her.

'I'm so glad I found you again.' he said

She looked at him smiled. 'Me too.' Her expression changed. 'Can you feel it, is there death in the air?

The doctor gazed at the cabin. 'No I can't.' he said.

'Good.'

'Will you tell me if and when you can?'

'Of course'

Chapter 50

Jezz, Becky and Tracy looked at the two cars parked up, and they could see the path that the others had taken. It seemed the only obvious way, yet they weren't sure what to do now. Tracy was wondering whether she had done the right thing. She had wanted to phone Goldstone, but the others had stopped her. Jezz wanted to go alone. Tracy wanted to call for the police. Becky wanted them all to go into the woods and find the rest of them. She was sure that Daniel would have found the two girls, and they would soon be home.

'The police will just mess it up.' said Jezz, because he really didn't want the police, as attracted as he was to the one that stood before him. He didn't trust the police. He didn't trust himself with them.

'What have you got against the police?' asked Tracy. 'Do you really want to know?' Jezz said. 'Do you really want to know? When I see them every day of my life, taking bribes, beating up no more than little kids. I'm black!' he said. 'You can't know what it's like being black, living in that place. The only way we can survive is by bringing them in on every move we make. Do you know who makes the most money out of the drug trade on my patch?' His eyes grew wide, he gritted his teeth.

Tracy didn't answer she didn't want to know though she could have guessed at the answer.

'Do you use, Jezz? 'she asked.

He was surprised at the change of subject, but he answered anyway.

'Not for four years. I'm clean.'

'For fuck's sake!' Becky shouted. 'Let's have the life story later. Are we going in, or what?' She was agitated. There was no time for this. She walked into the forest.

They both followed Becky into the woods, Jezz insisting they follow him, and he took over from Becky. The girls walked together, with Jezz in front.

'You know I would break your legs, if you ever touch my Daniel, copper or no copper.' stated Becky to Tracy, as they walked deep into the forest.

Tracy smiled. 'Well, the one thing I've learnt over the last day or so, is not to mess with the Fenton's.' She stroked the side of her own face. 'Even the women know how to punch.' Becky laughed.

Tracy touched her on the shoulder, as she walked. 'I'm not after Daniel. He's hot, but he's married to you. I'm no home wrecker.'

Becky smiled again, 'I love him to bits.'
'How did his brother learn to fly?' she laughed.

'I think Daniel taught him.' They both laughed...

Jezz urged them on to keep up, they quickened their pace. As they did, the rain came on, and the long arms of the trees looked as though they were going to reach out and grab them. For the first time that night, Tracy felt scared as she wondered whether the trees had swallowed the others in front of them, and were about to do the same to them. She held Becky's hand. Becky gripped it tight, for she too was scared.

Jezz just wanted to do one good thing in his sorry life. He just hoped he wasn't too late. He led with a determination to succeed, a feeling he had never known before, but it felt good, he liked it.

Daniel approached the cabin slowly, occasionally glancing back towards the group, to make sure he wasn't followed by them. They all stood watching, hoping, and praying.

He called out 'It's me, Daniel.' as he approached. He kept calling it, as he reached the cabin. The door was open, it was off its hinges. He could see that the cabin was empty. He stepped in, the log burner was still ablaze. There was a rucksack there, a saucepan and a kettle. He knew they had been here. He called the rest over, waving to them frantically, they all ran forward to the cabin, all except for Madison. Half way there she stopped, changed direction, and started jogging towards the hill. She wanted to see who it was standing on top of it. She could hear the others. They had all reached the cabin and were disappointed to find it empty. The heat from the burner was welcome, and now at least they would have a base to work from. They were all taking off their coats, hoping to get dry by the fire. Marie Rose lit her first cigarette of the night.

The Doctor looked around 'Where's Madison?'

'She was here. She was with us.' said Carol. She went to the door and shouted Madison's name.

'Shit!' exclaimed Daniel. 'I'll go look.' This was a problem he could do without. Where the hell had she gone?

'I'm coming,' said Todd, 'and don't you dare try to stop me.' They walked towards the direction from which they had just come.

Madison heard them calling, but she ignored it. She thought she could hear someone's thoughts again. As she stopped to listen, the thoughts had stopped, but it hadn't been clear. It was like it had been more than one thought. As she climbed the hill, her legs aching, she couldn't hear anything. As she drew nearer, she could see a man looking out over the sheer drop of

263

the hill, and in front of him was a wheelchair. Even from where Madison was, she could clearly see that there was someone in the wheel chair. She saw Todd and Daniel leave the cabin. She felt guilty, as she knew they were probably looking for her, and she had just added to their troubles. She couldn't shout out to them, as that would alert the man that she was there. She wasn't sure what she was going to do. Her young life had never experienced anything like this before. She walked towards the man and the wheelchair as they moved closer to the edge of the cliff. What was he going to do? She shivered as if someone had walked over her grave, when she realised that the man was going to send the wheelchair and its occupant, over the hill. She had to try and stop him. She had to do something. Was the man Bill Fenton? Was this her Father?

Bill hadn't noticed them arrive at the cabin. He had been too busy trying to get the wheelchair up the hill. Now he was at the top of the hill, looking down at the cabin, he could see Daniel and Todd running out of the cabin. He wondered what they were doing, running back. It had been a long time since he had seen his boys. He realised they were now men. For one moment he felt a tinge of sadness and regret. He wished them a better life than his had been. He looked out over the cliff, thinking what a wonderful view it was from up here. He reached the edge of the hill and looked down.

'Take a look, Katy,' he said, 'before I push you over. This is your destiny. This day was made for what is about to happen to you.'

Katy just sat. She wet herself. She didn't want it to end like this. She shivered. *Please let it be quick* she thought. She imagined herself bouncing against the rocks, strapped in the wheelchair, a certain death, but not necessarily a quick ending.

Then she heard a voice. It was a female voice. The voice of a young girl.

'You don't have to do that, Bill. Said Madison.

Bill wasn't sure at first, wasn't sure where the voice had come from. He thought it was Katy, but it couldn't be. The shock made him take his hands off the wheelchair, but it didn't roll over the edge. He looked to the side of him, not quite believing what he could see. He thought it was an angel or something. On the hill with him, no more than six feet away, was this beautiful young girl, an angel in the making. For the first time that night he was scared.

'Who the fuck are you?'

Madison will never understand what made her answer as she did.

'I think I'm your daughter. You're my father.'

Bill turned looked at her. At the smile which was now fixed on that innocent face. How can that be? Bill didn't say it, he thought it. For the sixth time in her short life Madison heard a person's thoughts.

'You and my mother had a one-night stand in Cardiff about seventeen years ago. I'm the result.' she smiled. She wanted to show him that she understood.

'Hello dad.'

Bill's mind drifted back seventeen years. He could remember it, although he wasn't sure why. He remembered waking up, and how the girl had changed from the night before, when she was up for it. In the morning all she wanted to do was to clear off as quickly as she could.

'It wasn't you.' She had been embarrassed. 'She don't normally do one-night stands.'

Bill was taken aback. 'How?' he paused, his shoulders dropped, what was happening?

'I can hear your thoughts.'

'Can you?' *You are so beautiful,* he thought

Madison blushed. 'Why, thank you.' she said.

Bill was confused. He couldn't focus. Something wasn't right. He felt like he couldn't cope. He wanted to jump off the cliff himself.

'Don't do that. Please don't.' she said.

Katy just sat in the chair, looking over the edge of the cliff, looking at what only moments ago was to have been her final destination. She could hear the girl, but couldn't see her. Would her life be saved? Tears came to her eyes. *I promise never to be bad again* she thought.

'Why? his voice croaked. He wiped his mouth. 'Why would you want to save me? he asked.

Madison smiled again. 'There's been enough hurt, don't you think?'

He did. Finally he realised there had been. He had had enough. *No more hurt* he thought *no more pain. Get a fucking grip!* said the voice in his head, the voice of his father.

Madison was confused. It shocked her. She almost shrieked. She gulped. There was a second voice, a second thought, but it was coming from Bill. Someone else was in his head.

'Who the hell is that?' she asked.

Bill smiled, his evil stare returning 'It's your grandfather.' he said, and continued smiling as his father spoke. *Push her. Push her, you coward.*

'He says I've got to push her.'

'Then don't listen.' she said.

'What?' said Bill, even more confused.

'Don't listen to him.'

Who the fuck are you, to tell my son what to do?, the voice in Bill's head said

266

'I'm Madison. Who the fuck are you?' she clenched her fists and gritted her teeth.

Bill's father's voice was confused. She had heard him. How could that be?

I'm your worst fucking nightmare, the voice said

Madison sniggered. 'Nightmare?' she said. 'You're just a cowardly voice. You don't even exist. You're just living off his memories. Just go!'

Kill her. Kill her, the voice raged. It was loud. Madison could clearly hear it.

'Dad.' she said. Bill stood confused in a trance. 'Dad!' she screamed.

He jumped, as if being woken from a dream. What was happening?, he wondered. He put his hands to either side of his head. It hurt like mad. There was too much going on in there.

Too many people, too many voices.

'Do you want to listen to your dad?' she asked.

Bill screamed, 'No. No, but I can't stop it. I have to do what he tells me.'

Kill them both, the voice said.

Madison walked over to Bill. She placed her hands over his, which were still holding his head.

'It's just a voice. We can make it go. Do you want it to go?' 'Yes.' he screamed.

'Get the fuck out of there!' she said, addressing the voice.

Kill her. Kill her. Kill them both.

'Noooo!' Bill screamed.

'Get out of his head! Get the fuck out!' and she pressed the side of Bill's head until it hurt. 'Go! Get out!' she screamed. She held his head to her chest, and stroked his hair. Somehow

267

she knew she had the power to do this, this was her gift. 'Go now,' she said softly, 'leave him be, and never come back.'

The voice in his head screamed obscenities, as it disappeared fading into the distance until it could no longer be heard. Bill knew he would never hear from his father again, and he wept as Madison held his head against her chest.

'It will be okay.' she said. 'He's gone now.' She held him for a further moment. 'Who is it in the chair?' she asked him. Bill raised his head. 'It's Katy.' He wiped his mouth with the back of his hand 'Tell her I'm sorry.' He took two steps back from the cliff edge. 'Someone has to die tonight.' he said. He turned and ran.

Madison pulled the wheelchair away from the cliff. It was heavy and the wheels didn't turn. She knelt before the chair, before the terrified girl who sat in it. She untied the gag from the girl's mouth. Katy took a deep breath, as if it was her last.

She coughed and spluttered, barely getting her words out. 'Thank you.' she said.

Madison worked at the tape around her legs and arms. Katy just sat there, letting her rescuer do it. She couldn't believe that she was alive. Yet she was still scared. She thought that she might remain scared for the rest of her life. Her life had been spared, but her fight had all gone.

'Who are you?' she asked the girl who continued working on the tape.

'I'm Madison, Todd and Daniel's sister.' she said. 'It's a long story, one I don't fully understand yet, but I'm getting there.'' she released Katy's arms.

How good it felt to Katy, as she touched her face with her own hands.

'I didn't know they had a sister?'

268

Madison freed her legs. 'Nor did they until very recently.' she said. 'Can you stand?'

'I think so,' she said, 'but I think I've twisted my ankle.'

'I could go and get some help.'

Katy grabbed Madison's sleeve and held it tight. 'Please don't leave me. He's out there. Please don't go.'

Madison smiled. 'I won't leave you. Come on. I'll support you somehow.'

She helped Katy to her feet. Katy put an arm around her shoulders.

'I'll tell you what.' Madison said.' I don't think much of my father or grandfather.' If Katy could have laughed she would have.

They hobbled down the side of the hill, one girl wondering what would happen next, and the other one just thankful that she was still alive.

Somewhere in the distance dawn broke, and the rain pounded down on the torso of Wendy Cross.

Bill Fenton walked the forest of Wentwood in a hazy daze. Todd and Daniel heard the shouting from Madison, and were so relieved that she was okay. As they ran towards her, both boys were going to chastise her for running off, until they saw her almost carrying another girl.

'Help me.' she said. 'I'm knackered!'

Daniel took the girl easily, sweeping her into his arms.

'What the hell?' said Todd.

'I've met your dad.' she said. 'Bit of a nutter, isn't he. I hope it doesn't run in the family.'

As soon as they got to the cabin there were a million of questions and answers, but first James got his bag out and treated Katy's wounds as best he could. He strapped her ankle. Then the others helped her out of what little damp clothes that she was wearing, and gave her a coat that had been drying by the fire. She lay beside the burner, warm and thankful to be alive. She told them as much as she could. No one was sure whether to love or hate her. There was certainly plenty of sympathy as they looked at the beaten girl. Yet wasn't she really the cause of all this. Still that would have to wait. They still had to find Wendy.

'So he just carried her out?' asked Daniel.

Katy looked exhausted. Tears streamed down her face. 'Yes.' she said.

'And she was alive?'

'Yes, I'm sure she was.'

'And he was gone for about thirty minutes.'

She thought again, wiping her face. 'I think so.'

'So she can be no more than fifteen minutes away!'

They split into two teams. Daniel and Carol, Todd and Madison, with James bringing up the rear. They would climb the hill on either side.

Marie Rose looked exhausted, as she stayed with Katy, who had her head in the old lady's lap. Marie Rose was now stroking Katy's forehead gently.   'If she dies, I'll never forgive myself.'

'They will find her sweetheart and she will be okay.' Marie Rose promised, as she stroked the broken girl's forehead. She hoped that she really believed what she had just said.

Chapter 51

If Bill Fenton had killed his father today, rather than all those years ago, and if Marie Rose had been a battered wife today rather than all those years ago, things may have been different. Authorities would have acted, organisations would have helped. Neither Bill nor Marie Rose would have needed to walk around with bruises and battered face. Teachers would have picked up on it, friends, neighbours, and others would have noticed. Support would have been given. Maybe mother and son would have stayed together and maybe, just maybe, Bill Fenton would not have turned out as he had. But that was a long shot, and everyone associated with the Fenton's would have known that. You can't legislate for evil, and Bill Fenton was evil.

No one had actually told Bill Fenton that his father was dead. Yes, Bill had pushed him down the stairs and left him for dead. When the police had arrived and taken Bill into care, and rushed his dying father, William, to hospital it had been five days before he came round, and a further three months before he left hospital, and after a further seventeen years before he was deemed well enough to be released from the mental facility where he had spent those years. He now resided in a residential home for the elderly, at the tax-payers' expense. Bill hadn't killed his father. William Fenton was still alive.

Bill knew none of this. The abused child had been hidden from his father's fate. It was better that Bill believed his father was dead, the authorities deemed. They didn't want the child to be haunted by the thought that his father was still alive, and would come after him. If he thought his father was dead, he would be able to remove him from his life, and maybe forget. How wrong can the authorities be?

Bill had spent all his childhood going from one carer to the next, from one foster parent to the next, believing that he had killed his father, and his father's soul would not let him forget that.

William Fenton was never charged for the offences that he had committed against his wife and his son. Most people would argue that Bill Fenton was born an evil man, because some people are just born that way. History tells us this. The man who had sired Bill Fenton, William Fenton, ergo had the same DNA as his son. Evil to the core. Bill's two sons carried his DNA. There were people who believed the two brothers would go the same way as their father and grandfather. They had genes which very few other people shared, unique in fact in the modern day world. People would always be looking at them for that reason. If they could see them now, they might have a different point of view.

The old man lifted his draught counter. His hand shook, as it hovered momentarily in mid-air. He had had a bad day, a very bad day and night. Picking the counter off the board seemed to take all his effort. The last twenty four hours had certainly taken it out of him. His hands hadn't been good lately. They always seemed to be shaking. His legs had grown weak, and he was finding it difficult to walk. The carers had noticed this, and in their minds, it was just that William Fenton was in decline. He loved to play draughts and he almost always won. He jumped his opponent's draughts and shakily removed them from the board. His eighty years of age was catching up with him, along with recent exhausting events.

'I didn't see that,' said Edith, an elderly lady in her late eighties, who sat opposite William, at the small draughts table in the communal room of the home. She had been there for four years longer than William, and they had become friends in some ways. William's cheekiness reminded her of her late husband, Frederick. She studied the table, looking for her next move. It would take her more than ten minutes.

The home was a good home. It met all the required standards that were laid on homes of this type, having passed all the inspections, and was not known for mistreating any of its residents. The staff members were well vetted and had passed all the relevant tests. Some residents did get shouted at, now and again, and William Fenton was not an exception, for he too had his moments. He was very rarely scolded for he appeared to have the foulest mouth on earth and he wasn't scared to use it.

He was generally a good patient, not deemed aggressive, just foul mouthed. He never gave the carers much stick, would throw a few lewd remarks at the younger ones, but they were trained to ignore it, and every night in his room, before bedtime, William Fenton would talk to his son, sometimes shouting at him, often swearing at him. Nobody questioned this, as almost half of the residents would talk to someone at night, a lost loved one that had passed on but they could never ever let go.

Residents were generally free to roam, walking the vast gardens, or even pop to the local shop. It wasn't a prison, but it had a smell about it. A smell which said, once you pass these doors, you will never leave. The antiseptic smell of death.

Today the carers were a bit concerned about William. Although he had never mentioned his son to the carers, today he did. In tears he told them that his son had died. They knew they would have to keep an eye on him, and try to get him through it, and hope he would make up another son from somewhere, or even a daughter.

Edith moved her piece. She was a dear old lady. 'Mad as a hatter.' William always said. Nearly every night they played draughts, and chatted at the same table. They would both miss each other when one of them had gone. William Fenton didn't think that would be long now.

'So you say, when you talked to him last, someone else was there?' asked Edith, as she wiped spittle from her mouth with the back of her hand.

William was making his next move. He was fed up now. Edith had asked the same question five times since he had told her. He wished the old bat would just shut up and play the game, He was 2-0 up, and it was the best of five. He wanted to watch the movie that would be on the communal telly.

'Yes. I told you, some girl.' he said angrily.

'Okay. Okay. Don't get your knickers in a twist.'

William tutted, then finally moved his draught with the same shaky hand. 'Your move.'

'And you say she spoke to you?' asked Edith.

William flipped the game board upside down. 'Stupid fucking game.' he proclaimed as the counters fell to the floor. Two carers looked on, monitoring the situation. Edith put up a shaky hand signalling that everything was okay. William leaned forward. Edith could feel the stench of his breath. William's eyes were now wide. He looked evil. 'She took me out of his head.' he said, and sat back in the chair.

'Nasty girl.' she said.

A carer came over, picked up the spilled pieces and set them on the table. Neither William nor Edith acknowledged her. 'How can you take someone out of your head?' asked Edith.

William slumped in his chair, breathing heavily. He had thought about this. He leaned close, and whispered, 'I don't know, but she's going to pay.'

Edith tried to reach down to her ankle, her frail body struggling with the task.

'Ooh, my corns are playing up.' she said.

Chapter 52

Todd and Madison walked together, a steady climb up one side of the hill, the rain still coming down, soaking them once again. There seemed no let up as the dawn broke, the weather seeming relentless with the attempt to deter them from their objective. The weather was really working against them by providing another challenge for them, but wild horses would not deter them, and Madison seemed to possess a strength way beyond her years and petite frame.

'She seemed a nice girl.' Said Madison, referring to Katy, as they walked.

Todd thought about that for a moment, she was, after all, a kidnapper.

'The jury's still out on that,' he said, 'and how can you know that. You saw the state of her, beaten, and god knows what else.'

'She was awfully scared.'

'I could see that.'

'She said she and Wendy became friends.'

'I will let Wendy be the judge of that.' said Todd. 'How come you know so much about her?'

'When we were coming down the hill, we chatted. All she could talk about was Wendy. It seemed she really cared for her.'

'If Wendy dies, the blood will be on her hands.'

Madison didn't answer. She could understand her brother's feelings, but she felt that Katy was genuine, and whatever she had done, surely she didn't deserve that.

They continued walking for a couple of minutes. They didn't really know what they were looking for. As Todd walked, he hoped it would not be he who found her. He didn't want to be

276

the one who found the body of his girlfriend. He didn't think he could cope with that.

Madison thought of home, her father, her real father, Morgan, not the biological one that she had just met. She wished Morgan was here now. He would know what to do, he always did.

Daniel and the rest were still in sight, some distance away. Carol was waving at them frantically. Madison heard Carol's thoughts telling her that they had found Wendy. As soon as she told Todd what she had heard they ran towards the others, Todd tripping and stumbling down. He shrieked in pain as he stood up again.

'My ankle,' he said, 'I've twisted my fucking ankle.'

For the second time that day and with great strength Madison used herself for support as they ran and hobbled towards the other search party.

Daniel, Carol and James could see her now. They could see her limp body laid out on the ground. She was no more than a few hundred yards away, the rain pelting her body, heavy and unforgiving. Her head was clearly visible, but most of the lower half of her body was covered by mud, wet and slimy as it slid down the hillside, covering her spread-eagled body. Mud still poured from the hill in mini landslides, devouring the landscape and all which stood in the way of Mother Nature. The three of them were exhausted now, as were Todd and Madison who were closely following them. The sight of Wendy had given them hope and renewed their strength. Daniel, holding the doctor up, as they tracked through the mud. The doctor fighting every ache and pain in his battered body, his hand tightly clutching the medical bag that he carried. He thought of all the patients that he had treated, mostly he thought of those patients that he knew whose life was ending. He prayed his gift would not reveal itself today. Today he did not want to smell death, taste it, even though he had never met this girl, he wanted to save her life more than any other, such was the magnetism of the whole situation.

The doctor stumbled, and both Daniel and Carol grabbed him before he fell. He grunted, and waved his arms, as if to say I'm okay. They carried on, no words were spoken. Wendy was yards away. They were almost there.

Carol looked back, seeing that Madison and Todd were not far behind. She could see that Todd was struggling, and Madison was supporting him. She marvelled at this young girl's strength, after all that she found out and been through in the last twenty four hours.

Carol wondered whether she would ever get over it. The five of them felt as if the whole party could only be stopped if death was borne down upon them. The same could be said of Wendy Cross, a fighter if there ever was one. It looked as though the fight had gone out of Wendy, as her last breaths faded away, and the life slipped from her, her last thought were of Todd.

Todd winced with pain on every stride that he took. His sister, whom he had only just met, supporting him all the way. Todd also wondered where she got her strength from, and what he would have done without her. For the first time he could see the girl that he loved, the girl that he adored, tied down to a hill, which had taken her.

As the first three reached Wendy's body, Daniel and Carol slumped beside her, scraping the mud away from her body and trying frantically to untie her. James checked for a pulse, anything, any sign of life. *This can't be it,* he thought, *not all this for nothing.*

'There's no pulse!' he shrieked. 'She's not breathing.' He paused. 'I think she's gone.' and he wept, the first time he had cried since his beloved wife had died.

Both Daniel and Carol shouted for him to do something, almost blaming him. The doctor now slumped to the ground still holding Wendy's hand, where he was trying to find a pulse.

'She's gone.' he said.

Daniel shook the doctor 'Did you see it?' he screamed, before we reached her, did you see it? Did you know she was dead?'

James wiped his lips with the back of his hand, letting go of Wendy's limp hand. 'No. No. I didn't.'

Carol broke down now. She was slumped in the mud crying, sobbing like a baby.

Fifty yards away. Todd had stopped. He told his sister to go on. Madison was reluctant to leave him, telling him she could support him the short distance to where Wendy lay, but he shoved her away.

He stood there now, the pain in his ankle gone, or not relevant anymore. He stood, arms outstretched in the air, looking up at the skies that poured rain down on him. He looked like some godly figure. He opened his mouth to scream, but nothing came. At least no sound that any human could hear. Four military personnel dressed in all black with no insignia looked from the distance.

There was no cry of pain, torture, anger or even fright, just a little light, hardly noticeable in the rain, floated, floated to where the group was as they cradled Wendy's body.

Madison had stopped and she was looking at Todd now. She saw the light, saw where it went. Still Todd screamed, with no sound.

It's not time yet. Todd heard himself say, deep inside his mind. *'You have too many songs to sing, Wendy.'* Arms still outstretched, his body silhouetted against the grey skies.

And you have too many songs to write, came the reply.

Madison could hear it. She could hear two people, just like with her father and grandfather. She could hear her brother, and she could hear Wendy.

I will still write them I will get them to you somehow.

I will sing them always.

I will sing them with you.

The doctor screamed, as if in agony as he picked up Wendy's hand.

'There's a pulse. I'm sure there's a pulse.'

Everyone sat up. There was a sign of urgency on their faces, the look of hope.

'Please, James. Please, God.'

The doctor checked again.

How can you Todd, you're leaving me.

I will never leave you, Wendy.'

Madison was looking back and forth, at Todd and Wendy. She didn't understand it, but she knew they were talking to each other. Madison cried.

Wendy's eyes flickered, and partly opened, not seeing anyone, not hearing anyone, except Todd. All she could hear was Todd. He had come to save her. The tears were now tears of joy, from the people who sat beside her as the doctor checked her over.

I will always be with you Wendy. Todd said to her

in person, or in memory?

In your heart, and in your soul.

Wendy's eyes were fully open now, although she didn't seem to notice the people around her. She sat up. The Doctor slumped in bewilderment he had never seen anyone come back like this. Carol and Daniel not really believing their eyes, not believing the miracle unfolding around them, only Madison knew it was no miracle.

Madison just stood there, totally transfixed, looking at the god-like figure of her brother, who suddenly appeared to be ten feet tall. The look on his face would be one she would never forget. She knew it would be in her dreams for years to come. She watched, as the angelic figure of her brother sank to his knees. She knew he was crying, as was Wendy. They wept like babies.

As Wendy's breathing got stronger, the person she loved more than anything in the world, was slipping away from her.

Don't go Todd. She told him. Only Madison heard,

I have to, Wendy.

I will always love you, Todd.

I will never stop loving you, Wendy. You are my life.

I'm scared, Todd.

Don't be.

Why are you leaving me?

To give us life.

I don't want to say goodbye. I need you, Todd.

I love you Wendy. Say hello, never say goodbye.

Wendy was alert now. She sat up, strength returning as she came out of her trance. No one could believe what was happening.

'Don't go Todd!' she shouted

As she spoke, what seemed to be lightning, struck Todd Fenton. They all turned to stare at the place where Todd had stood. All they could see was the earth underneath him. It was scorched.

'He just disappeared,' cried Madison, 'into thin air she said as she scrambled towards where Todd was standing digging the ground with her fingers as if he was buried there. There was a light. There was something, or someone, in the light. He's gone.' she cried as she stopped digging.

'He saved me!' said Wendy.

They all looked up into the sky. They could see a small light, fading in the distance, then it was gone. The clouds parted, and the sun shone brightly down on them. For just a moment, Wendy could have sworn she saw Todd, waving goodbye, but it may have been the clouds, playing tricks with her eyes. Daniel looked at Madison, and she at him. Daniel knew his brother was gone. He knew why. After all, it was his fault.

'Will he come back?' Madison asked.

Daniel looked at the skies. 'I love you, brother.' he said.

He took hold of his sister, hugged her, saying 'No, he's gone.' as he wiped away tears. They took the short walk down the hillside towards the Cabin.

Chapter 52

How much more can we take? Daniel thought, as he, Wendy, Carol, James and Madison stood by the door. Just inside the cabin, the sight before them was one of horror. Marie Rose lay on the floor. She had been knocked unconscious. There was a trickle of blood on her forehead. She looked old and frail as she lay there.

Mickey Bolan stood there. Katy was held in front of him with a knife held at her throat. Katy caught Wendy's eyes. Both had tears in their eyes.

'We were just about to leave.' said Mickey, his eyes wild, the knife hovering an inch from Katy's throat.

'I can't allow that.' said Daniel. He didn't care much about Katy, but thought she had suffered enough, and no way was this guy walking out with her.

He had just lost his brother. That was his fault, his mistake. He wasn't going to make another mistake today.

Mickey smiled. 'Think yourself lucky. I wanted both girls, but I'll just take my girl.'

'She doesn't belong to you.' said Wendy.

No one moved. Katy was staring out of the glassless window on the wall opposite her, and she understood what she had to do.

'Let me go with him,' she said 'I'll be fine.'

'I can't let you, Katy.'

'No, it's okay. It's my life. It's what I deserve. Mickey is the guy for me.'

As Mickey released the pressure on Katy, and lowered the knife a few inches, thinking that he and his girl would just walk out, Katy reacted by letting herself fall to the floor, and roll out of the way, just as the bullet came through the window, hitting

Mickey Bolan in the shoulder. It sent him sprawling to the ground screaming. Wendy and Katy ran to each other, embraced and kissed and cried. 'I thought you were dead.' said Katy.

'I thought you were too.'

'Where's Todd?'

Wendy just hugged her. 'He didn't make it.' she said.

James was attending to Marie Rose, as Tracy Bates, Jezz and Becky walked in. Jezz was still holding the gun with which he had shot Mickey. Both girls looked at him.

'Thank you.' Katy whispered.

Jezz had seen what was happening, as he approached the cabin. He had been able to catch the attention of Katy. As Marie Rose came round, Daniel hugged his wife. There wasn't a dry eye when they were all told what had happened. 'The police and ambulances are on their way.' said Tracy, and for once they were all glad she had got involved.

Chapter 53

Bill Fenton was back where he belonged, back to where the only harm he could do was to like-minded people. He had been caught an hour after the rest had been airlifted away in ambulances. He had been found, roaming the forest in a daze, saying something about she had taken him out of his head. He was back in Cardiff prison where he had spent his previous years.

As he was brought in after being processed, they didn't put him with the remand prisoners. He recognised some faces.
Some cons greeted him, some scorned him, but most hardly noticed him. He was no longer top man, so he had no relevance. There were plenty in there who wanted revenge, and some grinned like Cheshire cats, as they thought of ways to get their revenge. None of this bothered Bill Fenton. He wanted what he had left behind, which was being top dog. He didn't care how he got it. He had beaten people and been beaten since he was eight years old, and his mind was clearer now. He wouldn't have his father to muddle things up now, because he was gone forever. She had taken his father's voice from his head. Everything had worked out fine. He must thank her one day.

The moment the sound of metal upon metal entered his head, as the steel doors were closed behind him, he felt more at home then he had felt for years. After all that had happened this was where he belonged. This would be where he would be at his best.

He would be up in front of the judge tomorrow, but it would be a short hearing as he would be sent to prison, whilst awaiting his trial. He knew the score, it didn't bother him, nothing bothered him at all. He was back home.

Things had gone terribly wrong up in that forest. He had heard that his son, Todd, had died. That wasn't supposed to have happened. He had cocked up big time. He knew that, but he was always destined to be back in here, and for that reason, he wished he had killed them all.

He would start exercising again in the gym, get his strength and muscle back up, some of which he had lost since his release. He would befriend a few inmates, some that he could trust, some who had worked for him in the past and worked well. He would remind them how he always rewarded them, how he looked after them. If that didn't work, then he would beat the shit out of them.

He lay on the bed of a single cell, exactly the same as the one he first went to in his previous imprisonment. He would soon have a better cell because he was better equipped this time. He was happy, and he hadn't felt happy for ages. The same guards, the same cell, the same conditions, more or less the same people. He had made it to the top before. He could do it again. Bill Fenton is back.

It was ten pm. Lights had just been put out. He just lay there on the lumpy mattress, his cell in darkness. The light in the corridor sending an eerie glow into his cell. It wasn't silent. Prisons were never quiet even at night. There would always be someone shouting, screaming, claiming their innocence, banging on about the injustice. A few might be crying, scared, as it would be their first night inside. There was always somebody crying. He liked the criers. They were the easy ones to exploit. Tomorrow would be a new day. Tomorrow would be the day when he would announce his return. He drifted into a sleep, planning his many moves. He would dream tonight, he knew and they would be good dreams.

He only slept for about two hours, then he woke. No noise woke him for the prison was unusually quiet. It was also unusually dark. He woke, sensing something. He woke, scared. Bill Fenton was never scared.

He knew no one was in his cell, because if they had come in, he surely would have heard the clink of metal as the door opened. His eyes became adjusted to the dark, as he lay on his bed. He could see that the cell was empty, but he could see something he hadn't noticed before. He could see a light, not bright, but it was floating above him, hovering in mid-air. He suddenly felt short of breath as if someone was suffocating him. He put his hands to his throat, trying to remove what was choking him, but there was nothing there. No hands held his throat, no hands that he could feel. He gasped for air as he fought to breathe. He decided it must be a panic attack, so he tried to relax, but he was finding it increasingly harder to breathe. As he struggled, the light which hovered over him grew brighter. His hands started flapping now as he gasped for air, but that didn't last long, as the last breath was taken from his body. There would be no top dog for Bill Fenton. Just before he took his very last breath, and went to the hell that awaited him, just before he died, when the light was drifting away, he swore that he could see a face in the light. The autopsy would later reveal that Bill Fenton died in his sleep.

Chapter 54

Three months later

Todd's body was never found. The forest was searched as thoroughly as was possible, using over a thousand volunteers, most of them rave-goers.

The family never expected a body to be found. They hoped that somehow he was floating around the skies somewhere. Wendy certainly hoped that was the case, he would never be dead to her.

Mickey Bolan lived, and was charged with kidnap.

Sky News was there, they always were. It was a warm, sunny day even though it was mid-autumn. The skies really delivered today. The fields around Ashbourne were full of people. The roads had been closed except for those who were attending. Three months ago, the same people had attended for a rave. Today they attended for a service in honour of Todd Fenton. A lot of the people wore T-shirts of superheroes, written on the back was 'Todd the ultimate.' It would be the biggest service in Ashbourne's history, probably the biggest service in south Wales.

There were massive sounds systems around the estate, so that everyone could hear. They all hoped Todd was listening, they were sure he would be. The vicar's words were sincere and heartfelt, the song sung by Wendy Cross brought tears to everyone's eyes, as she sang a song about her Todd. It was as though the whole world paused as she sang. She had promised herself not to cry, but she broke her promise.

When she returned to her seat, Katy hugged her close.

'That was beautiful.' she told her as she smiled, showing a full set of perfect teeth.

The guests were unlimited, but there were certain guests who took the front pews.

Carol Fenton, the news of her ex-husband's death was the one good thing that came out of it. She would never mourn for him. She missed Todd deeply. Every minute of the day, she seemed to think of him, how much happiness he had brought. She would always miss him. In Madison, she had gained a daughter and she had remained extremely close to Marie Rose and James McCarthy. She had had the roof fixed, and was as close as she ever could be to Wendy, who she hoped would find someone to love again, but expected it would take a long time. Her home now seemed empty and she thought about moving to be near her elderly mum and dad. She had started dating again, well, not really dating. She had met a man, and had gone for dinner twice with him. She wasn't sure if she could let a man into her life again. Time heals, as they say. She would later marry this man, but she didn't know it yet. It would be a long time in coming. Life would be as good as it could be, considering that she had lost her son.

She looked as beautiful as ever. Today, even as the tears flowed, she still looked beautiful.

Daniel and Becky Fenton. Daniel missed Todd more than he ever thought was possible. The brother who used to annoy him, irritate him, pinch his beer, and never have any money. The brother for whom he would do anything, even die for. He wished he had died instead. It was only yesterday that he had seen someone doing a window round, and he almost got out to give the boy a hiding, telling him it was Todd's round, but he let it go. He had to. He had got the roof fixed on his mum's house, but at first he didn't want to get it done. He used to like standing in the street, looking at it, hoping Todd would come back. He never did. Life would never be the same again, without his kid brother. After all, it was all his fault. He had sworn to protect him, to hide him from the outside world. He had failed that task.

His Marriage to Becky grew stronger, even though she still blamed herself a lot. Their marriage would survive this. It had to, otherwise it was all for nothing. Today as they stood in church, neither of them was aware of the thing that grew inside her. Later, Daniel, inspired by the tales of Jezz and Katy, and the life they lived, would stand for Parliament, and try to make a difference. His financial life long past, together with all the dodgy dealings that went with it. They will call their son Oliver Todd. Daniel will always blame himself, not his father, not the kidnappers. It will always be Daniel Fenton who had lost his brother.

Marie Rose and Dr. James McCarthy, both have had a new lease of life. Both mourn the loss of Todd. Marie Rose sold up, and has moved down south to Marshfield, a place just outside Newport. James has done the same, and lives two streets away, having retired as a GP. They are very close to the Fenton family. Marie Rose enjoying the time with the one grandson she had left. She also felt responsible, and she would often think that it was all her fault for what had happened many years ago, and only ended months ago.

James' gift seemed to have gone for which he was grateful. He was now very close to his cousin. He was happy once more. He had a family again, and he would cherish it.

Neither will ever forget that day, nor explain it. They knew they had become a part of it, plucked up into the skies. They will both live to a ripe old age.

Jezz Dwayne and Tracy Bates. Tracy was sacked, but after seeing the events of that day it didn't really bother her. She worked as a receptionist at a solicitors in Newport, and, believe it or not, her closest friend is Becky Fenton, the one who once called her 'big tits' and decked her with one punch. They meet up regularly and often go out in a foursome with Jezz and Daniel.

Oh yes, Jezz, good old Jezz. He is on the straight and narrow now. He has moved in with Tracy at her flat, and he has got a job labouring at the moment, but he hopes for better things. They had fallen madly in love with each other. Jezz would never forget the friendship he had with Wendy and Katy, as he thought it was them who helped him turn his life around. Tracy regards Daniel as a big brother now. Jezz and Tracy will marry in two years' time.

Katy Harrison. She spent two weeks in hospital, and she had nightmares for a while. It seemed that every night in hospital when she woke up screaming, Wendy Cross would be there, holding her hand, telling her it would be okay. Wendy took her home when she was released, caring for her until she was well. She moved her into the spare room, found her a job at the same cafe where she worked, and went with her when she got her teeth done. And, as Madison Hughes told her after that, she really did scrub up well. Katy had become Wendy Cross' best friend, and soon became friends with the Fenton's. Her life had been turned round now. She was happy. She had a mother, as in Wendy's mother and life was good. It will always be hard for the likes of Katy Harrison to stay on the straight and narrow. She will try but whether she succeeds, who knows. She certainly deserves to, but those demons never completely go away.

Madison Hughes, the stunning Madison Hughes, was with her mum and dad today. They accepted her new family, but there were rules, always rules. Today they were here to support her at Todd's memorial. Madison will never ever accept what happened. She will go searching for answers, for as long as she can. She saw Todd. He didn't die, she would say, he just disappeared, and people don't disappear. Something took him. She would drive everyone crazy with that idea.

But Madison, the real hero of that day, was loved by everyone, especially by Wendy Cross. Maybe that's because Wendy wanted to believe the idea too. She remained up north with her mum and dad, but would visit almost every weekend, during the life in front of her. The beautiful Madison will break many a heart and the Fenton's will love her as a daughter and sister. Her parents will accept that, as she gently drifts from them. Madison will never reach her full potential, not until she has found the answers, and even as she's in church today in a memorial to her brother, whom she knew for less than thirty six hours, she has a feeling she knows where to start. She will see Carol as her second mum and grow very close to Daniel, who will always look after his kid sister. She hopes that one day he will help her find their brother, because, as Madison would repeatedly say 'He didn't die. There was no body.' All this couldn't have happened just so that she could watch her brother die. There was no sense in that. There was no justice. There were still answers to be found. There was no closure, not for the beautiful Madison.

Wendy Cross had only been in hospital for one night. She had been healed on that hillside as her lover drifted away. Todd had saved her after all. She had grown close to Katy because she thought that some good had to come out of that day, and

292

she needed someone to love. She needed something in her life. They had spent thirty six hours in hell together. That had to account for something. She loved Madison, loved her to bits, and wanted to believe her when she said she would get answers. But how could she believe? Wendy was there. She heard Todd say goodbye.

Although she was surrounded by people she loved, and they loved her, she often wandered round in a daze. As young as she is, Wendy Cross will never love another man.

The service was over and those special guests were on their way back to Carol's. The party started, but no one thought it would be like the previous one, as the thousands who had come were now making their way back, after paying their respects to a man who no one completely understood.

The special guests were now in Carol's house, eating food, drinking wine.

When Wendy told them she was going upstairs, only Carol guessed where.

Wendy stood in Todd's room in front of the old wardrobe, which was just too big for that room. The doors were closed, but soon she would open them. She just wanted to stand there for a moment, to breathe in the smell. She opened the doors, the inside looked huge, like looking into a bottomless well. She stepped into the wardrobe, sat down and closed the doors, pulling her knees to her chest. She sat like that for ten minutes, as she tried to stop her tears. She composed herself, drying her eyes on her sleeve. She licked her lips, then gulped.

'Are you there, Todd?' she asked.

'I'm here, Wendy.' came the reply.

About the Author

This is the first book I've ever written, something I wanted to do ever since I was a kid writing stupid poems and thinking I had a gift.

Why did it take until my mid-fifties? I don't really know, maybe I'm contented in life.

I enjoyed writing this immensely and those who know me well will see parts of my life in it.

I don't pretend it's a best seller, I wouldn't even say it's good.

But I wrote it, I do hope you enjoy it.

This book is dedicated to my darling wife Michelle, she pushed me to do it and I love her even more for it.

Printed in Great Britain
by Amazon